Cassia

Susan F. Craft

Susan F. Craft (signature)

HERITAGE BEACON

F I C T I O N

CASSIA BY SUSAN F. CRAFT
Published by Heritage Beacon Fiction
an imprint of Lighthouse Publishing of the Carolinas
2333 Barton Oaks Dr., Raleigh, NC, 27614

ISBN: 978-1-941103-73-9
Copyright © 2015 by Susan F. Craft
Cover art illustrated by Jacob Hägg [Public domain], via Wikimedia Commons
Interior design by AtriTeX Technologies P Ltd

Available in print from your local bookstore, online, or from the publisher at:
www.lighthousepublishingofthecarolinas.com

For more information on this book and the author visit: www.susanfcraft.com

Brought to you by the creative team at Lighthouse Publishing of the Carolinas:
Eddie Jones, Rowena Kuo, Leslie L. McKee, Ann Tatlock, Brian Cross, Paige Boggs

Library of Congress Cataloging-in-Publication Data
Craft, Susan F.
Cassia / Susan F. Craft 1st ed.

Printed in the United States of America

Praise for *Cassia*

Susan Craft has expertly crafted a superbly intriguing story. It starts calmly enough with a family on a ship, with hints of some misgivings and possible dangers. Until … Cassia. Then the breathtaking, unforgettable, page-turning journey really begins. It's a journey well worth taking.

~ **Yvonne Lehman**
Novelist Retreat director, author of 55 novels, including *Hearts that Survive*—A novel of the Titanic

Infused with lively history and the power of vivid storytelling, *Cassia* is an intricate and passionate tale of fierce determination, family love, and enduring faith. Author Susan F. Craft is masterful at blending days gone by with characters and events that will surely play over and over in the reader's mind and heart.

~ **Jayme Mansfield**
Award-winning author of *Chasing the Butterfly*

Susan F. Craft is known for her authenticity to historical detail (she won Book of the Year Award on Overcoming with God blog for *The Chamomile*) and she doesn't disappoint with this new novel. Fans of MaryLu Tyndall's pirate novels will enjoy this tension-filled book. Wonderful writing and sure to appeal to Christian historical fiction fans with a unique story line and setting.

~ **Carrie Fancett Pagels**
Award-winning and bestselling author

Suspense, adventure, history, and romance, *Cassia* has everything I love in a book! A true page-turner from the very first page, interwoven with family love and loyalty that will touch your heart, a sweet budding romance, danger at every turn, and an overarching theme of trust and faith in God through the hard times. Loved it!

~ **MaryLu Tyndall**
Award-winning author of the *Legacy of the King's Pirates* series

Acknowledgements

I owe so much to so many people who helped me bring Cassia to fruition. I couldn't accomplish anything without my family's support and encouragement, especially my dear husband. Thanks to my granddog, Steeler, who inspired me to include Cal. Though small in stature, he has the heart of a lion when it comes to protecting his family. Thanks to my "bestest buddy," Paula Benson, who serves as a sounding board and seems to sense when I require prodding forward. My sincere gratitude goes to the folks at Lighthouse Publishing of the Carolinas.

Above all, thanks to my Lord through whom all blessings flow, and whose robes, when He returns as King of Kings and Lord of Lords, will radiate the aroma of cassia (Psalm 45:8).

All thy garments smell of myrrh, and aloes, and cassia
Psalm 45:8, KJV

CHAPTER 1

April 1799

The *Merry Maid* pitched and rolled as a welcome wind curled into her mainsail, freeing the schooner from the doldrums that had held it captive for hours.

Lilyan Xanthakos, secure in the circle of her husband's arms as he steadied them against the rail, felt a stirring in her blood as the ship lunged forward. The lazy waves undulated and swelled gently as if God had grabbed the corners of a giant jade-green blanket and let it billow across the ocean floor. The clear, cloudless sky shone like a brilliant sapphire. She cupped her hand over her brow and craned her neck to watch crewmen descend the rat lines leading down from the billowing sails. The air crackled with their raised excited voices, the snapping of canvas, and the creaking of the rigging.

Needles of worry that had plagued Lilyan all morning danced across the back of her neck. She hated her uncanny intuitions, more so because they most times proved true.

"Thank heavens we're moving again. It doesn't bode well to

flounder in these pirate-infested waters."

The ship heaved, and she eyed her sons near the bow. Paul clasped his arms around his younger brother's waist, trying to keep Marion from falling overboard as he teetered on a barrel and peered through his spyglass.

"Paul, hold fast!" she shouted.

Digging her fingers into her husband's wrists, she twisted her neck around to look up at him. "Nikki, do something."

A wry smile curled his lips, and his topaz eyes danced with good humor. "Don't fret so, Lilyanista. They're strong, steadfast lads, and we've taught them well."

We have, she thought. But woodsmen's ways. Shooting a running deer will sour its meat. A purring, soft call makes the best wild turkey lure. Ginseng root provides energy. A sorrel tree leaf will slake your thirst. Some two-legged animals are more dangerous than the four-legged ones. Under their father's tutelage, the boys had learned all that and more. But this was the sea, another world altogether that could turn treacherous at a moment's notice.

She honed in on her sons again. At fourteen and thirteen, they were handsome lads, mirror images of their father with thick, unruly onyx-black hair and amber eyes, the deep tawny color of sap that rises up through the pores of fresh-cut pine.

Should we have brought the children with us? She felt a plummeting in her stomach.

Nicholas' breath warmed the side of her face when he dipped his head to whisper in her ear, "You're worrying about the last time you and I sailed, aren't you?"

"Yes." They both had almost perished in a storm, and the memories of their ordeal still held the power to disturb her.

She reached back and caressed his cheek before shifting her eyes to the helm, where their sixteen-year-old daughter, Laurel, conversed with Mr. Whitehouse, the first mate.

Laurel's titian red hair fell in waves down her back. A velvet hat the color of magnolia leaves framed her heart-shaped face and accentuated her eyes, which reminded Lilyan of dainty ferns that grew along the banks of mountain waterfalls. The wind blew open the hem of her long woolen coat and lifted tendrils of her hair from her shoulders.

"She's stunning, isn't she?" said Lilyan, making it a statement rather than a question.

"Stunning. Diamond of the first water. Like her ma." Nicholas spoke in a voice an octave deeper. "But does Mr. Whitehouse seem overly attentive to our Laurel?"

Lilyan studied Mr. Whitehouse, who stood straight and tall and looked quite dashing in his uniform. She had to admit there was something appealing about the combination of his charming smile and his rust-brown eyes the same hue as his curly hair.

She patted Nicholas' arm clamped tightly about her waist. "His expression is intent, and he seems to absorb her every word."

"The captain informs me that he's the son of a prosperous Baltimore shipbuilder. His father sent him out into the seafaring world to learn what he can before returning home to work alongside him."

"So, my dear husband, ever the vigilant father, you've already made inquiries."

He cleared his throat. "I take care of my own."

"'Tis only one of your many attributes I admire, dear man."

He clasped his arm tighter about her waist. "One puzzling thing. The captain let me know—and I'm sure it was a slip of the tongue—Mr. Whitehouse's family owns this ship."

"That could prove awkward."

"Yes, especially given the contrary nature of our captain. But despite the boy's glowing references, he stands too close to Laurel for my liking. He bears watching."

Lilyan couldn't help but smile at his protective stance. He had reason to worry. To her chagrin, men were beginning to take notice of Laurel. She knew she must speak with her about the consequences of such astonishing beauty. Their daughter would break hearts, for certain, but she must learn a lesson never to use her good looks for gain or harm.

"Nikki, have I been selfish, trying to prolong her childhood? I've delayed warning her about the pitfalls of her beauty. Have I failed in my duty as her mother?"

He turned her around to face him, delving into her eyes with his. "We stand together in our efforts to shelter her." He looked at Laurel and then back again, his eyes so close Lilyan could see the dark brown specks in his golden irises. "We almost lost her once. I will not apologize for keeping her close."

"Was it a good idea to bring the children?" She couldn't help voicing her earlier doubts.

"I'm a vintner, and as such, I expect my children"—he tapped her chin—"as their mother did—to learn my trade. In Roanoke, they'll see firsthand how the roots were shipped from Greece. On our journey home, I'll teach them to care for the cuttings." He gave her one of his most winning smiles. "Moreover, it's a grand adventure for the family."

But this trip wasn't only a learning expedition or an adventure. It offered a respite from dual tragedies that had struck their tight-knit family a reeling blow; the deaths of their youngest and their patriarch. It had been over a year, but Lilyan's arms still ached for her three-year-old boy, Francis, his sweet-smelling curly red hair and green eyes full of merriment that reminded her of her da. And Callum; he, too, still lived fresh in her mind. A craggy-faced, grouchy Scotsman and self-appointed protector of her and her brother, he had been an integral part of her life since she was born. Francis and Callum had died within months of each other, and the sting of their loss brought tears to her eyes.

Gazing once again at her daughter, she engraved the sight to memory, determined to paint a portrait of Laurel as she was at this moment. Her fingers itched for her brushes. The urge surprised her, for she hadn't been able to paint since Francis' death. Was her grief finally beginning to ebb?

"Ahoy! Ship two points off starboard bow," a sailor shouted from the crow's nest.

"Please, God, don't let it be pirates," Lilyan spoke under her breath.

Nicholas slipped her arm through the crook of his elbow. "You worry overmuch, my love. Before I booked our passage, I was assured that the few pirates who remain after the purge five years ago keep to the Caribbean."

"You speak of few. But it takes only one." She scrubbed at the gooseflesh that crawled across her neck.

Marion bobbed his telescope up and down and whooped. "First we've seen since we left Charleston."

Paul reached for the spyglass. "Let me see."

"All right, but give it back." Marion hovered next to his brother, his eager glance jumping from the ship to the telescope and back. "Finally, some excitement."

The barrel Marion stood on wobbled and so did Lilyan's stomach.

Her third child—now her youngest—Marion barely contained his zest for life. Among her children, he had taken the death of Francis the hardest and now seemed determined to give his parents his and his brother's share of tribulation.

Lilyan and Nicholas made their way to the boys, where Laurel joined them. To Lilyan's relief, Nicholas clamped his arm around Marion's shoulders and pulled him back from the edge.

"Looks like they've lost their wind." Paul glanced at his parents. "We're catching up with them."

Marion wrinkled his nose. "What's that smell?"

Lilyan breathed in, and coughed from the odor that assaulted her nose. Horribly familiar, it was something she hadn't been exposed to since she was a young woman growing up in Charleston—the unmistakable foul stench of unwashed bodies, blood, fear, and human misery. *Slaves.*

"Let me see." Laurel grabbed the spyglass before Lilyan could protest.

"Da!" Laurel clutched her father's arm. "They're throwing people overboard!"

"Give it to me." Nicholas took the spyglass, slid it all the way out with a *click*, and put it up to his eye.

Lilyan swallowed hard as her children gaped at her, their innocent faces registering their shock.

The first mate stepped into their circle and looked down at Laurel. "It's a slaver, miss. Disposing of the ones who succumbed to disease and death."

Laurel gasped. "Disposing?"

"They're dead?" Marion squeaked, his voice barely audible.

Nicholas worked the muscles in his jaws. Laurel's eyes brimmed with tears, and Lilyan's heart sank from the sadness she read in them. She threw a meaningful glance at her husband. He handed the spyglass to Marion and took his daughter into his arms.

"Come away, children," he said, a vein pulsing in his temple.

"But Ma!" shouted Marion, looking once more through the spyglass. He jerked back around and shouted, "They ain't all dead. One of 'em is swimming this way!"

CHAPTER 2

Her fingers trembling, Lilyan took the spyglass and trained it on the other ship's waterline. The *Merry Maid's* pitch and roll prevented a clear view, so she twisted the scope back and forth until she finally spotted a pair of spindly brown arms flailing against the churning waves. The water would soon win that fight. She turned her eyes away and after a shared glance with Nicholas, who continued to comfort their daughter, they sought out the ship's captain. He stood at the helm, his back as rigid as the mast grounded in the hull of the ship, his hands clasped behind his back, and his wintry eyes staring ahead as if oblivious to the desperate scene playing out before them.

"Captain Longstreet!"

"You must save them."

She and Nicholas shouted simultaneously.

The captain glared at them from underneath his bushy eyebrows that looked like giant black caterpillars; one lifted in a high arch and the other angled toward his bulbous nose. "I beg your pardon?"

Several of the crew hunched their shoulders and made a show of going about their business. One, an older man, his weather-beaten, pockmarked cheeks the color of tanned hide, turned his back to the captain and rolled his eyes. Winding a rope between the curve of his thumb and his elbow, he shook his head at her in warning.

Lilyan blinked at the sailor but pressed on, pointing to the ship that suddenly lurched forward. "Can you not see? Someone is drowning."

The captain deigned to glance toward the vessel and back. "My eyesight is excellent, ma'am. But 'tis none of my concern."

"What! In the name of human decency, sir…" Lilyan spun around and held her hands out to Nicholas. "We must *do* something."

Nicholas jutted out his chin and studied the captain with a determined look in his eyes. When he removed his arm from around Laurel's waist, she clasped her hands to her cheeks and swayed.

"Mr. Whitehouse." With a jerk of his head, Nicholas prompted the first mate to step close to their daughter and stand at the ready.

Nicholas took Lilyan by her elbow, and she had to lift her skirts to match his strides as they hastened to the bottom of the steps leading to the helm.

The captain glared down at them from his lofty perch, scorn in his beady eyes the color of bitter coffee. He drew himself to his full height. "Yes?"

Nicholas squared his shoulders. "You will help, of course. Send a rescue boat."

The crew, scattered about the deck, stopped any pretense of work and came to a standstill, intent on the unusual drama. The helmsman's knuckles turned white as he clasped the spokes of the ship's wheel and stared straight ahead.

Lilyan's glance darted back and forth between her husband and the captain. The tension between them crackled like ignited tinder before it bursts into flames. Would the captain relent? If not, what would Nicholas do? Her neck prickled in anticipation.

The captain curled his full upper lip, chapped from sun and wind. "There is no 'of course' about it. And no, I do not plan to help."

Nicholas balled his hands into fists. "As a captain, surely … surely … you are aware of the rules of the sea. Every master is bound so far as he can do so without serious danger to his vessel, crew, and passengers, to render assistance to everybody … even though an enemy … found at sea in danger of being lost."

"Do not presume to quote to me from the Black Book," the captain shouted, his arms rigid by his sides. "That"—he pointed toward the water—"is not a person, but cargo. And I cannot interfere with another ship's cargo."

Stunned by his cruel words, Lilyan sucked in a breath. She cast a furtive glance toward the castaway, who had stopped swimming and was now treading water. "Nikki, we must hurry."

He patted her arm, but his dour expression held no promise. "Captain Longstreet, as you can plainly see with your excellent eyesight, that ship is now leaving, abandoning the jettisoned cargo. To my reckoning, we are within the three-mile limit from shore. Therefore, according to South Carolina law, I claim the discarded cargo for my own." His back rigid, his legs braced as if for combat, he stared at the captain.

Although he kept his voice steady, Lilyan was alarmed by the Greek accent creeping into his speech; a sure sign of his anger. How would this confrontation end?

Nicholas crossed his arms over his chest. "It is my property, and you are obliged to help me now, sir. And if you don't, I shall take you to court."

"Blimey." A whisper made its way to Lilyan. "He's bamboozled him there."

The captain's usually bronze complexion turned crimson, and he cast a withering glance at Nicholas. "I'm obliged to provide you the means, but none of my men will assist." He turned his scowl upon the first mate. "Mr. Whitehouse, lower away a skiff for Mr. Xanthakos' use."

The first mate saluted. "Aye, Captain." He cupped his hands around his mouth and looked up toward the ship's rigging. "Lower away the skiff," he shouted, and a couple of the men scrambled down to work the skiff pulleys.

Nicholas, already removing his waistcoat, turned on his heel. "Paul. Marion. To me. We'll board the skiff. Hand your coats to Ma. Quickly, now."

The boys scrambled out of their waistcoats and draped them over Lilyan's extended arm. Paul's harsh expression bespoke his awareness of the danger. Marion handed his telescope to her, his eyes bright with anticipation of a great adventure. His cravat was rumpled, and strands of hair had escaped from the buff-colored ribbon at the back of his neck. Not desiring to embarrass him before the crew, Lilyan resisted the urge to hug her youngest. She hadn't felt this anxious about her boys since their first extended hunting trip three years past.

Please, Lord, I've already lost one child.

Nicholas squeezed her hand and gave her a reassuring smile. "'Twill be fine, *agapi mou*."

He and the boys dropped their hats on a nearby barrel and hurried over the side and into the boat that dangled from a pulley. Laurel joined Lilyan, and they leaned over the rail, hands clasped, watching the craft splash into the water below. Nicholas sat on the stern seat, took one of the oars, and pushed them away from the ship. As he began to row, Paul sat on the bow seat, and Marion settled between them in the hull.

Lord, a vast part of my joy is aboard that boat. Keep them safe, I beseech you.

A lump forming in her throat, she watched them close in on the place where countless bodies bobbed on the surface like corks. The gruesome sight made the blood rush from her cheeks, leaving them numb.

"Sharks!" came a call from the crow's nest.

With that, the crew ran to the rail and crowded around Lilyan and her daughter.

"Saw one of 'em swimming in our wake this morn'." The man's deep, grating voice evoked memories of folks gathered around bonfires spinning tales of haints and goblins. It made goose bumps run up Lilyan's arms.

The men groaned, and she threw the man a questioning look.

He tapped his knuckle to his forehead. "It's bad luck, you see, missus, for a shark to be in the wake. Means someone on board's gonna die."

She caught her bottom lip in her teeth and handed the coats to Laurel, who stared at her with eyes drowned in worry. She opened the spyglass in time to see her sons struggling to lift a nude person out of the water. The movement of the ship and the rolling of the waves kept her from getting a good look to see whether it was a man or woman, but the moment Nicholas pulled off his shirt and wrapped it around the poor creature, she suspected.

Her suspicions were confirmed minutes later when her unusually ruddy-cheeked sons hopped from the skiff onto the deck, followed by Nicholas, who strode toward her cradling a female in his arms. The muscles of his bronze chest and arms barely strained against his burden that couldn't have weighed six stones. The shirt he had slipped over the woman was drenched, sending rivulets of water down the front of his breeches. The transparent material clung to every curve and angle of the woman's form. When one of the crew made a coarse remark about the dark brown nipples, Lilyan grabbed Paul's coat from Laurel and draped it across the seemingly lifeless body.

In one terrible moment, Lilyan was wrenched back to the last time her husband walked toward her cradling a limp body in his arms. It was their son, Francis. Nicholas had taken the boys to the river to swim and for a fishing lesson. While standing amidst the rocks along the edge of the river, with his father not a foot away, their baby was struck in the neck by a timber rattler. The poison spread through his tiny body, and within minutes he was dead. A waterfall of agonizing emotions—pain, grief, anger—poured down on Lilyan's shoulders and threatened to bring her to her knees. The warmth of Paul's hand stealing into hers drew her back from her nightmare. She studied his amber-colored eyes and found them awash with misery. He was remembering too.

The crew closed in on Nicholas, and one of them sniffed in disgust. "Don't look human."

Another grunted in agreement. "More like a rack of bones."

Lilyan scanned the woman's long, bony legs and arms up to her head where the curly black hair had been shorn so close, she could see her scalp. The edges of the woman's full lips had turned the color of a day-old bruise. The blue tint set off alarm bells in Lilyan's head. Rubbing her fingers across the cold, limp hand, she lifted up a prayer. That prayer was immediately answered when the poor soul fluttered her eyelids and moaned.

"What is this?" roared the captain from the helm. "Bos'n. Get the crew back to work. Unfurl the stuns'l before we lose the wind. We've wasted enough time."

Nicholas frowned at the captain. "Beetle-browed jackanapes," he muttered.

"Nikki! Let's take her to our cabin. Boys, you bring me water for bathing her. Laurel, I'll need your help."

Nicholas regarded his daughter. "But—"

"No, Da." Laurel folded the waistcoats she'd been holding and put them alongside their hats. "I must do my part."

The momentary exchange between father and daughter was rife with meaning. Though Nicholas adored all of his children, Laurel held a special place in his heart. Not only was she their firstborn, but once they had almost lost her. A day after her first birthday, while visiting a Cherokee village, she and her aunt had been kidnapped by slavers. He and Lilyan had endured hellish months following every lead, every trail, before their precious daughter was miraculously returned to them. Nicholas shielded his own, and that living nightmare made him even more protective. When Francis died, Nicholas had flayed himself with guilt. His remorse and sense of failure to safeguard his son had nearly killed his spirit. It still haunted him, and Lilyan couldn't blame him for his hesitancy to expose Laurel to the unknown.

"Come, then." He shifted the woman up further onto his chest and led the way down the companionway belowdecks and through a narrow hallway. There, he waited for Lilyan to open the door to their cabin.

Inside, Lilyan lit the two tallow candles of the brass lantern bolted to the wall while Nicholas gently laid the woman on the alcove bed. Her emaciated body barely made an impression on the mattress.

Lilyan straightened the woman's frail arms and legs and patted her wiry hair. "Laurel, we'll need one of your chemises. Then, please pull the wet shirt from her while I find your da a dry one."

"No need. There's one here on a hook." Nicholas slipped on the shirt, tucked it into his breeches, and stood next to Lilyan, averting his eyes from the bed. "How may I help, my love?"

She cupped his face, drawing strength from his sturdy frame that seemed too large for their cramped cabin. "Supervise the boys." She hesitated and leaned in close. "Speak with them. They'll have questions. They are mountain boys. Unaware of slavery. Unused to such cruelty." She pressed her hand against the pain in her heart. "And the bodies."

Nicholas blew out a heavy breath, and lines of concern furrowed his brow. The bleak expression in his eyes gave a telltale sign that he too was deeply affected by what they had witnessed.

"Explain…" She shivered and glanced over her shoulder at Laurel. "Our dear ones have been exposed to much this day."

He pulled her to him and kissed the top of her head, then hugged her tightly. "Can you explain it to me?" he asked before closing the cabin door behind him.

CHAPTER 3

---

*"You may choose to look the other way but you can never say again
that you did not know."*

William Wilberforce, British House of Commons 1780,
abolitionist, evangelical Christian

After a light supper of biscuits and tea as evening neared, Lilyan and Laurel held a vigil, anxiously awaiting a sign from the still form that lay in the bed, her chest barely rising and falling with each breath. She had not stirred or made a sound, not even when Lilyan bathed the briny residue from her, rubbed oil into her parched skin, and clothed her in one of Laurel's lawn shifts.

"I need to feel for her pulse, but the skin on her wrists and neck are raw from the chains. She has suffered terribly, and I don't want to hurt her." Lilyan sat on the edge of the bed and gingerly slid her fingers underneath the gauze on the woman's left wrist. "She seems to be breathing easier."

Laurel, who sat in the only chair in the room, slid closer until her knees touched her mother's. "Ma, why is her belly so swollen?"

"It happens when a person has been denied food for a long

time."

Or, in an act of total desperation, denies herself food.

"Mother, please, may we desist referring to her as 'the woman' or 'her'? It makes us sound cold and unsympathetic. Can we not give her a name?"

Lilyan twined her fingers into Laurel's and smiled her approval. "You have something in mind?

"Me?"

Laurel studied the woman, who seemed dwarfed by the overlarge nightdress. The white lacy collar tied with a satin ribbon at her neck only partially covered a bandage that made a stark contrast against her dark skin.

"She fairly glows after the damaged skin sloughed off. Her color reminds me of cinnamon. I think we should call her Cassia."

"Cassia. The poor man's cinnamon? It suits."

Laurel let go of her mother's hand. "Until we know her real name."

If she lives long enough to tell us. Lilyan couldn't say the words aloud.

"Wasn't Da magnificent, handling the captain the way he did?"

"Magnificent."

"He was furious. I could tell."

"How so?"

"His accent. When he speaks normally, I can barely detect that he is from Greece. But it becomes obvious when he's angry."

Or passionate.

Laurel smiled. "It's very endearing."

Lilyan kept her eyes trained on Cassia. "Very endearing."

They grew quiet again until Laurel cleared her throat, drawing Lilyan's attention to her flushed cheeks.

"Ma? The scar below her ... breast?"

Lilyan braced herself. She had bidden Nicholas to speak with their sons. Now she must face her daughter's questions. "It's a brand."

"An animal brand? Made with a hot iron?"

"Yes." The horror in her daughter's eyes hurt so much that Lilyan massaged the skin over her heart. "On some occasions, when a ship is filled with slaves already purchased and bound for more than one place, the slaves are marked with their particular owner's brand. To more readily identify them when they reach America."

Laurel paled. "And the *VP* on Cassia?"

"I suspect it's for Violet Plantation in Mount Pleasant." Lilyan laced her fingers together and waited for her daughter to absorb the information.

"You grew up seeing this?"

"Regrettably, yes. Charlestown, as it was called in my youth, was a major port for slave ships. Because your grandfather was a trader and owned a warehouse—where my wallpaper shop is located now—I often saw slaves transported to shore. Although my da tried to shield me from it, I also witnessed the buying and selling of slaves in the market."

The memories roiled like undigested lumps in Lilyan's stomach.

Laurel's green eyes seemed to grow darker as a frown wrinkled her brow. "But our family was not a part of … that trade?"

"No. Emphatically, no. Your grandfather dealt in animal skins and mercantile goods for the backcountry settlers and the Indians."

Laurel's shoulders slumped in relief. "Why would someone want to own another human being?"

There it was. The question Lilyan dreaded. She thought back to the time when she was ten and had asked her father a similar question. He had explained it well. Could she do the same for her child?

She squared her shoulders. "I've heard many reasons in my lifetime. Slavery has been a part of mankind since the beginning. It's in the Bible. For some, it's a way of life, the way things have always been done. Something so familiar that they have no sensitivity to it, no sense of right or wrong about it."

"Even Christians who are taught to love their neighbors and to do unto others as you would have them do unto you?"

"Even so. It's our nature to assuage our guilt and diminish our wickedness despite our Christian teaching."

Laurel stared at Cassia's wrist lying so near her own. "But it's cruel," she whispered with a catch in her throat.

Watching tears gather in her daughter's eyes, Lilyan regretted her child's sudden and disturbing introduction to the harsh side of life. She barely managed to hold back her own tears as she searched for clarity. "For many, it's economics. A way for businessmen, far distanced from the horrible realities, to make a living. For plantations—like Violet Plantation—it's the cheapest way to cultivate vast acres of land and to maintain the resources to do the grueling work of growing indigo. But for those who live with slavery every day, it binds both slave and owner into strange familial relationships." She paused, resisting mental pictures of slave children running about in plantation courtyards, their faces mirror-images of their owners'. "Over centuries, slavery has become a terrible form of revenge among warring African tribes who sell their enemies into bondage."

Her tenderhearted daughter was so innocent, so unworldly. Would she spoil that with too detailed an explanation? She hesitated, choosing her words carefully. "And then there is the even darker side. It's a way for evil men to lord themselves over others and to act upon their basest feelings."

"Our vineyards take much labor, yet Father chooses not to have slaves."

"He never considered it an option. After the war, your father and I together read some of Mr. Wilberforce's writings. He is a British abolitionist. Later, when your father was invited to attend some meetings in Washington, he was among many—Benjamin Franklin, Alexander Hamilton, our own dear President Washington—who sought to abolish slavery."

Laurel's eyes widened. "Father went to Washington?"

"Yes. We went together. We traveled there with two of South

Carolina's most famous statesmen, Christopher Gadsden and Henry Laurens. Mr. Laurens was a great friend of your grandfather's. He and Mr. Gadsden spoke against slavery. But there were men—sadly, some of the most passionate of them from South Carolina—who wouldn't hear of abolition. They threatened the union of the colonies if they didn't get their way. A compromise—albeit a terrible one—was made."

"How did you come to know so much, Ma?"

If only she knew how little I know.

"I'm glad you think so, my dear." She crossed one ankle over the other and knit her fingers together on her lap. "But to answer your question, my father encouraged me to read. And I've done so all my life."

"You weren't fearful of being dubbed a bluestocking?"

A tap on the door made them both start. Laurel jumped up and opened the door to greet two sailors hovering in the hallway.

Lilyan stood, smoothing the wrinkles from her skirt. When the shortest man stepped forward, she recognized him as the one who had warned her not to press the captain about rescuing Cassia.

He pressed a knuckle to his forehead. "Sorry to disturb you, missus. Miss. I'm Carpenter's Mate Hennessy, and this here's Able Seaman Watson. Mr. Xanthakos made a request of the quartermaster for two hammocks."

Both men craned their necks to look past Lilyan toward the bed, until Hennessy poked the other man with his elbow, prompting him to give the women a salute. They unrolled two pieces of canvas and proceeded to string long lengths of hemp rope through hooks suspended from the overhead beams.

Hennessy stopped lashing the hooks to address Lilyan. "'Cause of the close quarters in here, we're puttin' 'em far enough apart where you won't toss each other out. And low enough so's ye won't break nothin' if you fall."

Watson guffawed. "You mean *when* they fall. 'Cause they're gonna."

Laurel sent Watson a quizzical look.

He grinned at her, exposing a mouth of missing teeth that reminded Lilyan of dropped stitches in a row of knitting. "Layin' in one of these takes practice, miss. They ain't easy to get into and harder to stay in." He chuckled. "I remember one time. The first night I served aboard a ship in the king's navy. Belowdecks they lined up all the hammocks nice and shipshape in a row. During the night, as the man next to me fell out, he grabbed hold of my hammock. I grabbed hold of the man next to me and … Whoosh! Like dominos, we all crashed to the floor. I was almost knocked senseless with such a pain in me head, I didn't know where I was."

Laurel laughed aloud at the man's antics, bringing an expression of such adoration to his face that Lilyan chuckled. The joy in his eyes at being able to make a young woman laugh was engaging.

Hennessy's suppressed laughter rumbled in his chest. "Get about your business, Watson."

Lilyan ran her hand across one of the hammocks. "It's not as heavy or coarse as canvas. What is it?"

"Dungri. A cotton cloth made in India. Sometimes used for sails. It's sturdy stuff, missus," Hennessy replied, cutting the end off a piece of rope that dangled from a hook and securing the grommets in place.

Laurel reached out and fingered the material, sharing a doubtful glance with her mother. "You say there's a knack to staying in it?"

Watson grinned at them. "Would you care for me to show ye?"

"Yes, please," Laurel answered and took a step back.

He spun around and turned his back to the hammock. "The trick is to do it all in one motion. Plant your backsi—yourself—midway and roll back and down, grabbing either side and folding yourself in." He followed through the motions and landed squarely and securely in the middle of the hammock.

"It looks easy, Ma. Surely we can do it. Let's give it a try, shall we?"

Laurel's keen expression brought to mind the time Nicholas

taught her to swim at the age of four. She'd been too impatient to wait for instructions. With an impish grin on her face and to her parents' astonishment, she jumped into the water only to surface seconds later sputtering and laughing as if she'd been swimming all her life.

Not in the least sure of her capability of making a graceful entry and exit from the hammock, Lilyan shook her head. "Maybe later, dear." She smiled at Mr. Watson, who had been watching their conversation with interest. "Very well. Thank you, sir. You've explained it ably."

He blinked rapidly, apparently unused to such praise. "One more thing. If the ship starts rollin' about and tossin' on a rough sea, just throw your—uh—limb over the side. Like this. You see?" He dangled his leg out of the hammock. "It'll settle you back in in no time."

Averting her eyes from the comical angle of the man's leg, which exposed tar-spattered shoes with a huge hole in the sole and tattered hose that stretched over a bony knee, Lilyan stifled a giggle. "We appreciate your kindness."

Watson slipped down to the floor in another practiced motion and bowed gallantly from the waist. "Happy to help, ma'am."

Hennessy secured the other hammock and grumbled, "That's enough, Watson. We need to let the ladies alone."

When the men had left, Laurel practiced several times getting in and out of the hanging bed. "It's rather comfortable, once you become accustomed." She pulled the sides around her body and draped her arms across her chest.

A moan from the bed startled them, spurring Laurel, in an awkward flurry of arms and legs and petticoats, to fall out of the hammock.

Cassia's eyes fluttered open and filled with panic as she glanced furtively around the room. She jabbed an elbow into the mattress in an effort to sit up, but too weak, she sank back down.

Lilyan gently touched Cassia's rail-thin forearm. "There, there.

You're safe with us. We mean you no harm."

Her calm demeanor had the desired effect; the terror in Cassia's huge brown eyes abated.

Lilyan pointed to her daughter. "This is Laurel." She tapped her index finger to her own chest. "And I'm Lilyan."

Cassia blinked her soft doe eyes that seemed too large for her face.

"Laurel, water, please." Lilyan made a motion of bringing a cup to her lips. "Water? Would you like some water?"

Cassia closed her eyelids and gave an almost imperceptible nod. Lilyan slipped one hand underneath Cassia's neck and held the cup to her lips with the other. Cassia drank so heavily that she coughed and sputtered, dribbling liquid down both sides of her mouth. Lilyan gently pressed the corner of the covers to the woman's lips and down her neck.

"Hungry?" Lilyan cupped her hand and tapped three fingers and her thumb against her own lips. "Food?"

Cassia curled up the corner of her lip.

"Laurel—" A knock on the door interrupted.

"It's Nicholas," came his muffled voice through the door.

Cassia's expression held such fright that Lilyan rubbed her fingers across her cheek and murmured, "It's fine. All is well. Don't worry."

Observing Cassia's eyes, she called out, "Come."

Nicholas opened the door and took a step inside.

"Carefully, Nikki." Lilyan held up a warning hand. "Keep your distance and try to keep your voice low. Cassia is frightened."

He raised an eyebrow. "Cassia?"

Laurel stepped across the room and curled into the crook of her father's arm. "'Tis the name I gave her until we can determine her real one."

"Lovely choice." He tapped the tip of her nose with his finger. "Before the boys and I retire, I thought I'd see if you have need of anything."

"Would you inquire of the steward for a cup of broth?" Lilyan started to move toward him, but Cassia gripped her hand and groaned.

He stepped back. "I'll not tarry. My presence seems to upset her."

"Thank you, dearest. Tell the boys that I love them and wish you all a pleasant sleep."

He looked at her with hooded eyes. "I shall miss you."

She would miss him more. Sleep eluded her when he was not by her side. The war and Lilyan's flight from bounty hunters for killing a British soldier, albeit in self-defense—had kept them apart much of their first two years as husband and wife. As a result, once they were reunited, they vowed never to be parted again. The vow remained intact, except for rare overnight hunting trips with the boys.

Before Nicholas turned to leave, he glanced at the hammocks and chuckled. "Sleep well, my ladies."

It wasn't long after he left that the steward brought the broth. This time, Laurel met him at the door before he could enter and disturb their patient. Lilyan settled on the side of the bed, and Laurel dragged a small table between them and handed Lilyan the cup.

"No spoon?" Lilyan wondered how she would manage, but she knew she had to get some nourishment into the poor woman or she wouldn't survive.

"No."

"Would have made it easier." Lilyan held the cup with one hand and spread a cloth underneath Cassia's chin with the other. "At least it's warm."

Cassia gripped the cup Lilyan held to her lips, the sleeves of her chemise sliding down to her elbows.

Laurel pointed to Cassia's arm. "Do you see the mark above her wrist? It looks like a dogwood flower."

Lilyan studied the birthmark. "It does. It looks exactly like a dogwood."

At that moment, Cassia's abdomen rolled and tossed, eliciting a gasp from Lilyan.

Laurel's eyes grew wide. "What is it, Ma? Why are you staring?"

Lilyan's heart hammered in her chest, and she clamped her hand to her forehead. How could she have been so dull-witted? "I was terribly mistaken."

Laurel couldn't pull her gaze away from Cassia's undulating stomach. "Mistaken?"

Lilyan looked from Laurel to Cassia and back again. "It's not starvation. I believe Cassia is with child."

CHAPTER 4

It is of the Lord's mercies that we are not consumed, because his compassions fail not.

They are new every morning: great is thy faithfulness.
Lamentations 3:22–23 KJV

The next morning Lilyan met Nicholas topside and broke the news to him as they strolled arm in arm along the deck.

He shook his head. "She looks no more than a child herself."

"I believe Cassia is older than I had first thought. Her frailty is deceptive. I'm worried she may be too frail … that she may not survive." *Lord, might I be of some comfort … for however long she is with us?* "For that same reason, I have no way of knowing how far along she is in her term."

Had the baby been conceived in love before Cassia's capture, or had the young woman endured the unthinkable aboard the hellish ship? If the former, where was the father now? Mourning Cassia's loss in Africa? Still aboard the ship? Or among the bodies tossed overboard? The troubling thoughts tumbled one over the other. Whatever the circumstances, it made Lilyan sad that life had been so unkind to the young woman. She was in awe of the courage it must have taken to survive. She was proud of the determination Cassia demonstrated as she fought against the odds to save herself and her child. How many women—or men—had that much gumption?

They stopped near the companionway to watch Marion show one of the sailors how to brace his longbow. The crew roared approval with each arrow that made its mark on a woven target hanging from the stern. Her son's every movement exuded confidence, and his face reflected his pleasure from the crew's praise.

Feeling the warmth of the sun on her shoulders, Lilyan pulled off her cape. "That bow is as tall as he is. How does he manage?"

Nicholas folded her cape over his arm. "He is stronger than you realize. Robbie taught him well."

Lilyan had first met Robbie Forbes when he and his father and brothers volunteered to search for Laurel when she had been kidnapped. A pleasant young man with auburn hair and merry dove-gray eyes, he had a reputation as a proficient archer and hunter. He visited their vineyard often and spent as much time with Laurel as he did with the boys. Though he was thirteen years older than Laurel, Lilyan wondered if the bond between them would grow into something more mature, more promising. Their relationship remained a puzzle, and she hadn't been able to read the glances that passed between them. This was another quandary to share with Nicholas.

Paul, who had been watching a seaman braid strands of hemp into rope, spotted them and hurried over. "Good morning, Ma."

He bowed and gave her a brilliant smile so like his father's that her heart tripped. Had he grown overnight? She studied his eyes, anxious to ascertain any ill effects from the previous day. Her serious child, he had only recently confided his desire to become a physician. Worried about disappointing his father by not wanting to follow in Nicholas' footsteps, he had determined to wait until they returned to the vineyard to broach the subject.

Paul cocked his head. "You look tired. Did you not sleep?"

"No. I did not. And how anyone can sleep in those—objects of torture—is beyond my understanding."

Nicholas' eyes twinkled. "I don't know. I found my hammock rather comfortable."

She harrumphed. "Can you imagine my surprise to be dozing off one moment and within an instant find myself on the floor, staring up at the ceiling?"

"Oh, Ma. You fell out?" Paul's topaz eyes lit with mischief, and she knew he wanted to laugh, but he was doing a yeoman's job of resisting, suddenly focusing on something interesting up in the sails.

She put her hand on her hip. "Twice."

Paul sputtered.

Nicholas sobered immediately. "You are not hurt?"

Lilyan rubbed her sore hip. "Only my ... pride."

A loud guffaw sounded a few feet away. It was Hennessy, standing arms akimbo next to a pile of coiled rope. "I've heard a backside called many a thing in my life, but never 'my pride'."

He threw back his head and roared and was soon joined by Lilyan, Nicholas, and Paul.

Just as Marion joined them to share in the joke, a muffled yell made its way to them from below.

"Pox! It's the pox!"

The voice grew louder until they saw Watson running up the stairs taking two at the time.

Hennessy pushed his way past the Xanthakos family to grab Watson by his shoulders. "Lower your voice, man. You want to start a panic?"

"But ... it's the slave. She's got the pox. Saw it with me own eyes when I was tucking in the hammocks."

"Stay here." Hennessey shook the frightened man to silence him and then stared straight at Nicholas. "You and your family stay put whilst I take a look-see."

He spun away so fast he nearly knocked Laurel down as she reached the top of the stairs.

Lilyan held her arm out and drew her daughter near. "Did you see any red marks on Cassia? Like mosquito bites?"

Laurel's bottom lip trembled. "There are places on her neck and arms. Her skin is very hot."

Lilyan and Nicholas shared a worried look and gathered their family into a tight circle.

The set of Hennessey's face as he took the last step back up to the deck told Lilyan all she needed to know.

Tamping down her dread, she waited for him to move closer. "You're certain?"

Hennessy dropped his gaze to the deck. "I know the pox. They don't call me cribbage-face for nothing, ma'am. " His cheek muscle quivered as he looked from her to Nicholas. "I'm bound to report it to the captain. I'm sure he'll bar you from the cabin."

Nicholas removed his arm from the small of Lilyan's back. "That won't be necessary. We're all immune."

Hennessy's eyes travelled across Laurel's smooth, rose-petal-colored cheeks. "All?"

"Yes," said Nicholas. "I was inoculated at age eight in Greece when my father learned about the procedure. Mrs. Xanthakos had smallpox as a child. Taking a lesson learned from General Washington, our children have been inoculated as well."

The gloomy-faced seaman blew out a deep breath. "'Tis a blessed relief. I can tell you. We've no doctor aboard." He slid his glance toward the forecastle. "Still, I know not how the captain will take this news."

As Lilyan suspected, Captain Longstreet didn't take it at all well. Once he understood the situation, he demanded to see the evidence of inoculation. Paul and Marion looked to their father, who nodded his consent. Nicholas removed his waistcoat, and the three of them rolled up their sleeves to expose the shiny cross-cuts on their forearms.

Pushing his sleeve back down, Nicholas faced the captain, who was eying Laurel. "Certainly, sir, you will accept my word of honor that my daughter has also been inoculated." His jaw set, he stood ramrod straight and positioned Laurel behind him to shield her from the captain.

The captain harrumphed and made a move toward Lilyan.

"You will not touch my wife!" Nicholas sprung forward and grabbed the captain's arm.

"Unhand me. Or I shall put you in irons," the captain bellowed.

Three sailors wrestled Nicholas to the deck and held him there.

Paul shoved Laurel and Marion behind Lilyan and took a stance in front of her.

Her heart in her throat, she searched around her for something, anything she could use as a weapon.

Nicholas yanked his arm away from one of his captors and was struggling to his feet when Mr. Whitehouse approached. "Please, Captain Longstreet. Is this really necessary? Surely Mr. Xanthakos would not lie about such things. To what end, sir? A man of his ilk would not voluntarily put his family in danger."

The captain's thick eyebrows shot up into an inverted *V*. "Keep to your post, Mr. Whitehouse."

"I mean no insubordination, sir. But I don't think my father would agree with what is occurring here."

The onlookers watched in stunned silence as the captain absorbed the fact that the first mate had invoked the name of his father—the owner of the ship and the captain's only superior.

Finally, Longstreet clasped his hands behind his back, swerved around, and stomped toward the forecastle. "Lock them in their cabin and station a guard outside. And no one is to go near them. Understood?" he ordered over his shoulder.

Inside the cabin, Lilyan checked Nicholas for bruises. "You were very brave, Nikki."

He stayed her hand from his brow and curved his fingers around hers. "I'm afraid I may have made our situation worse."

They shared a worried glance.

Laurel and Marion settled themselves on the floor, and Lilyan searched through her medicine chest for remedies to relieve her patient. Upon her instructions, using the candles from the lamp, Nicholas heated a tin cup of water into which she stirred chamomile tea leaves and herbs, aware that Paul hovered close by, concentrating on her every move. After concocting a paste, she spread it onto the quickly multiplying lesions on Cassia's body.

They had been cooped up an hour when Nicholas tapped on the door and ordered more water.

Within minutes, Hennessy entered, carrying a small keg. "Don't care what he says. I'm bringing this to ye." His grumbled *I'm sorries* and *It's not right*, as well as the wrinkles that dug into his forehead, confirmed his disapproval of his captain.

For what seemed hours, Lilyan pressed cold compresses to Cassia's forehead and the back of her neck in a futile effort to hold down her fever. Their vigil was broken once when Hennessey allowed them the use of the necessary and again when he brought them a keg and set it on the floor by the bed.

"What's this?" Nicholas faced Hennessey, his fists opening and closing at his sides, spurring Lilyan to stand beside him and slip her hand around his forearm.

"Hardtack." Prying off the keg top, Hennessey had the good grace to glance away.

Nicholas' arm muscles tightened beneath Lilyan's fingers. "This is all I am to feed my family, Mr. Hennessey? If so, it is beyond the pale."

Hennessey ducked his head. "Captain says no plates or utensils. A precaution, he says." Having spoken the pronouncement with much disgust, he reached into his pockets and withdrew three apples. "From Cook. For the children."

He extended his arms with an expression of such hesitancy Lilyan realized he stood prepared to be spurned.

She took the apples and handed them to Laurel. "Please tell the cook we appreciate his kindness, as we do yours, sir."

Hours later, Cassia's fever broke. She came to, panic growing in her eyes as they darted from one person to the next. While Lilyan fed her mush concocted of the salty crackers and water, she noticed the woman studying the boys, who sat in a corner quietly fletching arrows.

Laurel moved to stand beside the bed. "I wonder what she's thinking."

Lilyan dabbed Cassia's face with a cloth and placed the half-empty bowl on the table. "I would imagine—as I would be, finding myself in such a foreign place—she is sorting out her thoughts."

"Could we try speaking to her?" asked Marion, starting to uncurl from the floor.

Nicholas grabbed his son's arm and guided him back down beside him. "No. Boys, you must keep your distance. Our quarters may be close, but you must grant Cassia the privacy she is due as a woman. And, when someone is ill, we must needs keep our conversations low."

"Yes, Da," the boys whispered in unison.

Lilyan cherished her husband's genteel sentiments, and she caught his gaze and mouthed her thank-you.

Thank you again, Lord, for the gift of my beautiful husband.

Marion glanced at Cassia and, following his father's orders, he leaned forward and whispered, "How long must we stay here?"

Nicholas cleared his throat. "Until the captain comes to his senses."

The worry on her children's faces made Lilyan's stomach quiver.

Nicholas must have detected their uncertainty, for he clarified. "Not long, I'm certain."

Marion looked back and forth from mother to father. "What will happen to our family?"

"No harm. I promise," Nicholas spoke with assurance.

Marion's bottom lip trembled. "And Cassia? Captain Longstreet will not throw her overboard? Like the other captain?"

Nicholas threw his arm across his son's shoulder. "Let me sort that out, Son. You are not to worry about such things."

Lilyan retrieved her Bible from atop a chest in the corner of the room. "Shall I read awhile?"

To a chorus of *yes*es, she joined them on the floor and flipped through pages, choosing to read verses of encouragement about God's mercies. While she read, Nicholas replenished the candles in the lantern. When finally she closed the book, Marion stifled a yawn. It was then she noticed Laurel wilting against Paul's shoulder.

"Time for bed, my loves." Her pride in the way her children had behaved during their trial made a lump form in her throat.

Nicholas rose up onto his knees, bowed his head, and tented his hands. Lilyan and the children gathered into a close circle and followed his example.

"Lord. I look around this room and see the faces of my dear ones, who have endured much this day." Nicholas spoke in a low voice tinged with a slight Greek accent. "We are aware that our endurance comes from you. We are strong in your might. Oh, God of mercy, the young woman Cassia is suffering. We beseech you on her behalf, be merciful and bring her through this terrible illness. We bow before thee and invoke thy blessings in this time of trouble. We know not what tomorrow will bring, but ask in assurance thy aid as we are beset by foes, merciless and pitiless. Grant us a restful night, and may we enjoy your promise of new mercies in the morning."

Lilyan opened her eyes, and her attention was drawn to Cassia, who lay quietly staring at her with tears rolling down her cheeks.

Lord, she may not comprehend our language or our ritual. But she kens our feelings.

Lilyan leaned back against Nicholas, his strong, capable arms cupping hers. She twirled locks of Marion's hair as he rested his head on her thigh. Paul had already fallen asleep, lying on his back, his elbows bent, cradling his head in his hands. Laurel had curled into a ball, her back pressed against her father's leg.

She glanced at the empty hammocks swaying overhead. The children had chosen not to sleep in them. Instead, they gathered close, seeking warmth and security from each other.

Content for the moment, she dropped her head back and listened to the steady beat of her husband's heart and drifted off to sleep.

Hours later, she awoke to a knock and the creaking of the cabin door as it slowly opened. Nicholas steadied her shoulders and slid out from behind her. He carefully stepped over the children and met Mr. Whitehouse as he stuck his head around the door.

"I have bad news."

CHAPTER 5

*If I take the wings of the morning, and dwell in the uttermost
parts of the sea;
Even there shall thy hand lead me, and thy right hand shall
hold me.* Psalm 139:9–10 KJV

Two days later, Lilyan stood with her family on the beach
of a deserted island off the North Carolina coast. The wide
swath of white sands strewn with clumps of golden sea grass and
driftwood stretched as far north and south as she could see. The
salty aromas of ancient layers of sun-bleached shells wafting across
dunes evoked memories of Charleston, and she wished she and her
family had never left home.

Cassia and the Xanthakos family had been abandoned upon
the orders of Captain Longstreet, who had determined that they
presented an intolerable danger to himself, his vessel, and his
crew—in that order, Lilyan reflected. Nicholas had been livid and,
barely disguising his contempt, had spoken his mind in the most
scornful way possible. Sometimes lapsing into Greek, he enlisted
epithets she had never before heard. The one she did understand

brought heat to her cheeks, though the horrid captain deserved them and more.

Nicholas had threatened to sue the captain and the ship's owner, and he vowed that once he finished spreading the news of the captain's treatment of his family, no one would ever sail with him again. Despite Nicholas' protestations, the captain emphasized that his word was law on the high seas. Recalling the sneer on his face, Lilyan balled up her fists. As promptly as possible, he had abandoned them and all their belongings on the nearest stretch of land. At the determined behest of Mr. Whitehouse, the captain provided them with three days' rations, water, and tarpaulins for shelter, as well as a skiff and a map directing them to a nearby port.

With the heels of her shoes sinking into the crushed shells beneath her feet, she observed the crewmen unload the last of their possessions and dump them willy-nilly near the formidably dense woods of tall loblolly pine, red cedar, and scrub oaks. The cautious men kept their distance from Cassia, who lay in the shade on a mattress nearby. When they had completed their task, they lined up in a row, like a firing squad, facing the Xanthakos family.

Nicholas was the first to break the silence. "We thank you for your assistance, Mr. Whitehouse. You have behaved as a gentleman. Unlike your captain." He offered his hand.

A frown marring his handsome face, Mr. Whitehouse removed his hat and tucked it under his arm. "Beg your pardon. I cannot shake your hand, sir. Captain's orders. We are not to venture any closer than ten feet." He twisted his body toward the ship. "He's watching us. Any man who disobeys will be bent over a barrel, flogged, and thrown into the brig for the rest of our journey."

Mr. Hennessey harrumphed and shook his head. "It ain't right, I tell you. This is a dangerous place. Captain Longstreet shoulda picked some of us to stay with these people." He made a move to step forward. "By glory, I'm stayin'."

"Hold fast, Mr. Hennessey!" Mr. Whitehouse yelled. "Think what you're doing. Disobeying your captain's orders. You could be keelhauled. Or worse, he could hang you for mutiny."

The men on either side of Hennessey gripped his arms, and he struggled while they tried to reason with him. He surveyed Lilyan and her family, each in turn, his eyes mirroring his regret.

"Please, Mr. Hennessey," said Lilyan. "You've been kind to us. I couldn't bear to know that we had brought you harm."

He jerked his arms away from the men and grabbed his knife from his belt. "Here, boy." He motioned to Marion and threw the knife, which landed in the sand dead center between Marion's feet. "I can't stay and help ye, so I'm giving you my weapon. Keep it sharp, and it'll not let you down in times of trouble."

Marion bent down, wiped the blade on his breeches leg, and tucked it into his waistband. "I'm in your debt, sir."

It was a man's—a gentleman's—response, but coming from her young boy's mouth, it compelled Lilyan to regard him more closely. He had changed on this trip. They all had. None of her family would ever be the same after this.

After a round of good-byes, Mr. Whitehouse ordered the crew to wait for him in the dinghy. "Mr. Xanthakos, on behalf of my family, I offer my sincerest apologies for your abominable treatment aboard one of my father's ships. Rest assured, Captain Longstreet will no longer be employed once we reach Baltimore." He glanced at Laurel and cleared his throat. "I realize this is not the best time or place, but it's all I have, so I must speak. This was to be my last voyage before leaving the sea and helping my father with our business. It will take me about two to three years … That is, in three years I will be twenty-five and well established and able to consider matrimony and a family life."

He paused, and the dazed look in his eyes as he gazed at Laurel caused a lump in Lilyan's throat. She took a step closer to Nicholas and curled her fingers around his forearm.

The first mate continued, his face blazing red. "Laurel will be nineteen then. A good difference in age, don't you think?"

Nicholas had once spoken those very words to her. She sighed.

Another of her children was growing up.

Laurel, her hands folded demurely, glanced shyly at the ground, and then raised her head and bestowed on him a dazzling smile. His expression lit like a lighthouse beacon.

"You wish to court our daughter?" Nicholas asked gruffly. "In three years?"

Lilyan watched as many emotions—approbation, contemplation, sadness—played out in her husband's fine eyes. He turned to her with the unspoken question, and she nodded.

Nicholas cupped their daughter's chin in his fingertips. "'Tis your desire as well, sweet one?"

Her eyes teary, Laurel blinked, and her glance darted back and forth between her father and her new love. "Yes, Da. I should like it very much."

Her daughter's uncharacteristic shyness made Lilyan ache to clasp her in her arms and rock her the way she used to when she was a child. Where had the time gone? It seemed only yesterday that Laurel played with her dollies enclosed in a wagon bed while her parents worked nearby harvesting muscadine vines. Three years no longer sounded as far away as it once had.

Nicholas bent down to kiss Laurel's temple, then faced her anxious suitor. "You have my permission, Mr. Whitehouse. But as you yourself said, this is a bad time. Go. Return to your ship before there is trouble."

The young seaman slapped his hat back on his head. "I will write, Laurel. Uh, Miss Xanthakos. And you will write me too? I told you where?"

"I promise to write, Michael."

He seemed rooted to the spot by Laurel's use of his given name. Paul and Marion, who had been observing the exchange quietly, poked each other with their elbows. Paul snorted and jerked his head toward the beach. Deciding that they had seen enough, they ambled down the shore intent on finding a piece of wood to cut with Marion's new knife.

Nicholas chuckled. "Go."

With one last smile at Laurel, Mr. Whitehouse turned and trotted back to the boat.

Much later, after the *Merry Maid* heaved anchor and sailed north, Lilyan looked over her shoulder at Cassia lying on the mattress near the edge of the forest.

Notwithstanding the harm to her family, transporting the critically ill woman had proven the most heart-wrenching experience of all. Because the captain had refused to allow any of the crew near the family, it had been left to Nicholas and the boys to convey Cassia. They had enfolded her in a mattress, the boys on one end and Nicholas on the other, and with short, measured steps and as much care as they could manage, they carried her topside, across the deck, and into the skiff.

As Nicholas rowed them to shore, Paul had studied Cassia's face, alert to her smallest grimace or whimper. Lilyan watched her older son now farther down the beach stacking sticks of driftwood in his strong, capable arms.

He will make a fine physician.

She observed Laurel shoulder-deep in one of their storage chests retrieving the quilts, lap robes, and pewter ware they had packed. Marion chattered incessantly with his father and, employing his treasured knife, strung lengths of hemp rope between low-hanging limbs of oaks, over which they would drape pieces of mended sail for tents.

Her children had done well. *Lord, we thanked you when we arrived, but I'm thanking you again for blessing Nicholas and me with our dear children.*

She cupped her hand over her brow and shading her eyes from the late afternoon sun, she scanned the puffs of white clouds drifting across a peacock-colored sky that faded from brilliant azurite blue to violet. The weather was cooperating, no storms loomed on the horizon, and the wind wafting in from the sea had turned warm. *One good thing.*

She returned to a pile of kegs near the fire and sorted through their meager supplies trying to concoct something for dinner. She finally settled on boiled corn, bread, and cheese. Meanwhile, Nicholas and the boys erected two canvas shelters, closing off the sides with their baggage, leaving one end open facing west and the fire. With the same care as before, they carried Cassia inside one of the tents and laid her down, turning her so she could watch the fire. She had remained conscious the entire day, an interested, yet mute, observer.

After dinner, Laurel sat on a pallet beside Cassia and watched her brothers poke at the fire with sticks. The boys whooped with delight when sparks burst upward and curled into the plumes of the dark, pungent smoke. Each whoop was punctuated by a warning from Laurel to take care.

Nicholas held out his hand to Lilyan, and with fingers entwined they trudged over sandy dunes and around clumps of grass and spindly fronds of sea oats that bobbed their bowed heads in time with the breezes. They stopped at the edge of the water to gaze at the early evening stars poking one by one through gossamer veils of gray and apricot. Lilyan turned to face the ocean, amused by the tiny, stick-legged birds dancing on their tiptoes, just barely escaping the waves that pooled on the shore. A lone seagull screeched, caught in a crosswind that suspended it in motion. She spotted a ghost crab scooting across the sand, raising a set of its legs in the air like castanets. The thought of a crab playing castanets made her smile. Nicholas pulled her back against his chest and wrapped his arms around her waist. They stood quietly watching the full moon paint a golden pathway across the tips of the undulating waves.

She rested her arms on top of his. "What is our plan?"

"I've studied the map Mr. Whitehouse gave me, and I calculate, depending on the currents and if this weather holds, it will take us most of a day to reach Swansboro."

Lilyan loved the way his chest vibrated against her shoulder blades as he spoke.

"The craft is small. No room for baggage, except the essentials. When we reach Swansboro, I'll hire a schooner to return and retrieve our belongings."

"My medicine chest is essential. Yes?"

"Yes." He chuckled and then leaned down and kissed her temple. "It is so like you, *agapi mou*. Another woman might insist on her jewels."

"Humph. What are jewels compared to the health of my family?" She traced her fingers along his golden-brown arm. "It seems a long way to Swansboro. Will Laurel and I need to help row?"

"*Ah, diavolo!*" He grabbed her shoulders and spun her around. "No, a hundred times, no. And ruin these beautiful hands. It is unthinkable. We must keep them soft and smooth so that you will one day paint again. And"—his expression became tender—"to rock the sweet *mora* we will have."

He wants more babies. It was the first time he had mentioned having other children since Francis … Her heart leapt with joy. She longed for more children but hadn't said so, waiting for signs from Nicholas that he was healing from the loss of their dear little boy.

He kissed one of her palms and then the other and splayed her fingers across his chest. "And so that you may touch my body the way you are at this moment, *agapimeni mou gynaika*." *My beloved wife.*

She rose on tiptoe, eager for his kiss.

"Ma! Da!" Marion yelled.

"Come see," said Paul.

"The boys!" She could tell from her sons' voices that nothing was amiss.

Nicholas groaned, and Lilyan flashed him a wide smile. Grumbling, he took her by her elbow, and they walked to the dunes where Paul and Marion knelt in the deep, loose sand.

The boys had discarded their stockings and shoes, and Lilyan wondered where they had left them. The neat-leather shoes, purchased from a Charleston cordwainer, had cost a pretty penny. Nicholas had insisted the entire family be fitted with new shoes, but hadn't been prepared for the king's ransom they cost. When he received the cordwainer's bill, he complained that he hadn't intended to shoe the entire Continental Army. The astonishment on her husband's face still made Lilyan chuckle.

"Shhh." Paul put his finger to his lips and then pointed to the slowly growing mound of sand near his knee.

She leaned over and saw a turtle fanning her flippers back and forth digging a hole deeper and deeper, seemingly oblivious to her audience.

Marion's eyes grew so big, she could see the whites around the edges. "What is it?" he whispered.

Paul snorted. "It's a turtle, you addle pate."

"Your language," Nicholas warned.

Marion pursed his lips. "I know that. But it's huge."

Lilyan chuckled. "It's a sea turtle, dear. A loggerhead. You're used to our bog turtles that grow no bigger than the palm of your hand. These turtles live in the sea. The females come to shore about this time of year to lay their eggs. Though, this one is a bit early. Most will arrive next month."

"This turtle is nothing compared to the ones in Greece." Nicholas measured with his arms open wide. "Some grow large enough for you to ride upon their backs."

Paul's amazed expression mirrored Marion's. "Surely you josh, sir."

"I do not. When my brother and I were young boys, sometimes the turtles would allow us to hold on to their shells, and they would swim with us."

Lilyan draped her arm across Marion's shoulders. "Come away. We don't want to scare the mother lest she return to the water without laying her eggs."

With stars shining like burnished silver coins on a black velvet cloth, they returned to the campfire, where Lilyan read them the story of Jonah from her Bible. After kissing her children good night and checking on Cassia, who had fallen into a restful sleep, she spread pallets next to the fire. She and Nicholas settled on their backs, his arm curled around her. He laid a musket by his side and placed a tomahawk at his fingertips, a reminder of their unfamiliar surroundings. A breeze from the ocean rolled over them and swirled the flames of the fire until they crackled and popped.

She cuddled closer, twirling the string of his shirt around her finger. "Do you remember the first time we slept on the ground together?"

He clasped her hand to his heart. "I do."

"You were escorting me and Elizabeth to safety. Away from the bounty hunters."

He patted her hand. "You miss her still."

Sometimes the grief was as fresh as the day her dearest friend had died.

She drew circles in his skin that lay bare from his open shirt. "You had professed your love for me, and although we didn't know each other well, I trusted you with my life. Out in the middle of that ghastly swamp, lying on the black earth that smelled of overcooked eggs. You taught me which snakes to avoid and tried to teach me not to fear every crawly creature that ran across our path." She shivered, and he chuckled. "When I awoke one morning and found a beautiful white orchid next to me, I thought you the most wonderfully made man I had ever seen."

She traced her finger along a barely visible scar on his cheek where she had repaired a gash from a saber, using the smallest needle she possessed and making the tiniest of stitches with her finest silk thread. "Then came our time with General Marion."

She sighed. "Do you ever miss those days, Nikki?"

"I have worked hard to put them behind me. Though, I do miss the friendships. The hardships shared and the feeling that I was part of a cause much bigger than all of us put together." Nicholas' heartbeat trebled under her hand. "But I do not miss battle."

The war was long over, but the damage remained. Sometimes, without warning, the light in her husband's expressive eyes dimmed and he became pensive. He would stop whatever he was doing in the vineyard and seek out Lilyan, taking her by the hand and leading her deep into the forest. There, they would sit silently on a fallen log breathing in the fresh, clean air spiced with the scent of cedar and listening to the splashes of a nearby waterfall or the *caw, caw* of a crow on its way to feast on their grapevines.

One time when she saw tears pooling in his eyes, she hesitantly asked him if he wanted to share his burden with her. He had scrubbed away the tears with the back of his hand and shook his head. She reckoned his memories were too painful to speak about, even to her.

Nicholas blew out the breath he'd been holding in. "And now I find myself no longer the peaceable farmer tending to his vines, watching my children playing under their watchful mother's eyes. Instead, my actions have landed us here on this deserted … place. Forgive me."

Lilyan rose up, kissed him on his lips, and folded her arms on his chest. "There is no fault, so there is no forgiveness needed. I trust you with my life and the lives of our children. You are that kind of man, Nikki. Stalwart. Dependable. You will get us through this. I have no worries that you will deliver us to safety." Suddenly her empty stomach growled. "But let it be soon, dearest, for the bread and cheese are gone, and all that's left is hardtack and corn."

His stomach rumbled in agreement, and they laughed.

Settling her into the crook of his arm, he whispered, "Sleep now, my love. We have much ahead of us."

They prayed together, and then he pulled a quilt over them and they fell asleep wrapped in each other's arms.

Lilyan felt herself drifting awake, and she opened her eyes to a golden pink dawn. She shivered against a blanket soggy from the morning dew and snuggled closer to Nicholas until she felt a gentle shake on her shoulder and looked up to find Laurel, her tangled mass of red hair framing her face tight with anxiety.

"Ma." Her voice was hoarse and full of urgency. "Come. It's Cassia."

CHAPTER 6

Your eyes saw my substance, being yet unformed.
And in Your book they all were written,
The days fashioned for me,
When as yet there were none of them. Psalm 139:16 KJV

With the rising sun burning away the last smoky pink clouds of dawn, Lilyan huddled with Nicholas outside the tent, watching Laurel fan Cassia's face, shiny with perspiration. Every few minutes, Cassia's body would tense, and Laurel would cease fanning and massage her lower back.

Their daughter had met head-on the challenge of Cassia's care, expressing her desire to feel useful. But Lilyan sensed that was not Laurel's only compulsion. She was learning quickly her daughter's capacity for compassion. It was evident in her keen anticipation of her patient's needs, always at the ready with a wet cloth, and the way she carefully changed the bandages on Cassia's neck and wrists. Lilyan's chest fairly burst with pride in Laurel's maturity, especially at her tender age when most girls occupied themselves with what dress to wear to the next party.

Nicholas studied his only daughter, his eyes soft with affection. "She will grow up to be a fine woman." He pushed a tendril of Lilyan's hair away from her forehead. "I desired to shelter her from the bad things of this world. But I can see that I would have erred denying her this."

Deep in thought, he moved his attention to Cassia. "Her labor has started?"

"Yes." Lilyan mentally ticked off a list of necessary medicines and supplies.

"How long do you think?"

"I have no way of knowing. But she's young, which may mean a long time."

Nicholas frowned. "We will postpone our departure, then."

"Do you think that wise?" Lilyan clasped his forearm, not wanting to say what she was about to. "The sooner you leave, the sooner you'll return."

"*I* leave? You're suggesting I go without you?" The furrow in his brow deepened.

"It only makes sense." She glanced again at Cassia. "It may take all day. Two days. And there is no certainty that she and the baby will be fit to travel straight away. Our food won't last that long."

He rubbed his face with his hands and raked his fingers through his hair, which had fallen loose about his shoulders. "You're right. I don't like it. But you are right."

His hand on the small of her back, he guided her toward the fire, where they sat on upright kegs. She remained quiet while he added another piece of wood to the white-hot coals.

Crossing one ankle over the other, she winced. "Ugh. I should not have put my shoes back on without my stockings no matter how many burrs they attract. The sand between my toes is burning."

"Here," he offered, clasping her legs and resting them on his thighs.

He pulled off her shoes and knocked them together, dumping out the sand. When he started briskly rubbing her calves and ankles and massaging the bottoms of her feet, she sighed in bliss.

He smiled, enjoying her reaction. She arranged the folds of her homespun dress. Before leaving the ship, she and Laurel had donned the honey-colored linen dresses they had packed in anticipation of the wagon ride home from Roanoke. Not knowing the manner of journey that lay ahead—would they travel far … over difficult terrain … or in haste?—they had also dispensed with all save one layer of petticoats.

"You will need Laurel. Yes?"

They both watched Laurel hold a cup up to Cassia's lips and heard her gentle encouragement to take as much as she wanted.

"Yes," Lilyan answered. "Our daughter has proved herself to be a fine nurse."

Nicholas let out a breath through his nose. "Here is our plan. I will take Marion with me, as he tends to find trouble." He smiled, the lines in his cheeks crinkling. "I will tell him I need him as a rower and navigator."

She returned his smile. Marion would take pride in feeling useful.

"Paul will stay as protector. We will take only water and hardtack with us." He cocked his head. "'Tis a good plan. Yes?"

"Yes."

Apart again. Was she as confident as she professed?

She slid from the keg and onto his lap and wound her arms around his neck. Pressing her face into the crook of his neck, she twirled one of his ebony curls around her finger. "When?"

He ran his fingertips up and down her arm, sending goose bumps across her skin. "Right away."

"Oh." She gulped down her anxiety and attempted to put on a brave front. "We will care for each other until your return."

He didn't respond, other than to reach down and retrieve her shoes. "You have your stockings?"

She pulled her stockings out from her underskirt pocket.

He glanced over his shoulder at Laurel occupied in the tent

behind them and then scanned the encampment for the boys. Spotting them on the beach, he took the stockings. "Let me."

The warmth of his hands as he slid her stockings into place caused her heart to thrum. It wasn't a new gesture on his part, by any means—after all, they had been married seventeen years—but the fact that it was occurring out in the open and not in the privacy of their bedroom … the intimacy caused a hitch in her breath.

She stood and caressed his cheek, scanning his face rough from two days' stubble. His eyes held hers captive for a moment, transmitting heart-tripping emotions that spurred her to move around behind him, pull the ribbon from her braid, and tie back his hair with it. Her fingertips tingling from contact with his unruly, thick curls, she leaned over, breathed in the warm, salty aroma of his hair, and kissed his exposed neck just beneath his ear. What would she do without him?

He leaned back against her. "This is difficult."

She rested her hands on his shoulders. "It's time to tell the children."

He groaned and then quickly gathered the family to disclose the plan. Afterward, without a word, Paul stowed his father's musket and tomahawk in his tent and tucked a knife into his belt. Marion found a canteen in one of the trunks and filled it with water. He stacked a pile of hardtack into a square of burlap, tied the ends, and stashed it next to the boat seat with his bow and arrows.

In no time, Lilyan, Laurel, and Paul stood at the edge of the water waving their arms in the air in response to Marion's exuberant good-byes. Her children returned to their tasks while she watched the boat grow smaller and smaller before it finally disappeared. Blinking back her tears, with her chest aching as if someone had thumped her on her breastbone, she returned to the tent.

Cassia struggled for hours, moaning softly, stoically braving each wave of pain.

Outside, Paul lowered his head beneath the canvas and peered at them. "May I be of help, Ma?"

Lilyan placed herself between him and Cassia. "Thank you. No. This is women's business."

She knew he was curious, but he would find out early in his medical studies that doctors did not deliver babies. That was left to midwives and women like herself.

Several hours into her labor, Cassia's body seemed to sink into the mattress, and her chest became still.

"Ma?" Laurel touched Cassia's arm. "She's cold."

Had her heart stopped? What should she do? Lilyan jerked the covers away and pressed her fingers to Cassia's throat, digging her fingers into the skin, searching for a pulse. "Rub her arms and legs. Up and down, quickly," she ordered.

Massaging the skin over Cassia's heart, she beseeched, "Cassia, dear, please, have courage. Try. Please try. Not much longer."

Whatever made me think I could do this? Lord .... She couldn't even finish her prayer.

Moments later, Cassia sucked in a tiny breath. Lilyan pressed her ear to her stomach and heard the distinct, much faster heartbeat of the child. Mother and child had survived the ordeal. Lilyan's heart leapt with relief, and the tension eased from her shoulders.

"Dare we hope now, Lord?" Lilyan whispered, wiping away the perspiration beads above her lips and fanning her underarms, the material now clammy with sweat.

The pains increased in intensity and frequency until Lilyan lost track of time. Suddenly, Cassia's body arched and she threw back her head. Stark shadows of the noonday sun that painted the sands around them a brilliant white accentuated the strained cords throbbing in her neck. With her arms and legs trembling uncontrollably, she groaned and made one final push, bringing her daughter into the world.

Staring at the baby's wildly pumping arms and legs, Laurel gasped. "She's hardly bigger than Father's hand."

Lilyan sat back on her heels and counted the tiny nut-brown toes and fingers. "But she's perfect."

The baby scrunched up her face and gave out a mewling noise that sounded so much like a kitten, Laurel clapped her hands in delight. Lilyan, her spirits lighter than they had been in days, cleaned the exhausted mother and draped fresh covers across her. After she cleaned the baby, Laurel wrapped her in a piece of a cotton chemise they had torn for swaddling and nappies.

"Here she is, Cassia. Your precious baby girl." Sitting up on her knees, Lilyan leaned over to present the now quiet little bundle.

At first, Cassia's eyes seemed to devour her child, but she suddenly looked askance. She balled her fist and pushed her baby away.

Laurel knelt down beside the mattress, her lips trembling as she traced her finger across the baby's arm. "She refuses her?"

"I don't..."

Cassia, her face turning a startling gray, stared into Lilyan's eyes, placed her fist on her heart, and then pointed her finger toward Lilyan.

It took Lilyan a moment to comprehend, and when she did, an ache took hold of her, filling her body with such unspeakable grief, she found it difficult to breathe.

Gathering the baby to her heart, she tried to smile, but her lips quivered too much. "I accept your gift, dear Cassia. And I vow to love this little one as my own." A sob caught in her throat. "She will know how brave her mother was and what you suffered to bring her into this world."

Stunned by her mother's words, Laurel began to weep. Tears spilled down her cheeks and her shoulders shook.

Paul, who had been waiting patiently outside the tent, called out, "Ma. What's happening? Is all well?"

"Come in, Son." Lilyan held the baby with one hand and curled the other over Cassia's hand that still rested on her chest.

Paul scanned their stricken faces, and he stood behind Laurel, patting her shoulder. "Don't cry, Sissy."

Lilyan leaned back against his strong legs, and he bent down for a better view of the baby's face. "Pretty," he said in a voice filled with wonder.

Cassia flinched and clutched Lilyan's hand. Her face muscles tensed, and she lifted her head off the mattress. She moved her lips, her face a study of frustration. "Ca … Ca." She struggled. "Ca-sha."

Shaking, Lilyan cleared her throat. "I understand. You want her name to be Cassia."

The frail young woman dropped her head back and smiled. She exhaled a long deep breath and closed her eyes.

Her own pulse pounding in her neck, Lilyan held the sleeping baby in one hand and with the other she felt Cassia's wrist for signs of life.

Laurel's panicked glance bobbed from her mother, to Cassia, to the baby, and back. "She isn't?" Her face crumpled, unable to say the dreaded word.

Lilyan gingerly placed the sleeping baby on the end of the mattress and pressed her ear to Cassia's heart.

Nothing. Not a sound. Life had slipped away from the woman whose face, now in repose, seemed as content as Lilyan had ever seen it.

Had she understood me? Did I make myself clear? Did she leave this world knowing that her daughter would be cherished and cared for?

Lilyan put her arm around her distraught daughter. "She is gone, dear one. But know this: You made her last hours on Earth as comfortable as you could. You cared for her as diligently and completely as a mother would her own child. God was honored in what you did."

Laurel began sobbing in earnest, and Lilyan no longer tried to hold back the tears that streamed down her cheeks. Paul stood with his hands on their shoulders.

They buried Cassia in the woods underneath a canopy of pine trees. Using a spade from their supplies, Paul dug the grave deep enough so the resting place could not be disturbed by the animals that roamed the forest. Laurel held the baby while Lilyan and Paul covered the gravesite with pine branches. Afterward, Lilyan led them in prayer, witnessed by two white-tailed deer that bounded toward them and, startled, quickly fled away.

Halfway back to the campsite, Laurel stopped walking and faced Lilyan. "Ma, do you think Cassia knew about our Lord Jesus?

"We cannot know that."

"If she didn't, does that mean she isn't in heaven now?"

Paul came to a halt, also waiting for her answer.

Lilyan put her arm around Laurel's waist and took Paul by his hand. "No one can know what God is thinking, although he has revealed himself through nature and through the Scriptures. He created man with a will and a conscience. Only he understands the hearts of people, and I'm certain he wouldn't punish them for their ignorance. He would judge them, though, if they had knowledge of him and chose to turn away."

Laurel's face relaxed, and she smiled down at the babe. "I will imagine your ma in heaven, then."

Later, they sat together by the fire welcoming the cool, late afternoon breezes that made the tops of the sea oats bob like gentlemen in a crowded ballroom requesting a dance. Deep in thought, Lilyan held the baby and watched a flock of pelicans glide overhead in a lazy line. Seagulls dove into the ebb swells and rose again with tiny fish wriggling in their beaks.

The peaceful scene contrasted directly with the turmoil in her mind.

Baby Cassia began to stir, and once fully awake, she squalled as loudly as her little lungs could manage.

Paul clamped his hands over his ears. "Whatever is the matter?"

Lilyan put her little finger next to Cassia's tiny lips. She stopped crying long enough to suck on Lilyan's finger but soon became frustrated. Lilyan knew the fragile baby wouldn't last long without nourishment. "She's hungry, but I don't know what or how we're going to feed her."

Paul leaned forward on the keg seat. "Ma. Do you remember the time Aunt Golden Fawn took me to visit the medicine man of her village?"

"I do."

He had come back with his head full of knowledge about herbs and natural remedies and couldn't wait to write them in his journal, where he kept his drawings of every animal he had come in contact with.

"The shaman told the story of a Cherokee man whose wife died having their child. He was in the wilderness far from his village. To keep the baby alive, he cooked corn, chewed it up until it was almost liquid, then spit it into the baby's mouth."

Laurel huffed. "That's disgusting."

Paul snorted. "It's what mama birds do every day."

Laurel crinkled her nose. "We are not birds, Paul."

"He may have something." Lilyan pointed to a sack of corn next to the fire. "Laurel, find a tin cup and put a few spoons of water in it and some kernels of corn. We'll set it next to the fire until it boils down."

Paul hopped off the keg. "Let me."

"All right. Then, Laurel, let's tear a strip from the baby's cover. It will serve as a strainer."

With pitiful cries ringing in their ears, they soon had a cup of corn milk into which Lilyan dipped the piece of finely woven cotton cloth. She wrapped it around her little finger and put it in the baby's mouth. Cassia instantly began feeding on the makeshift nipple, amazing Lilyan with the strength of her jaws. Paul laughed at her suckling noises. Finally, sated or exhausted, Lilyan wasn't sure which, the baby fell asleep. Laurel carried her to one of the tents and laid her inside a small chest she had fashioned into a cradle.

The children sat on kegs nibbling salty squares of hardtack while Lilyan heated water for the last cup of coffee. When she stood, her cheeks felt so flushed she fanned them with her hands.

"Here, Ma. This will help." Laurel popped open her fan and started wafting it on Lilyan's face and neck.

Sweet girl. She should be at a dance, peeping from behind the fan, flirting with some dashing young man instead of here, cooling off her exhausted mother.

It felt so good, Lilyan closed her eyes and sighed. Hearing a rattling noise behind her, she turned around and was startled to find a group of men leaving the beach and heading their way. Her gasp caused Paul to spin around.

He studied the intruders. "Don't like the looks of them."

Watching them approach, Lilyan's pulse began to pound in her throat. Four of the men wore canvas doublets, breeches, and knitted Monmouth caps. The fifth wore a pair of breeches with garish violet stripes and a drop-shouldered shirt with billowing sleeves. He had tied a multicolored scarf over his shoulder-length stringy hair and topped it with a wide-brimmed felt hat. Some of their clothing was tattered, and all were covered with grimy streaks of dirt and grease. The flamboyant one wore a cutlass, and the rest had pistols and knives stuffed into their waistbands. Watching them slither in single file through the dunes—swaggering, arrogant, grinning—made the hairs on her arms and neck spring up like quills on a porcupine. Her spine straightened and the muscles in her stomach constricted.

She had come across men of their ilk as a young girl in Charleston. She had been visiting the tavern of a friend with Callum when two men, dressed in similar garb as the men snaking toward her, entered and sat at a nearby table. Even at age twelve she had sensed the heightened tension among the customers and worried when Callum swung his musket up and rested it across his arms. The proprietor grumbled as he served the men, warning them to drink quickly and leave. She made the mistake of staring directly at one of the men. He glared, his glistening eyes black as night. He sneered and winked, and for the first time in her life she knew what being in the presence of evil felt like—cold, dark, and vulnerable.

Paul leapt up and dashed toward the tent for the musket. Lilyan held out her arm and motioned for Laurel to come close.

"Who are they?" Laurel whispered, her eyes wide with fear.

Fear, like a bogle in the night, crept up her chest and clasped its bony fingers around her neck. "Pirates."

CHAPTER 7

"Don't come any closer." Paul leveled his musket at the marauders poised on the leeward side of the dunes.

The wiry, flamboyant man in the black hat made a mock salute and then pretended to yawn. "You have us at your mercy, lad." He grinned over his shoulder at his companions. "I do have an observation. You have but one shot, and there are five of us. What will you do?"

"You appear to be their leader. I'll shoot you first." Paul trained the musket at his heart.

Lilyan couldn't have been prouder of her son nor more frightened for him.

The man's jaw muscle twitched. "Someone taught you well, young fellow. Though you must learn to cover your flank."

Lilyan saw a flash of motion from the corner of her eye and watched in dread as a blackjack flew through the air and caught Paul with a *thwack* on the side of his head. He crashed to the ground, discharging the musket. Ears ringing from the explosion coupled with Laurel's scream, she dropped beside Paul and cradled his head in her lap. She trembled at the sight of the blood oozing from a gash above his right ear.

Dear Lord, let him be all right. She ran her fingers up and down his arms and pressed her hand to his heart. *He still breathed,* but he was too pale.

At that moment, the baby began screaming, drawing the attention of the men who had closed in on them.

"What in thun—"

"Cassia!" Laurel gathered her skirts and ran toward the tent, the men close on her heels.

Paul moaned, and his eyes fluttered open as Lilyan wiped away the blood with the hem of her skirt to get a better look at the wound. The three-inch-long gash wasn't deep enough to leave a scar, but it would take days to heal, if they could keep infection out. Looking up at the group of men who surrounded them, she shuddered with the emotions that roared through her—panic, hatred, fear. Her body could barely contain them. Most of all the fear, which left a metallic tasted in her mouth.

"It's not bad, Paul. Plenty of blood, but that's because it's a scalp wound."

He moved his head to agree, wincing at the motion.

She ripped a strip of cloth from her petticoat, folded part of it to form a pad, and secured it by wrapping another piece around his head.

Laurel, holding the baby tightly to her breast, returned and skirted her way through the men and stood next to Lilyan. "Is it bad?" Her voice quivered so much, Lilyan could barely understand.

"Ma says it's a graze. Don't worry, Sissy."

The man who had followed Laurel stroked his fiery red beard and leaned over to peer at Cassia. "Sink me. It's a babe. Haven't seen one o' them since—well—since I was one meself."

Another man, his forearms as big around as kegs, took one look at the bundle in Laurel's arms and scowled. "It's a blackamoor."

The leader lifted his eyebrows, rested his hand on his cutlass, and then bowed to Lilyan. "I've been remiss, madam. Let me introduce myself. I'm Bowen, first mate of the *Akantha*."

The Greek word for *thorn*. Lilyan felt a tingle across the back of her neck.

"This here, with the red beard, is Marteen. Next to him, the one with the barrel arms is Roche. The skinny one is Henreques, and olive-skinned one is Manuel. The one who thumped your young man is Cesare."

Lilyan swept a glance over each man as his name was called. Ignoring their bows and mumbled salutations, she thought it bizarre that Bowen was making introductions as if they were meeting at some social function. She had learned from Callum that men became pirates for various reasons. Many were press-ganged or sailors aboard captured ships given the choice of death or piracy. And then there were men like Bowen, who deliberately chose debauchery. Obviously educated, cultured, and taught manners at one time, men of his sort enjoyed danger and excitement and the freedom to indulge their basest impulses. Lilyan sized up the men and determined that among them, Bowen posed the biggest threat.

"Ha!" Bowen chuckled. "The woman stares daggers at us. If looks could kill, we would be dead three times counting."

Cesare snorted. "Come. Let's see if there's any swag to be had."

All but Marteen followed him and started tossing the contents out of the trunks that had served as a barricade for the makeshift home. Lilyan searched Paul's eyes for signs of concussion, but they were as clear as ever, only a bit sad.

"I'm sorry, Ma," he muttered and then took a quick look around. "Remember what Da says about capture?"

Try to escape early on. If you're caught, try again, and often. If you get away, good. If you don't, they might admire your gumption and let you live. But Nicholas referred to Indians, who had respect for courage and strength. Would the same reasoning apply to pirates?

She hunched her shoulders and dropped her voice low, "Choose wisely. I'll try to help."

Bowen sidled closer. "What are you two mumbling about?"

Lilyan looked up into what she had thought were black eyes; close up they were swamp-water brown. "Trying to see if he's ready to stand or if he needs help."

Paul pushed himself onto his knees and, leaning on one of the barrels, struggled to his feet.

Bowen, smirking, glanced back and forth between mother and son. "And now," he addressed Paul, "you are?"

Paul adjusted the bandage, which had fallen down on his ear. "I am Paul Xanthakos. This is my mother and my sister."

Bowen arched an eyebrow. "They have names?"

Paul set his jaw. "None that you would be privy to."

Lilyan's breath hitched. *Don't test this one.*

A sardonic gleam lit the man's eyes. "Careful, lad."

When Marteen moved toward Paul, Lilyan made a bow. "Lilyan. My name is Lilyan Xanthakos, and my daughter's name is Laurel."

Bowen swept his hat from his head and returned an exaggerated bow. "My privilege, ladies. I must say I haven't seen such beauties in many a passing tide."

The man's lascivious glances formed a knot of dread in Lilyan's stomach.

He clasped her hand as if to kiss it, but she jerked it away, and he chuckled. "Where is your most fortunate husband?"

When no one answered, he pulled a knife from his leather baldric and began to dig the dirt from underneath his fingernails. "I have only a small measure of patience. Is that not so, Marteen?" Quicker than a flash of lightning he pressed the knife against Paul's neck.

Paul curled his hands around Bowen's arm and pulled down, but couldn't loosen the viselike grip.

"Stop, please," Lilyan begged. "My husband has gone to find help."

"Much better." He removed the knife, leaving a bloody nick in Paul's skin.

Eyes blazing with hatred, Paul scrubbed the blood from his

neck with the back of his hand.

Bowen returned his knife to his belt. "How came you to be in this deserted place?"

"The captain of the ship we were sailing on discovered that my ... maid was ill. For his crew's safety—at least that's what he said—he landed us here."

"What kind of illness?"

"A fever. She had a fever." Lilyan bit her bottom lip, which refused to stop trembling.

He held up his hand and nonchalantly inspected his fingernails. "Where is she?"

Paul took a step toward Lilyan. "Dead. We buried her this afternoon. Yonder." Paul pointed toward the gravesite. "She died in childbirth. This is her baby girl."

Bowen frowned. "Unfortunate. Slaves bring a high price." He looked past Paul. "How goes the search?"

"Nothin' worth much." Cesare held up a pair of pantaloons and started to dance around. The others pointed at him and laughed.

Make all the merry you want. She had the satisfaction of knowing they hadn't discovered the false bottom in one of the trunks where Nicholas had hidden their money and her jewels.

Bowen stood arms akimbo and let out a belly laugh. "Bag what you can, then come here. We must decide what to do with our new friends."

Lilyan's heart raced. She held her children's hands, and they watched and listened while the raggedy crew hammered out their fate.

Taking a step back, Marteen yelled, "I ain't ever killed no babe and ain't about to start now."

The blood rushed from Laurel's face. "Surely, they would not..."

For what seemed an eternity, Lilyan studied the pirates. Cesare made a slashing movement with his hand across his neck that provoked Marteen to cuff him on his shoulder. The two of them carried on an animated conversation, Marteen becoming more and more agitated, shaking his fist in Cesare's face. Meanwhile, Bowen stood nonchalantly resting his hand on the hilt of the cutlass at his waist. The rest shrugged their shoulders as if they didn't care one way or the other.

Finally, Bowen moved away from the group and stood before Lilyan. "It's settled."

"Yes?" It was all she could squeak through her constricted throat.

"We take you back with us. The captain has standing orders. He gets first choice of female prisoners." He winked at her. "I'm willing to wager a chest of gold he'll take a shine to you."

Lilyan's skin crawled as if spider webs had trickled down her arms. "The children?"

"The young beauty will fetch a king's ransom at auction. The boy will be sold as well. If we can find someone to take him on." He chuckled, a malicious grinding sound deep in his throat.

Lilyan closed her eyes to the horror of what she was hearing. She swallowed hard. "And the baby?"

"It lives. For now. Unless it starts caterwauling."

His pronouncement twisted like a knife in Lilyan's stomach. It had been a while since Cassia's last feeding. "How far to our destination?"

"Two mile of walk and two mile of row to the next island. Not long," Marteen answered with a hesitant look at Cassia.

Maybe this giant of a man wasn't as cruel as the others. The thought was somewhat comforting.

Bowen whirled back to his crew, the crimson feather on his cap bobbing. "Heave anchor. We're done here."

Marteen grabbed Lilyan's elbow, but she pulled away. "Please, Mr. Bowen, may my daughter fetch my medicine chest and some things for the baby?"

Bowen pondered her request and then jerked his head toward the tent. "Hurry."

Leaning over to take Cassia, Lilyan whispered, "Leave a sign. You remember how?"

"I remember." Laurel ran to the tent and gathered the medicine chest, nappies, and the sack of corn.

To take the men's eyes off her daughter, Lilyan moved forward and feigned a trip.

"Steady, madam," Marteen said, clasping her arm.

Approaching the dunes, Paul staggered, causing the others to snicker. Lilyan wanted to encourage him but knew the sentiment would only provoke more derision. Though they had never faced trials like this before, her children were strong. Their father had made sure of that.

Nicholas, come find us. Soon, dearest.

Their walk took less time than Lilyan realized. Somewhere along the way, Cesare left the group, but he returned just as she spotted a skiff moored on the beach at the southern tip of the island.

"Please." Lilyan approached Mr. Bowen. "Before we board, may my daughter and I..." She hesitated, feeling the heat in her face. "May we have a moment of privacy?"

"What?" His expression changed from quizzical to derisive. "Yes. But don't go far. Hand the baby to your son. And don't dally about."

She handed Cassia to Paul and took Laurel's hand, and they hurried toward a thick patch of sea grass, ducking behind the barrier.

"We don't have long. Grab some shells and make an arrow pointing south." Nauseated from the nerves that heaved in her stomach, Lilyan peeked up over the grass to find the men busy filling the boat. She clasped Laurel's hand. "Paul contemplates escape. I know not when, but we must be alert. And dear one, know that your father will find us. Whatever occurs. If we are separated—"

"Oh, Ma." Laurel stopped placing the shells and gripped

Lilyan's hands. Her normally graceful body was taut with tension that accentuated the cords in her neck.

"If we are separated. Never despair. However long it takes, we will be together again." Lilyan gulped, unsure how much she should say. "If they harm you, remember it is your earthly body. God has made our bodies such that they heal wondrously. But he has made our spirits indomitable. No one can touch what belongs to the Lord. You understand?"

Her eyes wide with fear, Laurel worried her bottom lip. "I do."

Lilyan pulled her precious daughter into her arms and breathed her in—the trace of rose water in her hair, the sweat, and the sweet aroma so uniquely hers that permeated her clothing.

Lord, you gave this treasure to me. Spare her, please. Give her—give all of us—strength to endure whatever comes.

"Ladies, we await," Mr. Bowen yelled from the shore.

Holding hands, they walked down the beach, where Lilyan took Cassia from Paul and they boarded the skiff.

It wasn't long before Lilyan spotted a line of trees in the distance, and she reckoned they were nearing the halfway mark between the two islands. She caught Paul's eye for a moment and read the determination in his eyes. *This is it.* In an instant, he stood and dove into the water.

Caught off guard, the men scrambled about bellowing their confusion: "Where's my pistol?" "Why weren't you watching him?" "I'm on the oars, you fool."

"What the…?" Mr. Bowen grabbed a pistol from his belt. "Stop rowing!" he roared. "Cesare, keep a watch. The rest of you, pipe down. He's got to come up soon."

All was quiet, except for the squeaking of the oars against the iron rings. The wind itself seemed to stop blowing. Lilyan cast a reassuring glance at Laurel. What they knew, but these men did not, was Paul's extraordinary ability to remain under water for long periods of time. He had frightened the living daylights out of her and Nicholas many times on family swims in the river before they realized his skill. Still, Bowen was correct. Paul would have to surface sometime.

"There!" Cesare stood, rocking the boat precariously from side to side, and aimed his pistol at a disturbance in the water not fifteen feet away.

The men trained their weapons on the same spot until Bowen scowled and screamed out his frustration. "That's a dolphin, you chum bucket!"

While the others watched the shiny body of the blue-skinned dolphin curl up and down in the water, Lilyan scanned the sound between the two islands and spotted the moment Paul lifted his head out of the water and dipped back down again. Her heart tripped, but the others seemed intent on the dolphin, now accompanied by five or six others.

Startled, Cassia started squirming and began to squall.

The malicious gleam in Bowen's eyes as he turned toward her turned her skin cold. "Belay that. Or it'll soon join your son."

Knowing that Cassia would sense her distress, she gathered all her strength to calm herself. She began to coo and rock the child until finally she fell back into slumber. The time would come soon when cooing and rocking would not satisfy the babe. She prayed they would reach the pirates' port before then.

"He's gone. No one could last that long under the water." Bowen grumbled and sat back down. "Look at their faces. Is that hope I see? What say you if I told you that Cesare found your pitiful attempts to leave signals?"

Lilyan gasped.

"Cesare turned them in the opposite direction. When your husband returns and finds his family gone and sees your signals, he will head north." He grinned. "Clever, our Cesare. Yes?"

Disappointment washed over Lilyan like a tidal wave.

Cesare bowed from the waist, and Bowen threw back his head and laughed. "Heave to. And put some back into it."

They came aground on an island almost identical to the one

they had left. Two of the men hopped out and dragged the boat up onto the sand next to a small armada of dinghies and skiffs. Marteen was the only one to offer a hand to Lilyan and Laurel when they jumped from the boat. They had been slogging about a mile when Cassia started crying again.

"I warned you." Bowen squinted, his face resembling a dried out prune.

"She's hungry." Irritation filled Laurel's voice.

Bowen snarled. "So are the alligators."

Marteen clasped Laurel and Lilyan by their elbows. "Not far, now. Hurry on." He looked askance at Bowen. "We're coming to a cabin. It belongs to our carpenter, a freed black, and his wife. Her baby died a few days ago. She can nurse the babe."

Bowen snickered. "Well, Marteen, I believe that's the most words I've heard out of your mouth in a while. Have you gone soft on us?"

Marteen glared at him, the ribbons tied to the plaits in his red beard trembling with his ire. "I've warned you, Bowen. Leave me be, or I'll slice you from gullet to liver when you least expect it."

The muscles in the huge man's body radiated so much menace, the hairs on Lilyan's arms tingled.

Bowen grinned and held up his hands in mock horror.

She heard the hammering before she saw the tiny cabin tucked away beneath a stand of loblollies. At the cabin's entrance, a porch roof jutted out about ten feet, providing shade for a short, stocky black man intent on constructing a ladder-back chair. Beside him, weaving sweetgrass for the chair bottom, sat a rotund woman, her skin the color of café au lait. She was singing a song in the sweet Gullah language so familiar to Lilyan that it brought tears to her eyes. As a young girl, growing up in Charleston, she had loved to mimic the language, delighting in the mixture of Portuguese and English mellowed with the essence of the African Rice Coast.

The woman saw the group first and stood. "Samuel, cump'ny comin'."

The man, his onyx-colored face wet and the armpits of his homespun shirt stained with large dark crescents, put down his hammer and stared.

As soon as she caught the sound of Cassia's crying, the woman lifted her skirts and ran toward them, her bare feet kicking up sprays of sand. She stopped in front of Lilyan and peeked into the swaddling. Her eyes grew big and round when she spotted the tiny brown babe with skin a slightly darker shade than her own.

"Who be dish littleun here?" She clasped her hands to the front of her dress where two dark stains were spreading around her breasts. Her milk! Lilyan could have wept with relief.

"I be Lilyan Xanthakos. Dishyah my daa'tuh, Cassia."

The woman's eyebrows rose in surprise. "Oona Golla talk?"

Lilyan nodded. "She bin bawn one day. Nyam cawn milk."

Mr. Bowen closed in on them. "What are you two blabbering about?"

Without taking her eyes from the woman's face, she answered, "We're speaking Gullah. I told her this is my one-day-old daughter who has been eating only corn milk."

Samuel, barefooted and wiping his hands on the thighs of his canvas breeches, moved toward his wife. "I told you enough times to speak English. Gullah gonna get you in trouble."

Holding out her arms, the woman ignored his scolding. "I be Izzie. Gimme de chile." Clutching Cassia to her breast, she threw a scowl at Mr. Bowen. "Dat one wickit."

Wicked was too tame a word for Mr. Bowen.

She carried Cassia into the cabin, but when Lilyan and Laurel started to follow, Bowen shook his head. "Not you two. We leave it here."

"But—" Lilyan's protest was cut off by Bowen, who raised his hand as if to hit her. Instead, he shoved her away from the cabin so hard she stumbled.

Izzie called out from the doorway, "I puhtek dis gal. My pledjuh."

"T'engky, dear Izzie," Lilyan called out, thanking the woman for promising to protect the little girl. Cassia would have someone to care for her, but who was caring for her son? Where was he? Was he safe? It took every bit of strength Lilyan had to quash the melancholia that invaded her thoughts.

"Cast off, ladies. We have business." Bowen smirked. "You have yet the pleasure of meeting Captain Galeo."

Galeo. Greek for *shark*.

Lilyan cringed against the tingle crawling across the back of her neck.

CHAPTER 8

The motley group trudged the beach, passing an ever-increasing number of dwellings slapped together with lengths of rope and flotsam. The huts, listing like drunken sailors on their first night of shore leave, seemed poised to topple with the next hearty ocean breeze. As word spread of the captives' arrival, the occupants of those hovels sauntered through the gaping holes that served as doorways, where they observed the new prisoners, some yelling in languages Lilyan didn't understand.

One scruffy man, barefooted, shirtless, his canvas breeches shredded at the knees, and relieving himself beside a tree, called out, "*Hola, chicas.* Welcome to our little piece of hell."

Cringing, Lilyan wished she hadn't been able to understand that greeting. One glance at Laurel's pale cheeks and she quickly draped her arm around her waist. Her heart ached with longing for her husband and youngest, with anguish for her elder son, and with fear for her daughter being bludgeoned with obscenities and facing only God knew what. Her arms felt empty of the child who had nestled against her breast. Anxiety ran rampant through her body in alternating waves of cold and heat. Every step she took evoked a prayer for deliverance.

The farther they travelled, the more numerous the shelters became until they reached a town of sorts built on the edge of a crescent inlet, where two ships were anchored, both two-masted brigantines. Around the perimeter of the bay, more oddly fashioned dwellings with unevenly slanted roofs were attached one to the other, extending out from a large central building, reminding Lilyan of mud dauber nests. Women clad in only their stays and pantaloons slinked to the doorways or leaned against an assortment of pirates who yelled out wicked comments that stung like wasps, causing Lilyan to drop her head and stare at her boots.

An image of Nicholas came to mind, his expression serious, his words a warning. "When in danger, purge your heart and mind of all emotion. Anger, fear, and revenge will only cloud your judgment. Center your thoughts and hone your wits to needle sharpness. Observe everything—the lay of the land, possible escape routes, places where you can attack your enemies. Look for weapons. Sometimes a piece of metal or a splinter of wood is all that's needed."

Bolstered, Lilyan focused on her surroundings and took deep mental breaths to suppress the revulsion stealing through her body.

Following Bowen, their group shuffled across the splintered wood planks of a porch and entered a structure similar to a grand tavern in Charleston. Inside, it took a few minutes for Lilyan's eyes to adjust to the cavernous room illuminated by only a handful of lanterns whose candles had melted to the wicks, the dripping wax forming macabre stalactites. Men and women in the throes of drunken stupors draped themselves like rag dolls on tables scattered about the room. Overturned chairs, pieces of smashed kegs, empty mugs, and puddles of ale were strewn across the floor. It seemed oddly quiet for the number of occupants, except for the sound of snoring echoing through the rafters. The rancid odor of stale beer, vomit, sweat, and filth assaulted Lilyan's nose, and she clasped her mouth to keep from heaving.

Midway to a U-shaped bar that stretched across the room, Bowen stopped and pulled a lace handkerchief from his pocket and offered it to Laurel, who refused it with a shake of her head and pressed both hands to her nose.

"Very well." Bowen returned the handkerchief to his pocket. "Marteen, take our *guests* to the room next to the captain's."

Marteen, who carried Lilyan's medicine kit, jerked his head toward stairs at the back of the room. "This way."

Look for weapons, Nicholas said. Passing one of the tables, Lilyan spotted a knife stuck in the wood a few inches from the arm of a man who had passed out, his body sprawled across the surface. First, she glanced over her shoulder and then reached for the knife. The man's fingers twitched, and her heart stopped. She hesitated, her hand hovering over the weapon. The man stilled, and she grabbed the knife and slid it through the side of her skirt and into her underapron.

She and Laurel followed Marteen up a flight of stairs and down a dank hallway, relieved that air wafting through the open windows at either end of the hallway lessened the stench from below. At the end of the hallway, he opened a door and showed them into a room with the largest bed she had ever seen. The bedposts, as thick as pine tree trunks, spiraled to the ceiling. The mahogany headboard was carved with men and women posed in various stages of nudity. Not the classic renditions she had observed as an art student, these were prurient, evoking her embarrassment for the sculptor who had employed his talents in such a way. She watched Laurel for her reaction, but her daughter seemed focused on what looked like a door connecting to the next room, but without a handle. Lilyan quickly surveyed the rest of the chamber. Next to the bed stood a vanity table and a commode with a white porcelain pitcher and bowl. Trunks of all shapes and sizes ringed the edges of the room. Some were closed with the keys still in them, and some were open with dresses of every hue spilling out like disgorged silk rainbows.

Lilyan took the medicine kit from Marteen, noticing for the first time a scar above his eyebrows. "Thank you for your kindnesses."

"I am long past kind, madam." He paused, a brooding expression in his coffee-colored eyes. "Even so, I must warn you. Captain Galeo is named rightly. Speak carefully in his presence. And whatever you do, never—ever—cry in front of him. It sets him into a powerful rage."

The man's obvious apprehension of his captain set Lilyan's heart racing. "When shall we meet the captain?"

"Four. Maybe five days. He's away on a raid."

Laurel put her hand on his arm. "We thank you, Marteen, for the warning. You weren't obliged to."

The burly seaman, the wide black stripes of his shirt stretched taut against his chest muscles, stared at Laurel's fingers so pale in contrast with his sunbaked skin. He cleared his throat and headed for the door. "I'm to lock you in. Someone will bring you food."

The moment the door closed, Laurel ran to the only window. "Come see, Ma. The building backs up to the forest." She tested the window, which slid open without much effort.

"You remembered your father's words."

"Yes, but I must admit, at the time, I didn't think I would ever have to pay them heed."

Skulking to either side of the window, they watched two men saunter into the narrow clearing and sit on a fallen log.

Lilyan peered around the casement. "It's a long drop."

Laurel studied the roofline. "There's an overhang. See, just to the right. If we could make it to there, the drop wouldn't be as far."

"We'll have to wait until nightfall—"

The sound of a key turning made them jump away from the window. Lilyan plopped down on the vanity chair, and Laurel hopped onto the side of the bed. A woman walked in carrying a tray. Her dark, curly, shoulder-length hair was tied back with a red sash that matched the one around her tiny waist. The stays of her white cotton dress were loose, the strings dangling down her bodice. Her red shoes made tapping noises as she crossed the room and laid the tray on the vanity.

She glanced at the open window and nonchalantly strode to it and slid it shut. She flashed her grass-green eyes at them and waggled her finger. "I would not try it. The guards"—she slipped past a short, wiry man who had entered the room and doffed his hat—"will check on you. And it is farther down than you think. Someone will come for the tray and the chamber pots. Good night." She waved before the guard shut and locked the door.

They could hear the woman's sultry laugh as she walked away. Deflated, Lilyan picked up one of the wooden bowls, her mouth watering from the aroma that wafted into the room.

"Shrimp gumbo. At least someone here knows how to cook." She tore off a piece of brown bread and handed it and a bowl to Laurel, who had slipped off her shoes and sat back on the bed.

They ate in silence until they were both sated and then drank the goblets of water.

Laurel slid from the bed and studied the connecting door, running her fingers around the frame. "I wonder where this leads."

"Remember. Bowen said our room was next to the captain's."

"Do you think we could pry it open? Slip into the hallway and surprise the guard? Hit him over the head?"

"We could try." Lilyan joined her and pressed her ear against the door, straining to hear any noises, but all was silent. She pulled the knife from her pocket and guided it along the edge of the door on the opposite side from the hinges.

A bump sounded from the hallway, and they skittered to the center of the room. Eyes trained on the door, Lilyan held the knife behind her back. Trembling, they waited for the sound of the keys but were greeted with silence.

Her breath coming in spurts, Lilyan turned back around and tried sliding the knife at several angles around the frame. "All seems solid." Her shoulders slumped. "I don't think it's possible."

Defeated, Laurel returned to the bed, punched a pillow behind her, and sagged back against the headboard. Lilyan sat on the vanity chair and tried her best to avoid looking at the carvings.

"Ma. Do you think Paul is well?"

Lilyan swallowed hard. The thought had tortured her since she last saw the top of his head break through the surface of the water. "He's strong and resilient, and he's your father's son. I suspect he's making his way to Swansboro." She hoped she sounded more confident than she felt.

Laurel dropped her spoon back into the bowl. "He's his mother's son as well." She cocked her head. "I may be young. But do you think I'm unaware of your bravery? Do you have any idea how proud I am of you?"

Unexpected tears welled up in Lilyan's eyes, and she found herself unable to respond.

Laurel's bottom lip quivered. "How long before Father figures out where we are?"

Lilyan ran to the bed and swept her daughter into her arms. "Oh, my precious girl. Your father will search for us as long as there is breath in his body."

She cupped Lilyan's chin and kissed her lips. "Let's pray, shall we?"

They went to their knees beside the bed and began to pray. Suddenly, the door opened, and they turned to find Marteen studying them, his face devoid of expression. Without a word, he closed the door.

Laurel leaned in close. "How often do you think they will check on us?"

"It's hard to tell. So far, we haven't resisted them. If they think of us as two vulnerable females without much gumption, they may leave us alone."

Lilyan stood and returned to the window to discover a group of men, the full moon reflecting off their hats and shoulders, turning their faces into masks of white and black slashes. "Others have joined the men down there. I don't think they're guards. It looks like they're playing cards."

Laurel joined her. "Should we stay dressed?"

Lilyan sighed. "No. We need rest. Clear heads." She caressed Laurel's cheek, noticing the dark circles of strain underneath her eyes. "We need a plan, but we'll think better in the morning."

They stripped to their chemises, but when Lilyan turned down the brocade covers, Laurel shook her head and delved down into a nearby trunk, bringing up a stack of bed linens.

She unfolded one and proceeded to drape it over the headboard. "I'm sorry, Ma, but I don't think I could ever get to sleep with that awfulness behind me."

Her daughter *had* noticed the carving, but had been too much of a lady to remark upon it. Lilyan grabbed the other end of the sheet and between them they covered the *awfulness*.

Laurel put the other sheets on the floor next to the bed. "These might prove useful for climbing out the window."

As they crawled under the covers, Lilyan felt a rush of respect for her brave and resourceful daughter. They turned on their sides, and she rubbed Laurel's back until she felt slumber capture her rigid muscles.

Oh, Nikki, how proud you would be of our precious child.

Finally, she fell into a fitful sleep, and sometime during the night in a dream Nicholas' words came to her. "Be on your guard, my love."

They awoke the next morning to the faint sound of a violin. Perplexed, they ran to the door and pressed their ears against it.

Laurel raised an eyebrow. "The musician is quite good. Do you recognize it?"

"It's a concerto by Vivaldi. We heard it at the violin concert in Charleston. Do you remember?"

"I do."

The night before their departure from Charleston, Nicholas had given his family a treat by taking them to the Opera House. The enchanting music had swirled around her, lifting her into another place and time, teasing her imagination with visions of fireflies and fairies dancing through dark mountain woods. The effect on her family had been even more enchanting. Nicholas, his eyes closed, ran his thumb in circles in her palm. The glow in Laurel's eyes rivaled the candlelight from the magnificent chandelier reflected in the diamond tiara of the woman sitting in the front row. Captivated, Paul had slid forward on the edge of his seat. Even the rambunctious Marion, who had complained sorely about being dragged to a stodgy old concert, quit wiggling and remained silent until the performance ended.

The beautiful music growing stronger as it came nearer belonged in an opera house, not in this ugly, ramshackle place that smelled of bilgewater.

The key rattled in the lock, and they ran back to the bed and grabbed the covers to shield themselves. As soon as the door cracked opened, the violin playing swelled, and the same woman who had brought dinner carried in a tray and placed it on the vanity.

"I trust you had a good sleep." A heavy accent that Lilyan could not place flavored the woman's words.

"May we know your name?" Laurel asked, keeping the cover tucked up under her chin.

"It is Trezza." Not willing to share more, she started to leave.

"Wait," said Lilyan. "Did you cook our meal last night?"

Trezza stiffened, as if expecting criticism.

"I … my daughter and I … enjoyed it very much. It had an odd spice that we didn't recognize."

"Filé powder from ze leaves of the sassafras tree. I use it in all my gumbos."

Again, Trezza started to leave, but Lilyan stopped her. "Who is that playing so beautifully?"

Trezza smirked. "Paolo, show yourself," she called out.

The same wiry man who had stood guard during the night sauntered into the doorway and bowed from the waist, stroking out the last few bars of the song.

"Paolo is our ship's—"

"Catgut scraper," Paolo interrupted Trezza with a wide grin.

"Musician." Trezza cuffed the man on his shoulder. "His job is to calm ze crew in times of trouble and provide some fun when the hours drag by."

She walked past the guard, who folded his violin and bow under one arm and closed the door with the other.

Laurel harrumphed. "A musician to the pirates who can play Vivaldi. Extraordinary."

"Speaking of extraordinary." Lilyan fingered one of the silk dresses protruding from a trunk. "Did you notice these dresses?"

Laurel dug down into the pile of clothes. "Maybe we could find some day dresses. I don't think I could wear that filthy homespun again."

"Let's see."

They set about scrambling through the trunks and discovered a treasure trove of chemises, pantaloons, stockings, day dresses, hats, and fans in addition to several pairs of men's breeches, drop-shoulder shirts, and waistcoats. They found nothing to use as weapons. With escape in mind, they stowed the men's clothing in a chest of its own. Laurel chose a mint-green dress with a white muslin fichu and matching ruffled hat. Lilyan selected a lavender dress and a muslin fichu and mobcap. After they had donned the dresses, they released their hair from the plaits they had been wearing for two days and combed out each other's tangles with the brushes they found in a toiletry case. They braided their hair, put on their caps, and slipped their feet into their old shoes before sitting atop one of the larger trunks.

Lilyan picked up her medicine chest and placed it between them. The kit comprised several layers of sections and drawers that folded open like an accordion. After rummaging through it, she handed Laurel a glass vial about the size of her little finger. "Hold this up."

She opened several of the cork-topped clay bottles and with a steady hand, added the liquid from them into the vial drop by drop.

Laurel, who had watched her mother's every move, finally asked, "What is it?"

Lilyan took the vial, corked the top, and shook it. "A powerful sleeping potion. Two drops brings a calm stomach. Four drops, a long, peaceful slumber. Ten drops, death."

Laurel's eyes grew round. "You … we … plan to kill someone?"

Lilyan prayed to God it wouldn't come to that. "It may prove useful for sleeping." She placed the vial in the top compartment of the medicine kit, closed it, and stuffed it behind one of the casks.

They spent the rest of the afternoon nervously pacing the floor until Trezza brought them supper. The woman refused their attempts to talk and left silently after delivering another delectable dish, this time of turtle soup and yeast bread. Long after the sunset had painted the sky in a dazzling array of petunia pink and gladiola orange—they weren't sure of the time as they had no clock—they heard a commotion in the hallway.

"We just want a look-see," someone shouted, his words slurred.

"Yeah. A peek. We heard they was a sight to behold," came the drunken voice of another man.

"Heave to, you varmints."

Lilyan recognized Marteen's voice and dared to breathe a little easier.

With their ears pressed to the door, she and Laurel caught the sound of fisticuffs and the slamming of a body against a wall, followed by swears and grumbles that grew faint.

"What do you suppose—" Laurel began.

"Shhh." Lilyan held her breath, and her ears ached straining to interpret the silence.

When a tap came on the door, her head whipped up so fast, she wondered why her spine hadn't snapped.

"'Twill be all right now, ladies," Marteen spoke through the wooden barrier. "Rest now. I'm on watch."

Except for telling them they were free, Lilyan couldn't think of a thing he could have said to make her feel better.

Following another restless night and a morning of rambling through the trunks and staring out the window, they were startled again by the opening of the door.

Marteen, wearing a clean—well, cleaner—plain muslin shirt and sporting bright green ribbons in his plaited beard, stood arms akimbo in the doorway. He looked even larger, if that were possible, with several knives, a cutlass, and a pistol stuffed into his wide leather belt.

"Would you care to take a walk, ladies?"

CHAPTER 9

"Where?"

"Has—has the captain returned?"

Laurel and Lilyan's words collided.

Wringing her hands, Laurel gravitated next to Lilyan, who crossed her arms in front of herself.

Marteen smirked. "Did you hear that, Jamie? They're worried about Captain Galeo."

A man stepped forward from the hallway, so tall that his head barely cleared the door frame. "Aye. They've a right to be worried. He's the *Deil* himself," he answered, his words flavored with a thick Scottish accent.

Straight from the tales Lilyan's mother used to tell of the highlands, the man wore an open-necked pristine white shirt, a kilt, and knitted stockings pushed down and cuffing his ankle boots. The sleeves of his shirt were rolled up past his elbows, exposing his massive forearms. A sporran swung from the wide leather belt that encased his thick waist. The claymore at his side looked as ominous as the scar that slashed across the side of his neck and halfway down his chest. Other less severe scars crisscrossed his arms, and his right earlobe was missing.

Marteen made way for the giant. "Ladies, this is Jamie McDonald. Jamie, Mrs. Xanthakos and her daughter, Mistress Xanthakos."

The man bent from the waist. As he swept his arm in a formal bow, his shoulder-blade-length queue, the color of cattails in the fall, draped around his neck.

Should she return his bow? He was their captor. A pirate. Someone who meant harm to her and her daughter if they crossed him. Habit subdued her qualms, and she made a hesitant bow. Laurel followed suit.

"Jamie's a Red Leg." The corner of Marteen's lip curled into an imperceptible smile.

Lilyan lifted an eyebrow.

McDonald looked down past the blue-and-green hunting pattern of his kilt to his exposed, sunburnt limbs. "Too much sun, you see."

Laurel stifled a giggle and glanced away.

"How is it that you have the McDonald name but wear the Cameron colors?" Lilyan asked.

"You recognize the plaid?" McDonald perused her with his hazel eyes.

"My mother is a Cameron," said Laurel, leaning backward to face the giant.

"Should have guessed from the red hair and green eyes." McDonald's eyes lit with amusement. "As for the name, most here seldom use their real names."

He shared a sardonic glance with Marteen. "To find a lady of my clan ... well ... makes me even more *cantie* to have won the lottery."

Marteen snorted.

"A lottery? What was the prize?" Lilyan asked, intrigued by the obvious friendship between them.

"The privilege of guarding you ladies. We drew lots for the next three days." McDonald winked. "You have to understand. 'Tween raids, the life of a pirate is a dead bore. We wager on anything. If it's going to rain. Which bird swooping down from the sky will be the first to catch a fish. How many drinks a mate could down before he passes out."

Chuckling, McDonald pressed his hand to his chest, and for the first time Lilyan noticed a bandage wrapped around his hand.

"You're hurt." She stepped closer and put out her hand. "Let me see."

McDonald's face turned as red as his legs. "'Tis but a scratch."

"Scratches can turn septic. Laurel, my kit." She unwrapped the bandage to expose a bloody streak across the man's palm. "Knife wound? How long ago?"

"Aye." He dipped his head. "Last night."

Marteen snorted once again.

McDonald poked out his bottom lip. "Truth be told, I won the lottery for day after tomorrow. Didn't want to wait, so me and the winner for today had us a set to."

Lilyan rubbed ointment in the wound and reached inside her kit for a bandage. "We're out of dressings?"

"Yes, Ma." Laurel started to search through a chest. "Saw a cotton garment in here that should do. But I'd need a knife to shred it."

"How about the one in your mother's underapron?" asked Marteen.

Lilyan felt her face flush.

Marteen held up his hand. "Don't worry. Keep it. You might need it. But you won't never have to use it against Jamie or me."

McDonald chuckled. "I eat knives like that for me breakfast." He curled his fingers around the hilt of his sword. "Besides, 'twould be as good a weapon as a toothpick against my claymore."

She slipped the knife from her apron and handed it to Laurel, wondering what would have made the intimidating man allow a prisoner to retain a knife, even a small one. Of course, she realized, compared to their past opponents, she would pose no threat to them whatsoever. Eager to go outside, she made quick work of the new bandage, and soon they found themselves descending a steep stairway leading to the clearing at the back of the building.

Outside, they passed a handful of pirates throwing knives at a target.

When one of them pointed their way, Lilyan asked Marteen, "They don't mind us walking about?"

He shrugged. "It's none of their concern. We're guarding you today."

"They won't bother us?" asked Laurel.

"None will try. They ken who you belong to," answered McDonald with a scowl that dug deep furrows into his brow.

Lilyan rankled at being described as someone's possession but deemed it best to hold her tongue.

"Could we visit the baby?" She braced herself for rejection. Marteen had shown them some kindness, but she could only guess at his limits.

He shrugged. "As good a path as any."

Lilyan thanked him with a smile.

Keeping to the edge of the woods, they walked silently past the huts, the two women flanked by the men.

Lilyan wasn't surprised at the lack of people walking about so early in the morning. She supposed they were sleeping off the revelry of the night before; their bellows and screams had interrupted her sleep until the wee hours of the morning.

The farther they walked, the more she wondered why they weren't walking on the beach.

As if reading her mind, Marteen looked over her head at his friend. "McDonald, tell me? If you were trying to escape this place, what plan would you make?"

The Scotsman shrugged. "I'd wait till all had passed out but still give myself a couple of hours afore sunrise. Climb out the window and take our present course, north. Except deeper into the woods, but not so deep as to run into gators. Once past the last hut, I'd run like the wind toward the tip of the island."

"Hmm." Marteen traced his fingers up and down his neck and across his chin. "How soon?"

"Ach. The sooner the better."

Escape early on, Nicholas had said.

It took a few moments for their conversation to sink in, but as soon as it did, Lilyan's pulse throbbed so hard in her neck, she pressed her fingers to her skin. She shared an amazed glance with Laurel, and her heart skipped at the hope she saw in her daughter's eyes.

The two rugged, hard-living, frightening marauders offered them a way out. She would no longer think of them as guards but as guardians. *Thank you, Lord.* Still marveling at the epiphany, she followed them out onto the beach, where they heard Cassia crying. Lifting their skirts, she and Laurel bounded across the sand, but as soon as they reached Izzie's cabin, the crying stopped.

Inside Izzie cooed, her deep voice as sweet as molasses. "A strong sound from sech a littl'n. You don wormed your way into Aunt Izzie's heart and old Samuel's. Cept he'd never admit it. There. All nice and clean."

Lilyan moved up under the porch roof. "Izzie? We've come for a visit."

Ironic. How social I sound. A captive gone calling.

The rotund woman, her homespun dress and apron overskirt bleached a brilliant white from the sun, walked through the doorway. Cuddling Cassia next to her ample bosom, she smiled at her callers but looked askance at the men, who stood at the edge of the water, deep in conversation.

"A pleasure." She pointed to three ladder-back chairs. "Please."

When Lilyan sat on the recently fashioned seats, the aroma of sweetgrass brought to mind vivid memories of her girlhood in Charleston, circled by slave women sharing with her the ancient secrets of weaving passed from one generation to the next.

Aching to hold the babe, Lilyan stretched out her arms. "May I?"

Izzie gave Cassia to her.

Lilyan's eyes took in the tiny girl with her thick black hair and her light coffee-colored cheeks, blushing from a recent feeding. "Oh, see how healthy she already is. She's so small. But she never stopped breathing. Not once, like those born too early sometimes do. I suppose her size has much to do with the condition of her mother."

Izzie winced. "I can believe that. I got my own bad memories of coming over."

Laurel leaned over to get a closer look and traced her finger down the arm that wasn't much bigger than her thumb with skin as delicate as a magnolia petal and fingernails as thin as paper. "Ma. She has the same birthmark as her mother."

Lilyan studied the speck on the child's arm. "I'll be. Same dogwood pattern."

Izzie took a close look at the mark as well. "Tell me of her mother."

While Laurel recounted the trials of the past few days, Lilyan's mind raced over the revelation of Marteen and McDonald. Should she ask for their assistance? Offer the price of ransom? Though they had given advice about escaping, they had not gone so far as to offer to help. She understood. If caught, as ruthless as Captain Galeo was purported to be, they could face keelhauling or hanging. Why would they help, anyway? What would they gain? She and Laurel had to get away, but at what price to the person guarding them? Her head ached with the roiling thoughts.

Samuel rounded the side of the cabin, a pole resting on his shoulder, from which dangled about a dozen flounder. He placed the pole onto two Y-shaped sticks and slipped a creel from his shoulder. "Fish, crabs, and a chunk o' gator meat," he announced as if he deserved a prize.

Izzie stood and started pulling the fish from the pole. "I'll get to cleaning, and you build me up a fire. We gonna eat good today."

Curious, Laurel joined Izzie at a shelf built into the side of the porch. "Will you show me how?" She glanced at Marteen. "If it's permissible?"

He held out his hand, palm up toward the table.

Izzie grinned and handed her a knife. "We clean the white side first. That's where the meat's the thinnest. Slice a half circle behind the gills. Not too deep, mind you. We don't want to cut the bone. Then we cut down the center from that first cut to the fin. Turn it over to the dark side, and do it all over again."

Laurel followed Izzie's every move while the woman patiently demonstrated how to filet and skin the flounder. Meanwhile, Samuel cut the alligator meat into chunks and threw them along with onions, green peppers, greens, and garlic into a cast-iron pot hanging from a brace and hook over the coals. After placing the lid on the pot, he sat down on a sweetgrass mat and lit his pipe. "Stew will take a while. We'll wait to fry the flounder."

The pungent sweet smoke of tobacco swirled in the air, blending with the aroma of cooking onions. Lilyan's stomach began to growl, and she took the sleeping babe inside the cabin and laid her in a cocoon of covers fashioned for her crib. She returned to the porch and listened to Izzie answer Laurel's questions about her life.

"Samuel was born in Carolina. I was taken from my village in Africa long about the time I was twelve. Uh-hunh. The remembrances I have of that would make your hair go white. We was both bought to work at a plantation near Charlestown. We had jumped the broom about a year before the British came."

Laurel tucked her chin. "Jumped the broom?"

Izzie laughed, sliced another filet, and threw it into a wooden bowl along with the others. "Slaves ain't allowed to marry legal. We had our own ceremony—an old African way. Made our vows jumping over a broom together." She gazed off into the distance, captured by memories of younger days. "I was proud of my man. He was smart. Learned carpentry early on. And was good at it too."

She reached over and pulled the skin from a flounder Laurel was trying to cut. "Do it like this, honey," she instructed. "The British soldiers made our missus move out of the main house, and they moved in and took over. Two years it was before they was made to leave. Offered Samuel and me freedom, if we go wid them. We was soon on a ship bound for England."

She opened a wooden chest next to the cabin and pulled out a sack of cornmeal and some lard. "Samuel. Make yourself useful, man, and check that stew."

"You mighty bossy this day, woman," Samuel mumbled, lifting the pot lid and stirring the contents with a ladle.

Waggling a long-handled wooden spatula at him, Izzie said, "You don't know what bossy is."

He snorted and then winked at her with a smile. "I do know what riled is, though."

Their good-natured teasing made Lilyan miss her dear husband. Would they share such banter again? Would she ever catch him sneaking tastes from one of her freshly baked pies? She sighed as the aroma of garlic and onions mixed with the unfamiliar smell of alligator, something similar to roasted chicken, tantalized her nose.

Izzie dropped a dollop of lard into a skillet resting on the coals. "Where was I?"

Laurel wiped her hands on a cloth and sat in a chair beside Lilyan. "On a ship bound for England."

"Yes. Well, we wasn't two days out of Charlestown when pirates attacked. Thought they was going to sell us till someone told them Samuel was a carpenter. Seems they're scarce as feathers on a fish. That was about fifteen years ago. We been up and down the coast and all kinds of places in the Caribbean. Stayed here about two years now."

"You like it here?" Laurel whispered, glancing down the beach at the people who had begun stirring out of their cabins.

Izzie shrugged. "It ain't a bad life. Long as we stay out of the way of the mean ones." She pointed her spatula toward Marteen and McDonald. "Not speaking of them. They ain't as bad as the others. Hasn't had the rightness knocked out of them yet."

She dredged filet pieces in cornmeal and dropped them into the pan, where they sizzled and bubbled in the melted lard. A gentle ocean breeze wafted the delicious scent around them.

"Miss Laurel, if you'd get them wooden bowls from the chest there and some spoons, I'll start servin'."

After helping Laurel, Lilyan squatted beside Izzie, who was sitting up on her knees, stirring the stew.

"Do you ever think about leaving?" Lilyan asked in a low voice.

Sadness filled Izzie's usually bright brown eyes. "Three times. Each time I birthed and lost my babies."

Lilyan sucked in a breath and patted the woman on her shoulder. "I, too, have suffered such a loss. It's been over a year, but the pain is as intense as the day it happened."

A vision of Francis came to mind, followed quickly by one of Paul, wandering in the nearby woods. The image cut like a knife pressed against her breast. *Lord, keep my son safe, please.*

Izzie, her wise eyes filled with sympathy, patted Lilyan's hand.

Has this kind and generous woman already become attached to Cassia? I don't want to hurt her, Lord.

If she and Laurel escaped, taking Cassia with them wouldn't be an option. The baby would be safer staying with Izzie and Samuel. They'd have to come back for her. She would fulfill her promise. A thought struck her that nearly took her breath away. Would Cassia be better off with parents of her own kind? But then, what kind of life would she have growing up among pirates? Would Izzie and Samuel consider leaving and making a new life in North Carolina? She mulled over those disturbing notions as she summoned Marteen and McDonald with a wave.

Their guardians ate like hungry bears, each consuming two bowls of stew and mounds of flounder filets. Lilyan had to admit, despite the desperate circumstances, it was one of the best meals she had ever eaten—but during the meal her mind raced from one part of an escape plan to another. They would don the men's clothing from the chests and wait for the revelry downstairs to die down. They would climb out the window, enter the woods, and head north. At the northern tip of the island, they'd board a dingy or another of the smaller boats she and Laurel could handle.

Was two hours' head start enough? Three? Should they make their way back to the original campsite and hide in the woods and hope that Nicholas would return once he found they had not traveled north? As backwoods women, she and Laurel both had survival skills. They'd find water and provisions, but how long could they last? Wouldn't the pirates expect them to return to the campsite? If so, should they try to row around the island and make their way to Swansboro? Were she and Laurel capable of rowing that far? Either way, she was leaving too many details to chance. As thought after thought pummeled her mind, she recalled a conversation she and Nicholas had while they planned their trip to Roanoke Island and back. She had spouted question after question, worry after worry, until Nicholas laughed and called her "his little duck." Affronted, she asked him his meaning. With his eyes full of love, he explained that she always seemed so calm and serene like a duck floating on the surface of the water, but underneath, her feet were paddling like mad.

Lord, I pray for more moments like those with my dear husband. Please, may I have my family, my life, back?

When all had their fill, Izzie spread quilts on the sand in the shade of a palmetto tree. She, Lilyan, and Laurel sat on one quilt, Marteen and McDonald on another. Samuel went back to work under the porch, this time carving more wood bowls, which, Izzie informed her, he sold to the pirates. Lilyan, crossing her legs at the ankles and leaning back on her elbows, caught the sweet scent of the cedar shavings. The smell reminded her of Nicholas' hair after he had planed planks for their mountain cabin.

"Your expression is somber, madam," said Marteen, who sat on the corner of the quilt.

"I reflect upon my husband, sir."

Marteen rested his hands on his knees. "What sort of man is he?"

Lilyan brushed imaginary sand from her dress. "I would rather hear your story. How long have you and McDonald been acquainted?"

McDonald had removed his claymore and laid it next to him where he stretched out his long legs on the quilt. "We've been mukkers, well—"

"Too long, I think," Marteen interrupted with a smirk.

"Since about your age, lass," McDonald continued, leaning back on his elbows and making the queue of his hair sway between his shoulder blades. "Ten years ago, now. Captain Galeo captured both our ships within a month of each other. We were merchant seamen, you ken. The captain gave us a choice; sign the articles of piracy or die." He scowled. "We didn't mull it over long once we found out the captain's favorite way of dealing with the enemy was woolding."

Laurel pushed back a strand of hair loosened from her braid and curled it around her ear. "Woolding?"

Marteen stiffened. "Don't—"

McDonald held up his hand. "They need to know the kind of man they'll be facing if they don't get out of here soon enough."

His serious expression worried Lilyan, who felt she already knew how ruthless the captain was.

"Woolding is torture, plain and simple, used by the Spanish during the Inquisition. They'd take a piece of cord and tie it around a prisoner's head and then around a stick. Then they'd twist the stick until the prisoner's eyes would pop out of his sockets."

Laurel's eyes welled with tears, and she clasped her hand to her chest.

Lilyan grabbed her other hand and glared at McDonald. "That was cruel and unnecessary."

Watching Laurel's face turn ashen and her bottom lip begin to tremble, McDonald sat up. "Didn't mean to scare you, lass. But one must know his enemy."

"But, if he's so terrible, why have you stayed with him?" Laurel's voice cracked on the last word.

McDonald stood, donned his claymore, and looked down at her. "At first, we were young, scared lads trying to stay alive. As the years passed, it became a way of life. We became hardened to it all. We've lived this life longer than many. Most pirates don't last over ten years. It's only recently we've started to make plans—"

"That's enough, my friend." Marteen jumped up. "Time to head back, ladies. Thank you for the meal, Izzie. Best cooking I've had in a while."

Izzie cackled. "Don't let Trezza hear you say that."

"Speaking of Trezza..." McDonald jerked his head at the woman stomping toward them at the edge of the water.

Marteen blew out a breath. "I'll see to her."

He hurried to meet Trezza, who, obviously angry, slammed a fist onto her hip and jabbed her finger into Marteen's chest.

The small audience silently watched the altercation until McDonald addressed Lilyan. "She's jealous of you, you know?"

Astonished, she pressed her fingers to her chest. "Me? Why?"

He shrugged. "You exist. And..." He hesitated. "My friend speaks of you much in her presence."

Too surprised to respond, Lilyan observed Marteen raise his hands in a gesture of frustration and bend down to whisper something in Trezza's ear. Whatever it was, it caused the woman's body to relax, and she leaned forward, splaying both hands against his chest. The argument apparently resolved, she turned around to walk away, and Marteen playfully slapped her bottom, causing her to throw him a sultry look over her shoulder. He strode back to the cabin, deep in thought.

"Why the frown, my friend?" asked McDonald.

Marteen glanced back and forth between Lilyan and Laurel.

"Trezza says she overheard you planning your escape. She threatens to tell Galeo."

Stunned, Lilyan stammered, "Do you … do you think she would?"

Marteen stared at the ocean and suddenly straightened his spine. "We may know the answer sooner than we think."

"What is it?" McDonald followed his friend's gaze.

"The *Akantha*. Galeo has returned."

CHAPTER 10

*Give not that which is holy unto the dogs, neither cast ye your pearls
before swine, lest they trample them under their feet, and turn again
and rend you.*

Matthew 7:6 KJV

Back in their room, Lilyan and Laurel perched on the edge of
the bed, clasping hands. Lilyan's stomach muscles clenched so
tightly, she had to take slow, deep breaths to relieve the pain. High-
strung from tension, Laurel dug crescents into her own palms with
her fingernails.

Other than fervent prayer, how did one prepare herself to meet
evil incarnate? Would he come to them or have them brought to
him? And when?

The answer came within minutes when Trezza entered the
room with a message. "*Capitan* Galeo sends apologies. He has
much business. He asks that you join him for supper and requests
you choose from ze gowns."

"How long do we have?" Lilyan asked, uncomfortable with the
idea of dressing for a formal occasion and being put on display. But

dare they challenge his order?

"Two hour." Trezza shrugged. "Maybe less. I will come and get you." Her glance devoured the overflowing trunks, and her eyes gleamed. "I'm to select one, also."

She rummaged through a pile of dresses, choosing a violet gown embellished with black roses. When she discovered a matching mantilla, she gasped with delight. Greedily, she dug down into a box of jewels and retrieved a diamond-encrusted mantilla comb and an amethyst necklace.

Holding the dress up to her body, she gave them a sultry smile.

"It will look nice on you," Laurel said.

"Nice? Marteen will not be able to resist me." She twirled around and left the room in a cloud of purple satin.

She returned later, sweeping into the room like a grand Spanish lady on her way to the theater. In purple and black, she would stand out in any crowd; something Lilyan and Laurel took great pains to avoid. Lilyan had chosen a satin gown of pale cantaloupe with a double tucker of delicate ecru lace stitched across the top of her bodice and matching lace dripping from the elbow-length sleeves. In a deliberate understatement, she complemented her dress with pearl drop earrings and one string of pearls. Laurel chose to wear a pale blue brocade gown with a white stomacher trimmed in white lace. Her only ornament was a silver cross. Unable to find enough pins, they both wore their waist-length hair down, swept back from their faces with combs and tied at the neck with ribbons.

Lilyan beheld Laurel, comprehending for the first time that her daughter, her mettle tested by the recent dreadful circumstances, had taken the step forward from the brink of womanhood to stand before her now, no longer a child but a breathtakingly lovely lady. *You are altogether beautiful, my darling. And there is no blemish in you.* The words of Solomon drifted through her mind, warming her chest with pride.

Would that Laurel were attending her first fete, her heart light and eager to dance and to begin her search for that one person

God had waiting for her who would fill her life with joy. Instead, fear and anxiety spilled from her eyes, and Lilyan's heart trembled with dread at her daughter's being paraded before an audience of thieves and murderers.

Trezza eyed them and harrumphed. "Come, then. I've prepared a fine dinner. Afterward, Capitan Galeo has planned some 'very special theatrical entertainment.'" Her imitation of a Greek accent repulsed Lilyan, who refused to acknowledge any commonality between her beloved husband and the captain.

Walking down the hallway, Lilyan felt more like a condemned prisoner than a theater patron. At the top of the steps, she sensed the hush in the air, and she and Laurel drew closer to each other. There must be two hundred people in the room, all quiet, and all staring at them. But as they descended, Lilyan's attention was drawn to one man standing at the bottom of the staircase, his arm resting on the rapier strapped to his side.

Of medium height, he wore a chocolate-brown bombazine doublet with matching breeches and a beige brocade waistcoat, an impeccably tied white cravat, immaculate hose, and brown shoes with tall heels. His hair, tied back with a brown bow large enough that the ends peeked out behind his neck, was the same hue as his waistcoat but with streaks of gold as if bleached by the sun. His fashionable, though somber, appearance would make him welcome in any fine home in Charleston, causing Lilyan to wonder about the many fearful descriptions and warnings. Could anyone be that depraved?

He stood as if posing for a portrait, honed in on her face until she and Laurel reached the bottom step, when he made a formal bow. "Mrs. Xanthakos. Miss Xanthakos. Captain David Galeo at your service. For once, the stories I'm hearing have not been exaggerated. You are indeed two of the loveliest visions my eyes have beheld in many tides."

Close enough now to study his face, Lilyan's heart tripped. As a portrait artist, she always painted the eyes first, for they truly were the mirrors of the soul. If she captured their essence, then the rest would follow. The captain's eyes held such a flat expression, she wondered if they were alive. His charming manner did not reflect in those golden-brown orbs, which were not the warm honeyed hue of her beloved's but the brittle ocher color of ice that forms at the edge of a muddy stream. He studied her too—cold and calculating as a cat calmly licking its paws and casting sidelong glances at a cornered mouse.

The indwelling spirit that abided within her stirred and whispered a warning. *Know this. You are in the presence of evil. Gird yourself.*

This man was as depraved as she had been led to believe, and her body recoiled with that realization. Only one other person in her life had elicited such a dreadful response at first sight, and she had killed him. Would life repeat itself? She shuddered at the thought.

The captain's glance swung to Laurel, dipping to the cross resting against her pale skin, and his lip curled slightly.

Lord in heaven, arm us with your strength. Give us wisdom as we confront this evil.

The moment she and Laurel stepped down to the floor, the captain crooked both elbows and indicated he would escort them. Swallowing her revulsion at having to touch the man, she barely rested her fingertips on his arm. His sleeves stretched taut over the well-defined muscles of his arms. His fit physique filled out his doublet—no need for form-enhancing bombast. He guided them toward a table that faced the center of the room. Though long enough to seat ten, it was set for three. The middle chair, made of mahogany, had a tall back that came to a point at the top with ornate patterns of ivy, reminding her of a judge's chair she had once seen in a Charleston courthouse.

Captain Galeo seated her first and then Laurel. As he settled between them, Lilyan noticed for the first time his—not unpleasant—scent of lime and bay rum. In response to a sweep of his hand, several women approached the table with bowls and a lustrous gold tureen the size of her laundry tub back home. Severely underdressed compared to Lilyan and Laurel, they wore caraco jackets over layers of petticoats that clung to their forms in the absence of farthingales. The women filled the bowls, from which wafted the familiar aroma of Trezza's turtle soup. One who served Lilyan sported the French á la victime hairstyle: bobbed and combed forward with strands of hair dangling over her eyes, the way the executioners cut their victims' hair. She had painted a beauty spot at the corner of her scarlet lips.

Before Lilyan picked up her spoon she lifted up a prayer and afterward wondered if the captain would roar with laughter if she requested a blessing. Stifling a nervous giggle at the ridiculous picture, she almost choked on her first taste. She kept her eyes on her spoon but felt a movement at her side.

"It is to your liking?" asked the captain, his face close enough for her to see a faint scar that ran from his earlobe to his chin.

Though she wanted to spit the food into his leering face, her good sense prevailed, and she tamped down her anger and swallowed. "Delicious."

"It pleases me to hear it."

The captain indicated to one of the servers to come close, and then he whispered something in her ear. A few minutes later, she returned to hand him a silver necklace with a sapphire pendant the size of a grape.

He stood behind Laurel's chair, unfastened her necklace, and handed it to the server. "Let's be rid of this."

After clasping the sapphire around Laurel's neck, he returned to his seat. "Much better," he said, readjusting the gem to lie between Laurel's breasts.

Lilyan gripped her dinner knife and tried with every ounce of strength to keep from stabbing the hand that had dishonored her daughter's person. She gritted her teeth so hard she gave herself an instant headache. How she made it through dinner, she wasn't sure.

Astounded that the food made its way past the knot in her throat, she kept trying to see Laurel, but the captain blocked her view. His voice when addressing Laurel was so low, she couldn't hear what he was saying, nor could she hear her daughter's responses. Frustrated, she scanned the people gathered around tables and spotted Trezza's purple gown. Marteen and McDonald were seated on either side of her. Eyes downcast, feigning shyness, Trezza leaned in toward Marteen, curling her arm through his. Lilyan observed them for a while, but they never looked her way. The crowd noises increased proportionally to the amount of liquor being consumed.

The trivial conversations with the captain made her feel like an actor in a play. Had they been treated satisfactorily, he asked. They had not been harmed, she answered. What she wanted to say was, "You cannot be serious. We've been kidnapped and live in fear of being raped or sold into slavery."

Finally, the meal ended, and Lilyan watched in surprise as the revelers pushed back tables and kegs, clearing the center of the room. A small band—a snare drummer, a fifer, and the violinist they had met earlier—entered playing a lively tune.

Captain Galeo poked her with his elbow. "I have something quite special for you." He looked from her to Laurel and back, his expression expectant. "You may not know, but a pirate's life can be boring on the sea and the land. So, we often hold mock trials to pass the time."

And what of the punishment for the guilty? Lilyan gulped at that unsettling premonition.

He lifted his hand as a signal, prompting a man who strode forward holding a three-spiked staff. Dressed like the newspaper cartoons Lilyan had seen of macaronis during the war for independence, he wore garish pink-and-purple striped breeches and a lavender waistcoat. His white wig stood a foot tall and was topped by a ridiculously small black tricorn. A nosegay of poppies was pinned to his shoulder. Lace, at least a foot long, spilled from his cuffs.

The man rapped the triton on the floor. "Ladies and gentlemen—not that there are any present among us."

Loud guffaws exploded from the crowd.

Captain Galeo cleared his throat.

The man tapped his fingers to his mouth. "Ah. My apologies." He made an exaggerated bow toward Lilyan and Laurel. "Ladies."

"I am Verdin and I will be your guide, as we have before you this evening the trial of Captain William Kidd, a most esteemed brethren of the coast."

The crowd cheered as one.

"The year is 1701. The captain has been captured, brought from New York in the English ship, *HMS Advice*, and thrown into Newgate Prison on the charge of murder and piracy upon the high seas."

"Boo! Boo!" yelled someone from the back of the room.

"He was transported from Newgate to appear before the House of Commons, where he insisted that he held a commission by King William under the Great Seal of England, which would vindicate him. But these papers have not arrived. Craven chicken hearts as they were, the House of Commons returned the captain to Newgate."

He pulled a silver box from his pocket and in a grand gesture, pinched some tobacco leaves and sniffed. "Presently, he was brought to the bar and summoned before a grand jury of seventeen, who stood together to be sworn in."

A short man dressed in a black robe ran to Verdin, clasping the wig that threatened to fall off his head.

Verdin swept his arm toward him. "Meet now the Clerk of Arraignment as he swears in the grand jury."

A group of men jostled forward and formed two lines.

The clerk bowed and addressed them. "Raise your right hand"—two of the men held up their stumps—"if you have one, that is."

People screamed with laughter. One rotund woman, her gray frizzy hair reminding Lilyan of a scrub brush, laughed so hard, she fell off her chair. All about her pointed and roared even louder as she rolled around in a flurry of petticoats. One man made a gallant gesture of offering his hand, but she slapped it away and yelled something that set everyone off until she settled in her chair once again.

The clerk continued, "The king's majesty commands la-la-la."

The band struck up a ditty, and the grand jury began dancing a jig, grabbing each other's arms and forming a chain. When the music stopped, they all yelled together, "We swear."

"Gentlemen, be seated," ordered the clerk.

Suddenly there came a whir of tapping from the drummer, and two men hurried forward to place four ladder-back chairs into a square beside the jurists.

Verdin rapped his staff again. "It is now my great pleasure to introduce"— the drum roll grew loud and steady—"Captain William Kidd."

A man, almost the same height as McDonald, sauntered forward, wearing a white shirt, a black waistcoat, black leather pants, and hip boots. He removed his black felt hat that sported a red feather and bowed to the four corners of the room before standing in the center of the witness box of chairs.

The miscreants went wild, slamming their tankards against the tables and stomping their feet. Some whistled and some cheered, "Huzzah!"

"And now to the testimony," announced the clerk.

The musicians struck up a tune, and the audience joined in, tankards swaying to the beat of the drum. The atmosphere seemed so hostile, so foreign, Lilyan longed for the reassurance of friendly faces. She searched for Marteen and McDonald, but they were nowhere to be seen. Trezza, her shoulders slumped, rested her chin on her hand, and as if bored with the theatrics, ran her finger around the rim of her tankard.

When the music faded, the clerk bowed to the jurists. "Members of the jury, it's time to deliberate."

Captain Kidd pounded his fists on the chair and shouted, "But my papers. I need my papers. They haven't come."

The members of the grand jury mumbled among themselves, nodding, winking, and poking each other in the ribs.

"Mr. Foreman, have you come to a decision?" asked the clerk.

The jurists prodded one of the men to stand. "We have—guilty as sin. Hang 'im."

The clerk smirked. "Tut-tut. Mr. Foreman, that is for a jury to decide. It's your duty to give an indictment."

The foreman scratched his head. "Well, that's what I thought I was doing."

The clerk waggled his finger. "Mr. Foreman?"

"Well, all right, then." The foreman held up a piece of paper and began to read. "The jurors for our sovereign lord the king do, upon their oath, present that William Kidd, late of London, mariner, not having the fear of God before his eyes, but being moved and seduced by the instigation of the devil—"

Before the foreman could finish, a short, stocky bald man swept into the room, twirling his red cape with a flourish, and stood behind Kidd.

Someone in the crowd yelled, "It's the devil himself!"

No, he is sitting next to me.

The foreman stood at attention. "The thirtieth day of October, in the ninth year of the reign of our sovereign lord, William the Third, by the grace of God, of England, Scotland, France, and Ireland, king, defender of the faith, by force and arms, upon the high sea, near the coast of Malabar, in the East Indies, and within the jurisdiction of the admiralty of England, in a certain ship, called the *Adventure Galley*, one William Kidd did make an assault upon one William Moore, with a certain wooden bucket, bound with iron hoops, of the value of eight pence, which he held in his right hand"—getting pink in the face, he paused to draw a suitably deep breath for one who delivered such a momentous pronouncement—"did violently, feloniously, voluntarily, and of his malice aforethought, beat and strike the aforesaid William Moore upon the right part of the head. In short, William Moore kicked the bucket because Captain Kidd hit him across the head with one."

To the delight of the audience, the devil pantomimed hitting Kidd on the head and ran from the room.

Fearing the heightened tension in the room, Lilyan bit down on her trembling lip. The back of her neck tingled, but she resisted the urge to rub it. Captain Galeo seemed captivated with the mock trial, chortling along with the others.

"Thank you, Mr. Foreman. Captain Kidd, what do you plead?" asked the clerk.

Captain Kidd pounded his fists again. "But my papers. I need my papers. They haven't come. My lord, I insist upon my papers. Pray let me have them."

"Come, sir, what do you plead? Mr. Kidd, I must tell you, if you will not plead, you must have judgment against you, as standing mute."

Captain Kidd yelled, "I want counsel."

The foreman's face turned red. "Answer my question you puling, shindly beanrake! How sayest thou, William Kidd, art thou guilty of this murder whereof thou standest indicted, or not guilty?"

"Not guilty, then."

"Not guilty, not guilty," the crowd chanted.

"How wilt thou be tried?" asked the clerk.

"By God and my country," Kidd answered, slapping his hat to his chest.

Verdin held the triton high over his head. "And now, with your indulgence, a pause in our proceedings as we set the scene for the trial."

Each word, each gesture, each howl of laughter whirled Lilyan's acutely perceptive mind toward visions from her past—the days she had endured in the vermin-infested dungeon that reeked of urine, vomit, and sweat—awaiting her own grand jury trial and the gallows swaying out over the docks of Charleston Harbor.

Premonitions of where this mockery was heading bludgeoned her. She knew … felt it in her bones as clear as the trail signs one left for others to follow in an impenetrable forest … something terrible hovered in the air. Wilted from her prophetic thoughts, she slumped back in her chair. How much more of this farce could she endure?

The captain turned toward her, his glance colliding with hers. "You are enjoying the farce?"

Had he read her mind?

"'Tis interesting," she managed to squeak through her tight throat.

He chuckled. "A tad more bawdy than you are accustomed to, one would imagine."

A server bent down to refill her wine goblet, and rather than responding to the captain, Lilyan shook her head and placed her hand over the cup. Galeo turned his attention to Laurel, and Lilyan desperately tried to think of something to say to divert him.

With trepidation, she tapped him on his shoulder. "Are there always this many people here in port?"

He turned around, lifting a derisive eyebrow. "Not usually. No." His sinister smile that wrinkled the suntanned skin at his temples did not reach his eyes. "Many have come for the auction."

"Auction?"

"For your daughter, my dear. Word has spread, and we will have many more ships anchoring within a fortnight. She will fetch a king's ransom. Are you not proud?"

Lilyan's stomach contracted as if he had socked her. Like a specimen speared with a pin on a slab of wax, she yearned to fly away from this living nightmare; but she was trapped, destined to finish out a macabre charade of someone else's diabolical imagination.

Why, oh why, had she insisted that she and Laurel take an extra night to rest?

She sucked in a deep breath. The sound of the gavel falling

made her jump in her chair. In her distress, she hadn't been aware of the staging of a courtroom with a jury box, seats for the jurors, and a chair similar to the captain's, in which a man sat wearing a scarlet robe and a wig that looked like spaniel ears lying on his chest.

Verdin turned to the audience. "Ladies … and the rest of us … I recognize the twelve-member jury and introduce you to Lord Chief Baron Ward, the trial judge. We meet again the clerk of arraignment, and another new player, the solicitor general."

The actors bowed as he called their names.

The clerk stepped forward. "Gentlemen of the jury, the prisoner at the bar, William Kidd, is indicted for the murder of William Moore, and whether he be guilty of this murder or not guilty, it be your part to determine on the evidence given. Captain William Kidd, you are now to be tried on the bill of murder. The jury is going to be sworn. If you have any cause of exception, you may speak to them as they come to the book."

Kidd scanned the jury. "I shall challenge none. I know nothing to the contrary, but they are honest men."

One of the jurists hollered, "Honest men, me arse. Thorough, bilge-sucking renegades all."

The crowd's raucous laughter made Lilyan dizzy, and her heart pounded so hard, she felt ill.

Emotion clouds thinking, Nicholas had warned.

As long as they remained a spectacle at the table, she and Laurel were vulnerable to the crowd and to the whims of the monster seated between them. *I must get my sweet Laurel away from here. Should I feign illness? Ha! That would require no acting, as I am sick unto death.* Somehow she knew Galeo would not sympathize but would take great pleasure in her discomfort. She promised herself, if they lasted out the drama, the second they were returned to their room, she would plot their escape. *No more waiting.* Pressing her fingers to her temples, she worked to get herself under control by no longer viewing the pirates en masse but as individuals.

She discovered that most of them had been mangled in one way or another—scars, severed digits, missing limbs. And that, she conjectured, was not counting their mangled spirits and souls. Several of the women were with child, making her wonder what chance their children had to know decency. What circumstances had brought the women so low? She spotted a boy who reminded her of Paul and his plans to study medicine in Europe. Once he was back in her arms, would she allow him to travel that far? That she was still thinking in terms of a bright future, any future, somehow reassured her. Hope flickered like a firefly in a mountain cavern.

She focused on a young woman in her twenties sitting on the lap of a dark-skinned man who looked twice her age. She was still beautiful with shoulder-length golden curls and eyes as blue as a robin's egg. What was her story? Where were her parents? Had anyone ever shared the gospel with her? Or had she heard the message and turned away? Did these people realize that despite anything—anything, no matter how dastardly—they had done in their lives, salvation was theirs for the asking? Did they care about such things or were they too debauched?

She had been so intent on her ponderings she had missed the testimonies of several witnesses and was shocked to hear the judge's pronouncement. "Gentlemen of the jury, to make the killing of a man to be murder, there must be malice expressed or implied. The law implies malice, when one man, without any reasonable cause or provocation, kills another. You have heard the witnesses make it out that William Moore was a healthy man, and they are of the opinion that the blow was the occasion of his death.

"If you believe the blow was done without reasonable cause or provocation, then he will be guilty of murder. If you do believe him guilty of murder, upon this evidence, you must find him so. If not, you must acquit him."

The musicians struck up another tune as the jurists pretended to deliberate.

The clerk put up his hands to quiet the onlookers. "You have reached a decision?"

The foreman held up a piece of paper and shook his fist. "We find Captain William Kidd guilty."

The drummer began to beat a dirge on his snare drum, the pounding growing louder and louder. Lilyan sensed the tension in Captain Galeo's body as he leaned forward. He glared at her for a moment and then turned his attention to the judge. The malevolence in his eyes stunned her more than a slap in the face.

The Lord Chief Barron placed a black cloth on top of his wig and rapped the gavel. "Captain William Kidd, having been found guilty of murder and piracy on the high seas, I sentence you to death by hanging."

The clerk pointed to a pirate standing nearby with a rope draped across his arm. "Look to him, Keeper."

The pronouncement sent the crowd into a frenzy of dancing and shouting and screaming. The sneers, the growls, the rancid stink of unwashed bodies twisted into macabre positions—couples kissing and fondling each other with lurid, abandoned expressions. Ensnared in a nightmare of Sodom, Lilyan stretched forward across the table, seeking Laurel, who stared down at her lap and the napkin she had twisted into knots. The ache for her child thrashed its way through her body, bruising her from head to toe.

Captain Galeo, his elbows on the table and resting his chin on his fingertips, chortled.

Something terrible is about to occur. Lord, protect us.

One of the jurists jumped up onto his chair and yelled, "Now comes the real entertainment."

CHAPTER 11

Therefore take unto you the whole armour of God that you may be able to withstand in the evil day, and having done all, to stand.
Ephesians 6:13 KJV

The keeper unwound ropes from his waist, fashioned them into two nooses, and threw them over a low-hanging ceiling beam. One by one, candles were extinguished, blacking out the perimeters of the cavernous room and transforming the occupants into ghoulish cypress knees. The ropes swung to and fro and two lanterns on either side of the gallows cast eerie shadows on the floor. Someone shoved a footstool underneath the nooses.

Though horrified, Lilyan couldn't make herself look away.

Verdin stepped forward and slammed his staff against the floor. "On the twenty-third of May, 1701, the day of his execution, Captain Kidd was goaded into drinking so much brandy and rum, he couldn't stand up. He was thrown into a cart and paraded through the streets of London. The crowd mocked him and jeered."

As if on cue, the audience began to mumble among themselves. Above the din, Lilyan caught the sound of muffled whimpering, and every muscle in her body tensed, prepared for flight.

The captain leaned forward and trained his ear toward the whimpering sound. "Is someone crying? I cannot abide sniveling. Such a disgusting display of emotion." He leered at Lilyan. "It would serve you well to remember."

He sprang from his chair to stand beside Verdin, where he held up his hands to hush the crowd. "People, I have arranged for some special entertainment."

His eyes, gleaming with malevolence, honed in on Lilyan. "As you see, we have two nooses. One is to honor Darby Mullins, the lone crew member who remained loyal to Kidd. He was hanged beside his captain." He swept his arm toward the dangling rope and then to his audience, holding a mock cup in his hand. "I say we raise our glasses in Mullins' honor."

Those who were not too drunk stood and held aloft their mugs of ale and beer. "To Mullins," one man shouted, "the stupid bloke. I wouldn't dance with Jack Ketch for nobody."

"We're told that the first attempt to hang Captain Kidd was not successful," the captain continued. "The rope broke and he landed in the mud, where he wallowed for a time."

Suddenly, a figure catapulted from the darkness and landed in a heap at the captain's feet. The man, his head covered with a sack, began to sob and shake. The hairs on Lilyan's neck and arms tingled.

"We have before us a prisoner." The captain poked the man with his toe. "Someone who has *volunteered* to play the part of Captain Kidd for our final scene."

"Please. No," the prisoner begged.

A thought struck Lilyan so hard she sucked in her breath. She knew. She heard a gasp from Laurel, who hung her head and stared down at her lap. *She knows too. Heavenly Father, we are in a deep and dark valley. Draw near.*

Captain Galeo motioned to the keeper, continuing his monologue, "Kidd was helped to his feet and pushed back onto the gallows for a second time."

The drummer's steady dirge intensified as the Keeper hauled the prisoner up onto the stool and slipped the rope around his neck.

With her heart hammering against her breastbone, Lilyan stared at her daughter and noticed her lips trembling. "Laurel," she hissed.

Laurel's head snapped up, exposing tears pooling in her eyes.

Captain Galeo watched them like a bird of prey preparing for its dinner.

"Do. Not. Cry." Lilyan spoke the warning in Cherokee.

She slid from her chair and helped Laurel to stand, never taking her eyes from the pain-filled orbs.

With the drum pounding in her ears she leaned toward Laurel, keeping her voice low, speaking in Cherokee. "We will take our minds from this place. Answer only in Cherokee."

Lilyan knew how much her daughter would have to concentrate to obey, but they had to distance themselves from the horror playing out only yards away.

Laurel gulped.

"Remember your Aunt Golden Fawn? How she taught us about healing? What herbs and medicines to use?"

The prisoner lifted a mournful cry, and Laurel's shoulders sagged. She trembled so hard, the sapphire nestled against her chest captured the fire from the lantern light, but she managed to nod.

Lilyan clasped her daughter's freezing hands. "What is the treatment for stomachache?"

"C-chamomile tea." Laurel's teeth chattered.

In the background, the crowd started to jeer and whoop, the sounds running goose flesh up and down Lilyan's spine. "And for snakebite?"

"The roots of jack-in-the-pulpit."

"Where is the best place to find the roots?"

"Thick, moist woods, bogs. Bottomlands."

The drumming ceased. A sob echoed through the hushed room, and a raucous cheer rose up. Laurel jutted her chin in a defiant gesture so like her father that Lilyan breathed easier.

"And, now, Mrs. Xanthakos—Lilyan—if you would join me." The captain swept his arm toward her.

Fear clawed at Lilyan as she gave Laurel a quick hug. Then, on legs that wobbled like rubber, she stepped away from the table and approached the captain.

"You did well, my dear. You and your daughter have mettle," he whispered his congratulations as if they had passed some sort of test.

He took her hand and turned them both to face the subdued audience and the dangling, still-twitching corpse. "Brethren, may I introduce Lilyan." He drew her hand to his lips and kissed her knuckles. "A new member of our merry band of thieves."

His moist, soft lips ignited an explosion of revulsion in Lilyan's stomach.

"Huzzah!" came a shout followed by a round of toasts and congratulations.

The woman who earlier had fallen off her chair blew her a kiss. "You're his now, dearie. Branded by Captain Galeo."

Lilyan blanched and recalled the horrible brand on Cassia's chest. The woman's owner had seared her flesh with his sign. Did this rakehell really think he could mark her in such a way?

The captain bowed, bringing his face close, staring deep into her eyes. "You have experienced much this day. You and your daughter may retire."

His words, coming from someone else would signify compassion, but Lilyan saw past his façade, as transparent as snake skin, and as easily shed and discarded.

His eyes skimmed the ruffles at her neckline and slowly travelled down her breasts to her waist. "I regret that I have a great deal to occupy me, but I would request the honor of your presence at dinner tomorrow. In my quarters."

He pivoted to Laurel, ducking his head to whisper in her ear. "You are a lovely, dainty bit of frippery. You will fetch a huge purse from those who enjoy the young and untouched. I, however, won't be involved in the bidding, as I prefer maturity and experience." He slid his eyes toward Lilyan and back. "Enjoy your last evening together with your mother, my dear. As of tomorrow, she will remain with me."

Laurel cast a helpless glance at Lilyan.

Courage, my love.

"Good night, then." The captain motioned to Mr. Bowen, who came forward and escorted them upstairs.

As they climbed the stairs, Lilyan curved her arm around Laurel's waist. She might be a "dainty bit of frippery" to the likes of Captain Galeo, but not many girls her age could have withstood the horror they had both been subjected to. She considered his inability to discern her daughter's depth of character a blessing.

At the door of their room, Lilyan waited for Laurel to enter. McDonald's absence worried her, and she chewed on her bottom lip before venturing to ask his whereabouts. "Mr. Bowen, I understood Mr. McDonald was to guard us this evening. He isn't unwell?"

"No. He's as well as could be expected under the circumstances." He chuckled as if responding to some secret joke.

Lilyan's heart tripped. "Yes?"

Mr. Bowen curled his lip. "Seems a jealous little bird spoke to Captain Galeo upon his return and mentioned the walk you took with Marteen and McDonald this morning. The captain didn't take well to your spending so much time with them. Unfortunately for them, he ordered them to the *Salamander*. They're to careen her tomorrow." He wrinkled his nose. "Worst job there is for a seaman."

Lilyan caught Laurel's conflicting expression and raised eyebrows, knowing that she was thinking that being hanged for your captain's deviant pleasures far outweighed scraping barnacles and filth from the bottom of a ship.

Marteen and McDonald's punishment for granting their prisoners a reprieve was a nasty chore, and Trezza's snitching had earned her a dress and jewelry. But what else had the jealous little bird revealed?

Inside, after Bowen closed the door, Laurel crumpled to the floor. "I cannot bear this, Ma." She buried her face in her hands and sobbed.

Lilyan dropped down beside her and pulled her onto her lap. With tears spilling down her face, she rocked her precious girl to and fro.

"Shhh, sweet girl. Ma is here and I love you more than my life. You witnessed something dreadful. But it is a memory we both must push to the back of our minds, for we have work to do."

Laurel gulped and moved her hands from her face.

"We are getting out of here. Tonight."

* * *

Hours later, according to Lilyan's plan, Laurel took her place at the end of the bed.

Earlier as they prayed for deliverance, they had heard the muffled voices of the captain and a female in the next room, but all had grown quiet. Double checking, Lilyan pressed her ear against the connecting door. Silence.

She crept to their door and tapped her knuckles softly against the wood. At the appearance of Bowen in the doorway, Laurel wilted her body against the bedpost and held a hand to her forehead.

He lifted a quizzical eyebrow. "Still awake?"

Lilyan held out her hands, entreating. "Would it be possible for us to have some brandy, Mr. Bowen? My daughter is distraught, and I think it would help her relax."

He stared at Laurel. "She looks ready to cast up her accounts.

S'pose I could bring it to ye."

Minutes later, they heard the scraping of a key in the lock, and Bowen entered with two goblets filled with crimson liquid. He put them on the vanity, and without a word, left the room.

Having already retrieved the vial of potion, Lilyan measured some of it into one of the cups. Laurel quickly changed into the men's garb they had found and then jumped under the covers.

Lilyan undressed to her shift, which she loosened and let drift down onto one shoulder. She tapped on the door once more.

Upon seeing Lilyan's dishabille, Bowen's expression turned from sour to interested.

"Mr. Bowen," Lilyan spoke his name sweetly and then draped her hair across her shoulder and let it fall over her breast to her waist. "Laurel has fallen fast asleep. So you see, we didn't need the brandy after all." She gazed at him from underneath her fluttering eyelashes. She thought it a silly gesture, but it seemed to please him. "Won't you share a drink with me?"

She retrieved the goblets, careful to offer him the one filled to its brim.

He grinned, his eyes twinkling. "Don't mind if I do."

Her heartbeat pounding faster, Lilyan sipped the fiery liquid, more potent and bitterer than the palatable wines Nicholas produced from their vineyard. She feigned disinterest as Bowen knocked back his drink.

"Will you be guarding us all night, Mr. Bowen?"

"'Tis my orders. Someone will relieve me at dawn."

She studied his eyes that seemed to have lost some of their glow. "So you will not get any sleep?"

He shrugged and jerked his head toward the door. "Once you're asleep, I'll bunk down in one of the other rooms across the hall." He swallowed hard.

"What if someone comes by and sees that you're not on duty?"

He chuckled. "They're all passed out by now. I'll leave my hat on the chair in the hall, so's they'll know I'm about."

She took a step closer and played with the buttons of his vest, distressed to see her fingers trembling. "I cannot tell you how thankful I am for all your kindnesses."

He curled his hand around hers, blinking rapidly. "No thanksh." He wrinkled his nose and stifled a yawn. "Not nesheshary."

He staggered, and Lilyan slipped her arm around his waist. "Whatever is the matter, Mr. Bowen? Are you unwell?"

"Can't sheem to shtand up."

"Here. Let me help you to sit. We wouldn't want you to fall."

She guided him across the room, where he proceeded to slide down the wall and land on the floor, his head lolling to the side. Lilyan untangled herself from his arms and ran to close the door.

Laurel shot out of the bed and searched his pockets for the key, retrieving that and a knife he had stashed in his vest. Lilyan hurriedly donned men's breeches and a cambric shirt that billowed to her knees. She tucked the shirttail into her breeches, pushed her arms into an oversized black waistcoat, and stashed her purloined knife into one of the inside pockets.

Bowen sighed, snatching a gasp from Laurel. "Should we tie him up?"

Shaking her head, Lilyan pulled on her boots and stood looking down at him. "No need. The potion will keep him asleep through the morning." She stuffed her hair up under a Monmouth cap.

"You are sure about the dosage?" Laurel skirted around Bowen's legs.

"I am sure. We'll be far away before he wakes."

After binding her hair with a scarf and sliding a knife into the waist of her breeches, Laurel skulked to the window. "No one is about."

"Ready?" Lilyan's throat muscles stretched tighter than the springs of a wine press.

The moment they stepped toward the door, a thud sounded from the captain's room. They froze as if their feet had been nailed to the floor.

Once Lilyan felt she could breathe again, she cracked open the door and stuck her head out. "Grab Bowen's hat," she whispered.

Laurel leaned down and picked up the felt hat with its flamboyant red feather. In the hallway, she locked the door, shoved the key into her boot, and dropped the hat on the guard's chair.

On legs that shook like gelatin, Lilyan crept along the hallway and down the back stairs, flinching with each creak that seemed louder than a pistol shot. Laurel was so quiet, Lilyan had to look over her shoulder to make sure she was following. At the back entrance, in the gloom of the moon that danced behind a scrim of clouds, the distance from the building to the woods seemed vast. She took a timorous step onto the grass. Confidence building, she made a few more strides until the sound of someone coughing brought her to a sudden halt.

Laurel slammed into the back of her. "Umph!"

Gathering her courage, Lilyan grabbed her daughter's hand and they flew so fast across the clearing and into the woods, she wondered if their feet had touched the ground. They had run a few more yards into the dense forest, when she made a sharp left turn.

"Ma!" Laurel whispered. "Wrong way. We want to go north."

"False trail."

Laurel's eyes lit with understanding.

They continued south a few minutes, stomping their footprints into the ground. Determined that they had traveled far enough, they stopped to gather branches and, pivoting north, they trod lightly, brushing the ground across their tracks. A steady breeze pushed the dark clouds away allowing fibers of moonlight to brush a luminescent glow amidst the thick foliage. Seeing their way more clearly, they took off running like deer fleeing a forest fire, their trousers freeing them to jump over logs, around trees, and under limbs that slapped at their faces, constantly keeping within the sound of the ocean waves breaking on the shore. Bounding over a fern, Laurel almost landed on a mama raccoon that hissed and growled. The chattering of her frightened cubs echoed throughout the forest.

With every pore of her skin alert to danger, Lilyan sensed the presence of other wildlife. Ignoring the dread of snakes harbored in the thick vines she shoved out of her way, she converted her fears into energy for sprinting even faster.

"Ma, we've got to stop. I have a stitch." Laurel massaged her side and took gulps of air.

"We're here anyway. At the end of the row of cabins."

They both dropped down on all fours and inched toward the edge of the woods. Lying on their stomachs, they scanned the beach and picked out Izzie's cabin.

The plaintive whistle of a plover floated to shore on warm, salty breezes that feathered across the fronds draping over the sides of thatched cabin roofs. *Kroow, kroow* called an egret that had risen early to feast on sand crabs before the greedy, squawking seagulls crowded them away. Moonlight lit the tops of lazy waves that curled over and spilled onto the shore, ebbing farther and farther back into the sea.

Compared to her life-and-death battle, the tranquility of the scene astounded Lilyan.

"Cassia?" Laurel asked between gasps.

A deep sadness washed over Lilyan. Would she see her baby girl again? The melancholy thought scratched her heart like sandpaper. The wound seemed so real, she pressed her hand against her throbbing chest. But right now getting Laurel to safety was paramount.

"Can't take the chance. Might get them in trouble."

Next would come the task of finding Paul. *Dear Lord, where is he? Please let him be safe.*

Emotion clouds thinking, came Nicholas' warning. The vision of his dear face renewed her. Mentally shaking herself, she grabbed Laurel's arm, and once again, they shot through the woods like a cannon blast. They arrived at the northern tip of the island, where they shuffled through deep, wet sand and dunes piled high during the night by encroaching ocean waves. Their clothing was bloody and tattered, and globs of spider webs clung to their faces. Lilyan, her arms stinging from scratches and mosquito bites, thought her lungs would burst as she pulled in ragged, painful breaths. In the shelter of the dunes, they peeked through banks of sea oats, hesitant to cross the wide open area between them and a small armada of boats pushed far up onto the beach. She pointed to a dingy and scurried toward it, her shoulders tingling with anxiety, waiting for someone to order them to halt. Digging their boots into the sand, they shoved the boat across layers of shattered shells soon to be covered, along with their footprints, by the incoming tide. They jumped into the boat and each took an oar and quickly established a rhythm that had them gliding through the calm waters.

Things had gone smoothly. Maybe too smoothly, she worried. Had anyone awakened to discover them missing? No, of course not, sunrise was at least an hour away. She imagined that even the women who rose early to cook breakfast were still fast asleep. Her self assurances didn't prevent her from looking over her shoulder every few minutes.

By the time they reached the spot in the sound where she lost sight of both islands, her hands were already starting to blister.

Laurel groaned. "This is about where Paul jumped overboard. Isn't it?"

"Yes."

Where was Paul, she wondered. Had he caught up with Nicholas and Marion? Were they safe and well? Somewhere near?

"We're halfway, then?"

"About another hour."

"Ma." Laurel glanced at the sky. "We can't let them catch us again. The captain is a monster. There's no telling what he will do to us."

What horrors had been occupying her daughter's thoughts?

The memory of the pirates shooting at Paul caused her to jerk and miss the water with the oar, sending a pain shooting through her shoulder.

"Worry will drain us, dear. Concentrate on the matter at hand. Row. Row hard."

She spotted the outline of the island lit by the backdrop of the moon, now shining brilliantly across the tops of the rippling ocean waves.

By the time they reached their campsite, the pain in Lilyan's arms, like a thousand needles ripping through her muscles and stitching them together, made it difficult to move. Her palms were wet from numerous popped blisters. The determined expression on Laurel's face couldn't disguise her pain. They managed to land the boat, and Laurel flopped down on the sand and groaned. Lilyan sat beside her, glancing at the horizon that was slowly turning the clouds a light peach, extinguishing the stars one by one.

She looked over at Laurel, who had flung an arm across her forehead.

"It will be dawn soon."

Laurel remained silent, not moving her arm.

"We must check the tents. See if there are any water kegs or food."

Laurel rolled up slowly, brushing the sand from her palms. "You don't think Da is still searching north, do you?"

"It's possible. It's only been a couple of days since we left."

"Seems like a lifetime." Laurel stood and helped Lilyan up, wincing from the effort.

Lilyan turned Laurel's palms up, distressed by the puffy, angry skin. Why hadn't she thought to bring her medicine kit?

"We'll need bandages, too."

The campsite hadn't been disturbed, and Lilyan was happy to discover a keg of water and a small cask of hardtack. Rummaging through the tents, they found one of Cassia's diapers, which they tore into strips to bandage their hands.

The tiny piece of clothing evoked Cassia's curly black hair and velvety brown skin. It amazed Lilyan how little time it had taken for that baby girl to become a part of her life. She missed her terribly.

They decided against remaining at the campsite but, instead, determined to take their chances finding Swansboro. Lilyan brought to mind the map Mr. Whitehouse had given Nicholas. From what she could remember, further north lay a much larger island. If they turned west in between the two islands, they would have to navigate through a series of channels to reach Swansboro. Nicholas had said it was a day's row.

After loading the dingy with supplies, Lilyan led the way to Cassia's gravesite.

Laurel crossed her arms around her waist. "At least it hasn't been disturbed."

Lilyan sighed. "Time to go." They had almost reached the tents when she stopped and cocked her head. "Do you hear that?"

"Men's voices." Laurel's eyes lit and she picked up her pace.

"It's Da. I know it," she said and took off running.

"Laurel, wait," Lilyan called out and hurried after her.

As they burst through the trees, to Lilyan's horror, she spotted three pirates tramping across the dunes. One of them looked straight at her and pointed.

She grabbed Laurel's arm and spun her around. "Run!" she screamed.

CHAPTER 12

For I reckon that the sufferings of this present time are not worthy to be compared with the glory which shall be revealed in us. For the earnest expectation of the creature waiteth for the manifestation of the sons of God.

Romans 8:18–19 KJV

They took off, Lilyan leading the way north, deep into the forest. Branches reached out like bony fingers, scraping her arms and plucking the Monmouth cap from her head. The pounding of boots hot on their trail echoed the hammering of her heart. The stench of hot sulfur bubbling up from a nearby bog singed her already burning lungs.

Laurel sped up beside her, her eyes wide with fear. She glanced over her shoulder, stepped into a hole, stumbled, and fell.

"Ma!" she screamed, her cheeks pinched with pain.

By the time Lilyan grabbed her under her arms and stood her up, their pursuers had them surrounded. Crouched back-to-back, facing the three men, they drew out their knives.

A short, beefy man guffawed. "What you going to do with

those? I pick my teeth with bigger knives than that."

He lunged at Laurel, who raked her blade down his arm, ripping it open from shoulder to elbow.

"Sink me! The hellcat sliced me," he bellowed, staring in disbelief at the oozing gash in his skin.

His face turned as red as the blood dripping down his arm, and the veins in his temples bulged as he bounded forward and slammed his fist into Laurel's jaw. Her head snapped back, and she crumpled to the ground.

"Laurel!" Lilyan screamed, stunned by the sight of her daughter splayed unconscious across a thick pile of leaves and pine straw.

The others, who had been keeping their distance, waiting for their chance, pounced on Lilyan, grabbing her by the arms. As she struggled with every ounce of strength she had, she couldn't keep her eyes off the pitiful sight of her daughter's face already swelling and turning blue. *She's still breathing, thank God.*

"Stop fighting us, woman," yelled one of the men, who squeezed her wrist tighter and tighter until tiny black spots swam in front of her eyes and she let go of her knife.

She kicked him in his shins, and he yowled like a dog. Her satisfaction was short-lived when her arms were yanked behind her so hard, she felt like her shoulders were coming out of their sockets.

The man she had kicked rammed his ugly face close to hers. Her stomach turned from the stench of his breath. "You want to play it that way? Do ye?"

He unwound a rope from his belt and twisted it around one of Lilyan's wrists. Dragging her by her hair, he pulled her toward a tree. He threw the rope over a limb and tied her other wrist. As she hung there, her nose touching the tree trunk and her toes brushing the ground, every muscle in her body screamed in protest.

Standing behind her, panting heavily, the man clasped the collar of her vest and wrenched down, tearing the garment in half and sending a lightning bolt of pain shooting up her spine and across her shoulder blades.

"Oh-h-h!" she cried out.

"Screaming already? You ain't felt nothing yet."

He sounded gleeful, as if anticipating her pain.

Thick fingers jerked her shirt from her pants. He stuffed her shirttail and her braid up around her neck, exposing her back to his hot, sour breaths. "The captain told us you might come this way. Said you weren't a stupid woman. He'll be pleased to know his hunch paid off."

"What you doing, Wallace?" one of the men asked.

"Gonna teach her a lesson," Wallace answered, backing away so that Lilyan no longer felt the heat from his body.

"Not the belt. Captain said we could do what we want with her. Just don't break or scar nothing."

Wallace's chuckle was followed by the snap of leather. "I won't use the buckle." He leaned in, breathing in her ear. "After I beat you, I'm going to take you like I've been aching to do since I first laid eyes on you."

She steeled herself, desperately stifling a moan. She might be helpless to prevent him, but at least she could endeavor to deny him the pleasure he took from hurting her. *How long can I hold out?* She twisted her neck, trying to look behind her, but to no avail. Every muscle in her body contracted. Every hair bristled. Waiting. *God give me strength.*

"Avast!" a voice yelled.

Marteen. Weeping with relief, she dropped her forehead against the tree trunk.

"Come to join us?" Wallace asked.

"Come to stop you."

Lilyan heard a knife whir through the air, a groan, and a body thudding to the ground.

"You turncoat," roared Wallace. "Always thought you wasn't one of us."

A pistol shot rang out, making Lilyan's ears buzz. Desperate to see what was happening, she pushed her toes into the ground and angled her spine, but the rope held fast.

"You too, McDonald?" asked Wallace. "Well, come on. See if one of you can handle the two of us."

Only one. Where was Marteen?

"Aye. Let's see, shall we?" growled McDonald.

Her senses alight and ears still ringing, she was able to distinguish the clashing of swords, grunts and groans, and shuffling feet. *Was that a wail? Another body falling? Another?*

"Mama," came a gasp followed by a moan.

The pitiful cry knotted the muscles in her back as if she had been struck by Wallace's belt.

Finally, all was deathly quiet except the heavy breathing of one man. She heard his footfalls, plodding her way. Slowly. Steadily. He stopped behind her. *Why won't he say something?* Arms slipped around her waist, and her body went rigid.

"'Tis all right, Mrs. Xanthakos. You are safe," said McDonald.

She whimpered with relief, and hot tears slid down her cheeks, burning the open cuts on her face. He cut the rope, and her arms dropped down, the numbness in them making way for the sting of a thousand bees, and she fell against his rock-solid body. She wanted to thank him, but her ragged emotions held her throat captive.

"Step away from her," came a voice from behind them.

At the sound of the familiar, dear voice, she whirled around to find her son Marion, his bow drawn tight, the arrow pointed at McDonald, ready to hit its mark.

"No, Marion. He's a friend," she managed to squeak.

Over Marion's shoulder, she spotted Nicholas sprinting toward her. Joy burst its way through her with such force, she pressed her hands to her chest to prevent her heart from leaping out.

On the run, he scanned the battleground of bodies. Spotting Laurel, who had come to and was moaning and curling her palm to her cheek, he blanched. "Marion, to your sister."

Lilyan's knees buckled, but he took her up into his arms before she could hit the ground.

"*Agapimeni mou*. My love. My heart," he murmured, pressing kisses all over her face and hands, frowning at the bandages wrapped around them.

"Nikki. You're here. You're real," she managed between sobs. "You found us. I prayed my heart out."

"I heard the pistol shot and prayed it would lead me to you."

She started to cry, deep gulping keening, as she let go of the tension and fear that had gripped her body for days. He tightened his arms around her and lifting her and pressing her to his chest, he strode away from the carnage. Cradling her, whispering wonderful sweet words in Greek, he sat down and leaned back against the trunk of a palmetto tree.

"Lilyanista." His voice shook. "We've been searching everywhere."

"They—the pirates—moved our trail signs. Sent you in the wrong direction."

"Pirates?" He scanned the woods.

The feel of his arms easing from around her caused a panic that shook her to her soul. "Don't let me go," she begged.

Bereft, she gripped his collar. Her hands ached. Her teeth chattered.

"Shhh. *Agapi mou*." He nuzzled her hair. "I'm going to give you my shirt."

He removed her tattered vest and pulled off his shirt. Gently, as he had done many times with their babies, helping them don their nightshirts, he slipped the garment over her head and guided her arms through the sleeves. The material, warm with the smell of his body, cocooned her. She snuggled her face into his neck and cupped his cheek in her hand. *In the arms of my beloved. I am safe. Home.*

"The children," she murmured. "Laurel. I must see to her."

Her cheek pressed against his thundering heartbeat, she cuddled in his powerful arms as he stood and carried her back to find their children leaning against each other, surrounded by a group of strangers. She tensed.

"Nothing to fear," said Nicholas. "Men from Swansboro who came to help."

"Ma!" Marion's faced crumpled, but he didn't let go of his sister.

With Nicholas helping her to stand, she embraced her children, delighting in the smell and feel of them; kissing one and the other and then the other again. Laughing, crying, she traced their beautiful faces with her fingers like a sculptor learning their features for the first time.

Nicholas wrapped his arms around his family, and they stood quietly until he whispered, "Thank you, Lord."

He stepped back and scanned the area, a frown furrowing his brow. "Where's Paul?"

Lilyan felt as if he had belted her in her stomach. "He's not with you? I thought he might be ill. Back on the ship?"

"Our son is not on the ship."

Her pulse quickened. "But he escaped. The very first day. He was making his way to you."

Nicholas groaned, and she pressed her hand against his heart and felt it thud.

Breathe. Remember to breathe.

She clutched his shirt. "Nikki. We must find him. He might be hurt. Sick." She gulped in ragged breaths, refusing to say *dead*. "Promise me you'll find him."

"I promise, Lilyanista, but we must get you and Laurel back to Swansboro."

"No. We don't have time. He's been … out there … three days."

Nicholas let out a deep breath and closed his eyes. "All right. We have about twenty men. We'll organize and search for him. But…" He looked at her steely eyed, his jaw set. "You and Laurel will stay aboard the ship."

She wanted to protest, wanted to help in the search, but she realized that her body shook with the effort to stand. Her legs that felt like lengths of rubber could barely hold her up. She'd only slow them down. Nevertheless, it was frustrating to give into her weakness. "We'll stay aboard the ship."

McDonald crouched next to Marteen, who lay on the ground, his life oozing from a bloody hole in his side. McDonald met her stare, a tortured expression in his eyes.

She looked at Nicholas with an unspoken question, and he helped her as she limped to Marteen, sat down, and put his head in her lap.

The young man, his naturally olive skin pale and beaded with sweat, gazed up at her. "You are safe," he whispered.

She clasped Nicholas' hand. "I am."

He took a deep breath and groaned. "McDonald and I. Our lives would have been much … different … if we had had someone like you. Someone good. Kind. Brave."

She brushed a leaf from the side of his face. "You are those things, Marteen."

His body shuddered. "Do you think … God will see me that way?"

His question pierced her heart. "If you ask him in the name of his Son."

"It's that simple?"

"It's that simple," she answered.

"Then I ask." Each sound he uttered seemed to rack his body. "You will put in a good word?"

Her lips formed a tremulous, encouraging smile in direct contrast to the sadness that pervaded her body.

Death snuffed out the light in his eyes, transforming them to glassy brown marbles. In a breathtaking instant, he had crossed over. What was he seeing now? *Please, Lord, let it be your marvelous face.*

Gently, she closed his eyelids with her fingertips, and a sorrow permeated her body with pain far more intense than any of her physical wounds. She wept for the young man cradled in her arms, for his circumstances, his regrets, and for his life's choices. Except for his last choice. That one soothed her pain. Spent, she reached for Nicholas, who lifted her into his arms.

"Nikki, you don't have to carry me. I can walk."

"I want to hold you close." The yearning in his eyes coiled around her heart like a grapevine spiraling around a trellis. "You will not deny me in this."

She traced her thumb across his bottom lip and wilted her body into his.

"There are others close by?" Nicholas asked McDonald.

The giant Scotsman, his eyes moist, his bobbing Adam's apple closing off his words, simply nodded.

"We must leave here quickly." He leaned down, still holding Lilyan, and kissed their daughter on both of her tear-dampened cheeks. "You are safe now, dear one. Pa is here."

Laurel tried to take a step but gasped and stared at her bulging ankle; the swelling skin strained against the boot leather like a bellows on a bagpipe.

"I'll carry her." McDonald plunged his claymore into the ground, cleaning the blood from the tip, and then slid it into its scabbard.

He scooped up Laurel and cradled her in his arms. "Which way?"

Nicholas stared a moment at his daughter wrapping her arms around the pirate's neck. Lilyan felt him tense. He wasn't frowning. He wasn't happy about it either.

"To the beach. We have a schooner."

Sitting in the rowboat headed for the schooner and cradled in her husband's arms, Lilyan scanned up and down the shore.

Please, God of heaven. Where is our son?

CHAPTER 13

Lilyan sat at the captain's table of the schooner, *Virginia*, among the men gathered to hear Nicholas explain his plan to find Paul. Bathed and wearing one of her own muslin dresses, she was beginning to regain a sense of her old self, except for the incessant itching from the cuts on her arms from her flight through the woods. In the absence of a ship's doctor, the cook had bandaged her deeper wounds. Her nose wrinkled from the camphor-based ointment he had applied to the scratches on her face. She was impressed by the extensive supplies in his medicine kit—jalap for purging, mercury salves for the Foul Disease, autumn crocus and meadow saffron for gout, and St. John's wort for insomnia, all carefully wrapped in oil-soaked paper. She missed her own kit she had spent years assembling and wondered if it remained in the room where she and Laurel had been held captive. The memories of that place threatened to revive her headache, which was finally easing after taking a dose of the mixture the cook had concocted from willow bark.

Her gaze traveled up Nicholas' muscular arms to the strong column of his neck above his cambric shirt, which he had donned in their cabin while she and Laurel retrieved clothes from their luggage and prepared for their much-anticipated baths. Since boarding the ship, now anchored in a sound to avoid detection by the pirates, they hadn't had a chance to talk. They had taken one quick moment to embrace before he hurried away to organize the search, leaving her longing for more.

Nicholas fanned out a compass and stuck its point into the map laid out in front of him. He glanced up as the men crowded around the table leaned in close. "We're here. At the northern tip of Bear Island."

He walked the compass down the length of the green land mass. "The island is approximately three and a half miles long and one mile wide. We've already searched the upper half. Our son jumped from the pirates' boat in the middle of the sound ... about here"—he pointed to the words *Bear Inlet* on the map—"between Bear Island and the one the pirates inhabit."

Captain Hawkins, the schooner's master, who was seated to Nicholas' right, brushed his hand across the map. A tall, slender man with a shock of white hair that stood out from his head like a porcupine's quills, he carried about him an aura of confidence and steely resolve, which had gained the obvious respect of his crew and the volunteers and—most important in Lilyan's eyes—of her husband.

The captain leaned back in his chair, forming a steeple with his hands, tapping his fingertips together, and then pressing them to his chin. "You say that was three days ago?"

Nicholas caught Lilyan's attention, and she nodded.

Drawing his bushy eyebrows together into one white slash across his forehead, the captain studied the map. "If he was travelling north—and I'm assuming he avoided the tidal creeks and marshes on the western side of the island—"

The man to Lilyan's right harrumphed. "Let's hope so. Lest he wants to run into alligators and snakes."

"Aye," another man chimed in. "Dangers aplenty there."

Paul would have had the good sense to avoid it. Wouldn't he?

The captain's expression was dour. "Three days is ample time to reach the campsite and the northern tip of the island. Our search party should have run across him already. Or at least his trail."

"Unless he went deeper into the woods than we did. Or went too far west to Huggins Island," said the first mate, who sat to the left of Nicholas.

"If he ever reached shore," mumbled one of the men gathered behind those seated at the table.

His words struck a blow, and Lilyan flinched.

The captain cleared his throat. "Let's not consider that just yet."

"Well, we must consider what we know," the man continued. "He was swimming, dodging bullets from what I've heard. He could have mistakenly gone to one of the barrier islands."

The captain's clear blue eyes regarded Lilyan with kindness and concern. "Sorry, Mrs. Xanthakos. No one means to worry you."

She said nothing but smiled at him, though she knew most of the volunteers in the room had already convinced themselves that the search was futile. They could speculate all they wanted, but she would never give up hope. She locked eyes with Nicholas and saw in his the same resolve.

"Captain Hawkins, how many men are needed to remain on board?" Nicholas asked.

"Five and myself."

"That gives us sixteen men for our search party." Nicholas dropped the compass and scanned the men, who waited for his instructions. "We'll split into four groups of four and comb the island from the campsite to the southern tip. If we don't find Paul, we'll sweep across the closest barrier islands."

"What about the pirates out there looking for your missus and daughter?" asked the first mate.

McDonald moved to stand next to Nicholas. "Mrs. Xanthakos and her daughter did a good job of throwing them off their trail. Most think they've gone south. The ones who attacked the ladies were there because they had been ordered by Captain Galeo, who sometimes has an uncanny ability to predict his enemies. Marteen and I came north on a hunch ourselves."

Some of the men at the table looked askance at McDonald. Lilyan sensed they were not sure whether to fully trust the word of someone who so recently counted himself as one of the brethren of the coast.

"And when Galeo realizes the group he sent hasn't returned?" asked Nicholas.

McDonald shrugged. "Galeo doesn't care a fig for them. He's changed his plans and will leave here in four days' time. Taking his ships and most of his men to Key West for a parley. He'll auction off his prisoners there."

To think, we might have been among them. The thought ran gooseflesh up and down Lilyan's arms. "He said Laurel would fetch a king's ransom. He'd give up that easily on something that valuable?"

McDonald wouldn't acknowledge her but instead looked askance at Nicholas. "He's a vile man." His brows knit as he turned to Lilyan. "Your escape drove him to fits, and he told us he hoped the alligators were feasting on the both of you."

Lilyan gasped. *Vile* was a perfect word.

Nicholas worked his jaw and crumpled the edges of the map in his fists.

"The timing of the captain's departure fits in well with our other plan," said Captain Hawkins.

Nicholas looked puzzled. "Other plan?"

"We—the people of Swansboro—have had our fill of pirates. Pillaging, kidnapping, boarding our ships and stealing us blind. Why, once Galeo blockaded our city and wouldn't leave till we gave him what he wanted—medical supplies."

"More valuable than gold," commented one of the men, and the others mumbled in agreement.

The captain addressed the men hovering around the table.

"We'll give the search three days. After that, we're going after the pirates. We've got more ships on the way. One holds a contingent of local marines and some who fought as partisans in the war. Two are gunships that plan to blast the scoundrels out of the water or send them away with their tails between their legs, never to return. Anyone left on shore … we plan to burn out."

What of Cassia, Izzie, and Samuel? And Paul, if he's near? Lilyan cast a panicked glance at Nicholas.

"What's the lay of the land?" Nicholas asked McDonald.

McDonald pointed to the cove on the map. "Three ships are anchored in the port, though one's been stripped, ready to be careened. There's a cluster of buildings at the top of the horseshoe cove with about twenty cabins fanned out from it either way." He met Nicholas' stare. "Cassia is in the northernmost cabin."

McDonald had been thinking about Cassia too.

The captain scraped his chair away from the table and stood. "How many men are we talking about?"

McDonald shrugged. "Two hundred."

Nicholas stood and shook the captain's hand. "We'd best get started."

While the men filed out, the captain took Nicholas aside. Curious, Lilyan fidgeted with the folds of her skirt. They spoke for a while, and then Nicholas helped her out of her chair and escorted her from the room.

In the hallway, Lilyan stopped and placed her hand on his shoulder. "What did the captain say?"

He looped her arm through his. "Told me it would be a good idea to leave someone on board to watch after you and Laurel."

Lilyan understood the captain's request. In the threat of attack, the skeleton crew's first concern would be the safety of the ship. Passengers would come second.

He guided her down the gangway stairs to the lower level passenger quarters. Before opening the door to their cabin, he surveyed both sides of the galley way, pulled her into his arms, and claimed her mouth with a hunger and a sense of urgency that she answered with abandon. She didn't care where they were or who saw them. He was hers, and she was his, and they had been separated far too long.

Finally, he broke their embrace and leaned against her, pushing her body into the door. He placed a hand on either side of her face and gazed at her with eyes of molten honey. "At last." He tucked a tendril of her hair back inside her mobcap. "I have missed you, *agapi mou*. My stomach turns to gelatin when I think I may have lost you forever."

He curled his hands around her cheeks, and his warm breath fanned her skin as he rained kisses across her forehead, down her nose and on her eyelids, tenderly avoiding the scratches. She stood on tiptoe and slid her arms around his neck, nuzzling her lips against the pulse that thundered at the base of his throat.

He moaned his pleasure, and his body shook with wanting. "I must leave now, Lilyanista, but when we have our son back … when we have Cassia back and are all at home again safe and sound … I swear to you, I will never allow you to leave my sight again."

It was a lovely promise, but Lilyan knew a great many things had to come about before they could return home. She kissed him again, loving the way their bodies fit together perfectly like pieces of a puzzle.

Reluctantly, he opened the door to the cabin to find Marion, his bow and arrow in his lap, looking at them with somber anticipation.

He seemed so mature. A man in a child's body.

She put her hands on his shoulders. "You have done well, my son. Da and I couldn't be prouder. And we have decided to honor your request to join the search for your brother."

Marion grinned, his eyes alight with pride. "Thank you, Ma. Da. I won't let you down."

"May I give you my blessing?" Lilyan's throat nearly closed on the last word.

He leaned forward, and she hooked her finger under his chin

and angled his face to study his eyes. She kissed his right eyelid and then his left. "May God be with you while we are apart..." She kissed his lips.

"One from the other." They spoke the last words together.

Nicholas, who had watched them with his arms folded across his chest, turned away and started rummaging through one of the trunks they had brought on board. He pressed against a panel of wood in the lid, popping open a hidden compartment that held a set of pistols, a long knife, and a leather pouch stuffed with currency and Lilyan's jewels.

"Pleased to see the pirates missed this." He shoved the knife and one of the pistols into his belt.

Lilyan helped Marion stuff arrows into his rabbit-skin quiver. "Where is your sister?"

"On deck. Mr. McDonald took her topside. Her ankle seems better, but she still needs to lean on someone."

Lilyan moved to stand close to Nicholas. Laurel and her ordeal had left them both in need of someone to lean on, and not only physically. The brush with evil had sapped Lilyan's self-sufficiency—a stark reminder of her need for God's strength and comfort.

"I need to speak with him." Nicholas put his arm around Lilyan's waist. "Let's all go."

Topside, they found Laurel sitting on one barrel with her foot propped up on another. She and McDonald were laughing.

Nicholas approached the Scotsman, who stood and regarded him, a nervous tick above his right eyebrow.

"McDonald—"

"Excuse my interruption, please, Da." Laurel smiled up at him, her green eyes soft with entreaty. "But his name ... his *real* name ... is John Cameron. Could we address him as such instead of his pirate name?"

Nicholas' right eyebrow shot up toward his hairline, and he glared at the young man, who had taken a defensive stance, his arms crossed over his chest. "It's your wish?"

"Aye."

Nicholas offered his hand. "All right, then, John."

John glanced at Laurel and then shook Nicholas' hand. "Thank you, sir."

Nicholas stood tall and tucked a thumb into his belt. "I have a boon to ask."

"Ask."

"The captain recommended leaving a guard for my wife and daughter. Should there be trouble, his men will be seeing to the ship and not its passengers."

John met his stare. "Aye. You have my bond. I will guard them with my life."

The men studied each other a few moments and then shook hands.

Lilyan had been watching a gamut of emotions play across Laurel's face. She was beginning to care for him. Her daughter had endured much in the past few days, but she was still an innocent in many ways. John had witnessed so much more of the underbelly of the world, so much more of the darker side of man. She could only imagine … didn't want to know … all he had done in his life. Would Nicholas allow a union with a reformed pirate? Or would he favor Mr. Whitehouse, the son of a prominent shipbuilder with a promising future?

Watching Nicholas tip Laurel's chin and kiss her temple made Lilyan wonder who she was fooling. Their beautiful, courageous daughter had her father wrapped around her pinky finger. He would allow her choice no matter who it turned out to be.

"Boats are ready," the first mate yelled.

As the others climbed down the side of the ship and into the awaiting vessels, Lilyan found herself swept into her husband's arms for one more kiss. Next she hugged Marion, who glanced around to see if any of the sailors were looking. Once he and Nicholas had boarded the boats, Lilyan, Laurel, and John leaned against the ship's rail and waved good-bye.

The weight of worry settled in her heart like a sack of lead bullets. *Saying good-bye. Again. Lord, please, if it be your will, let them find our Paul.*

Anxiety remained with her the rest of the afternoon and into the evening as she stood with Laurel and John watching the sun dip into the ocean. During the dinner with the captain in his quarters, she half listened to the banter between him and John. She knew the jocularity was for her and Laurel's benefit, and she tried to show her appreciation, but she couldn't let go of the strain that had every muscle in her body in its grip. Her facial muscles especially hurt trying to smile and laugh at their jokes. The playacting exhausted her, and yet later in bed she was unable to sleep. After a restless night of counting the planks in the ceiling, she spent the next day pacing the deck, periodically peering over the water through a spyglass.

That evening the captain invited them to his table again, though his duties kept him away. Once the cook's assistant served their plates with swordfish steaks and yellow rice, Lilyan, who sat at the head of the table, asked John if he would bless their meal.

John dropped his glance to his plate. "I'm not a religious man, Mrs. Xanthakos."

Laurel, who was sitting across from John, reached for Lilyan's hand. "I'll do it, Ma."

After Lilyan spoke an amen with Laurel, she took a few bites of the fish and then put her fork down on the edge of her plate. "John, I will not discomfort you, but, though you say you're not a religious man ... have you heard the gospel?"

He swallowed a forkful of rice. "Aye. My ma was Presbyterian and took great pains to educate me until I left home at age ten."

"Why did you leave home so young?" Lilyan asked.

Sadness flitted across his face. "Because my father's religion was found in a whisky bottle and his fist."

Lilyan studied his stoic expression and the way he braced his broad shoulders as if prepared for a blow. She caught a glimpse of what he must have looked like as a boy, and she covered his hand with hers. "'T'isn't easy believing in a loving heavenly Father when your earthly one brings you pain."

"I've brought pain to many. Done things…" He clamped his jaws until the muscle in his cheek quivered.

Lilyan's eyes roamed over the scars that marred his neck and hands. "I understand, John. I do. I was once where you are now. Wondering if God could forgive me for what I did."

He frowned. "Ach. You, Mrs. Xanthakos? 'Tis not possible. You are a vintner's wife and the mother of three children."

Laurel sat forward, her expression fierce. "Don't be fooled by my ma's genteel demeanor. As a young woman with deceased parents, she took care of herself and my Uncle Andrew as a successful painter and wallpaper artist. She joined a Patriot spy ring and was wounded helping rescue Andrew from a horrible prison ship. When she married my da, a partisan with General Francis Marion, she became a camp follower. She patched up the wounded, hid in the swamps, and endured the same hardships as the men." Gripping the edge of the table with her hands, and with fire in her eyes, she added, "To save her friend from ravishment, she killed a British officer, and for over a year was tracked by bounty hunters."

Look at her. A lioness. She's proud of me. Lilyan's eyes misted.

Watching John's eyebrows shoot up and his expression grow more and more astonished, all she could do was bobble her head and smile.

John's eyes held a new respect. "Marteen and I spoke of your gumption, but we never imagined the depth of your bravery. Now I know where Laurel gets her feistiness." His face turned red with that last admission, and he grabbed a fork and made quick work of eating the pile of rice on his plate, scooping up the remaining few grains with a slice of bread.

After supper, Lilyan went topside and gazed out over the calm ocean swells, listening to them breaking on the distant shore.

Laurel and John walked toward her, illumined by the soft glow of ship's lanterns swaying overhead and hanging from ropes strung around the captain's deck. Leading the way, he cupped his long, tanned fingers under her elbow. She stood beside Lilyan and tilted her face to the sky and the partial moon. A gentle, humid breeze teased tendrils of her hair into filmy corkscrews. Some of her longer tresses clung to John's shoulder.

He followed her gaze. "It's called 'God's thumbnail.'"

"Yes. At home we say, since the points are turned up, it means it won't rain because the water will be caught in the curve of the moon."

He chuckled. "Aye. We seamen say the same."

"John," Lilyan ventured. "You told us that you became a pirate because your ship was attacked by pirates who gave you the choice betwixt joining them or dying. Why did you stay?"

"I was only fourteen, and in the beginning, I was scared witless. At first, until they were sure of me and Marteen, we weren't allowed to go ashore." He considered for a moment. "We became known as the 'Pesty Boys' because we were so often put on rat detail, combing the ship and ridding it of rats and spiders while everyone else enjoyed shore leave."

Laurel wrinkled her nose. "You never tried to escape?"

"No." He braced his shoulders and leaned against the rail. "But three years ago, Marteen and I started making plans. Decided we'd had enough of pirating … enough of the sea. We saved our share of the booty. Stashed it away in our quarters aboard the *Salamander* in hopes of one day buying a place—a banana plantation. Or trying our hands at shipbuilding. Maybe marrying ladies who'd get along with each other as well as we blokes did. They were dreams, mostly."

He pressed his lips into a grim line, and his shoulders drooped. Sorrow dulled his eyes.

Lilyan had been studying his face and caught the moment that grief trounced his fond memories. His sadness gripped her heart. "You miss him."

"Aye, that I do. He was the only true friend I ever had." He balled his right hand into a fist, and then, with a deep sigh, he opened it again.

Laurel caught his shirtsleeve in her fingertips. "It heartens me to know that you had such a friendship in your life. Though our acquaintance was short, I liked what I knew of Marteen. You were fortunate to have each other. I grieve for your loss."

Their eyes locked until she pulled hers away to look up at the sky. "It's a marvelous night. I don't think I've ever seen so many stars.

"Sail off the larboard!" came a warning from the crow's nest.

Laurel's breath hitched. "Pirates?"

"Come. To the captain," John ordered, urging them toward the upper deck. They huddled beside the railing, while crewmen first stood as still as statues and then ran about gathering pistols and swords. Tension crackled in the air as the captain reached for his telescope. Lilyan's heart hammered so loud, she thought her ears would burst. Could everyone else hear it too? She leaned into John and slid her arm around his back, discovering that Laurel had already draped hers there. He tucked them both in close and stood like a giant, sturdy tree trunk. Huddled in the shelter of John's arms, she recalled her husband's trust in the young man, but though she felt some measure of security, he was not her Nikki.

"Ma?" Laurel's voice quivered.

The ship drew nearer with each passing minute, and Lilyan's body shook so that John tightened his hold on her.

The captain peered through his spyglass, lowered it, then looked again. "Anyone recognize her?"

"No, sir," said the sailor nearest him. "By the looks of her, though, she ain't been long at sea. Riding the waves high. Newly built. Ain't no pirate ship either, I'll wager."

"Stand down," the captain ordered, taking the telescope from his eye. "I recognize her. It's the *Lapis Lazuli*. You've a good eye, Smith. I saw her being built a few weeks ago. One of the

Whitehouse line."

Lilyan let out the breath she'd been holding, and her shoulders wilted in relief. Her hand ached from gripping John's shirt. She and Laurel let go of him and clasped their arms around each other.

"Ahoy!" came a shout from across the water. "Permission to board?"

Laurel ran to the rail. "I recognize that voice, Ma. I think it's Daniel."

"Permission granted," Captain Hawkins yelled through his cupped hands.

The crew surrounded Lilyan, Laurel, and John and watched with them as a dinghy was lowered from the *Lapis Lazuli* into the water. The moon spread a gossamer mantle over the heads and shoulders of the occupants of the boat and sprinkled diamonds across the waves in their wake. In a short time, the crew boarded their vessel and headed straight for the captain.

Lilyan recognized Mr. Whitehouse as he bowed and made introductions.

"I knew it was him," Laurel called over her shoulder as she hurried to the captain's deck.

Lilyan and John joined her. The puzzled expression on the Scotsman's face tugged at Lilyan's heart.

The skirt of Laurel's dress bobbed as she waited impatiently for the men to finish their conversation. "Daniel?"

The young man spun on his heel. "Laurel! Mrs. Xanthakos! I cannot believe it. The very ones I've come to rescue." He took the steps from the deck two at the time and stood before them. He glared at John. "I am too late, I see."

John glared back. "Much too late."

If they had used a ruler, they could not have taken each other's measure more accurately.

Mr. Whitehouse proffered his hand. "May I introduce myself. I'm Daniel Whitehouse, first mate of the *Lapis*.

John hesitated so long before finally accepting Daniel's gesture,

Lilyan was afraid he would refuse.

"John Cameron, former first mate of the *Salamander*."

"A pirate?" asked Mr. Whitehouse.

Laurel stepped between them. "Former pirate. He saved Ma and me from Captain Galeo."

Mr. Whitehouse darted glances from Laurel to John and back again, and then bowed. "Forgive my manners, Mrs. Xanthakos. Miss Xanthakos. 'Tis so very good to see you alive and safe. You cannot imagine what manner of thoughts I've had about you these past few days. I had hoped to find you in Swansboro. So imagine my shock at seeing you aboard this ship." He looked over their shoulders. "Where is the rest of your family?"

"It's a long story, Mr. Whitehouse. A nightmare that refuses to end." Lilyan laced her arm through his. "Come, let's sit over here."

They gathered on a cluster of barrels that the crewmen relinquished while Lilyan relayed the story of their capture and rescue. Her heart fluttered once again as she relayed the terrible adventure and grew sad with the telling of Cassia's death. It tattooed like a drum when recounting Paul's disappearance and the search for him.

"An amazing story." Mr. Whitehouse shifted his body toward Laurel. "And you bore it all with such courage."

Laurel blushed.

"Aye," John said. "She's a right fine lass."

Mr. Whitehouse raised an eyebrow.

Fearing raised hackles, Lilyan stood and took Laurel's arm. "It's time we bid you good night, gentlemen. It's been a trying day. We must rest to face another day of unknowns."

Grapevines have been known to extend an inch or two a day, and the way the following day dragged on, Lilyan felt she would have seen faster progress watching the vines grow. The mounting animosity between John and Daniel didn't help. It was almost embarrassing, the way they flitted around Laurel like bees swarming around a flower. Several times Lilyan saw members of the crew poke each other in the ribs and smirk at the drama being acted out before them. Though it was a diversion, it wasn't enough to keep Lilyan's mind from her *men*. She couldn't call them boys anymore. They had endured too much.

Finally, at the end of supper when they were gathered at the captain's table, they heard a call from the crow's nest.

The group of them—the captain, John, Daniel, Laurel, and she—scurried up the gangway stairs and waited by the rail as the lifeboat headed their way. Using a spyglass she caught a glimpse of Nicholas in the prow of the boat. His grim expression soured the food in her stomach. When the boat bumped against the ship, the crewmen directed Lilyan and Laurel away from the rail as they scrambled around, putting the pulleys in motion.

"Hoist the swing," one of the men shouted.

In a few minutes, Lilyan thought she heard a baby cry. Puzzled, she glanced up and, to her amazement, she saw Izzie perched on a swing out over the water to the side of the ship, an anxious expression on her shiny brown face. Lilyan clapped her hands in delight when she realized that Izzie clutched Cassia in her arms.

"Oh, my!" Lilyan shouted and ran toward Izzie, barely able to wait for the men to maneuver the swing onto the deck.

The moment Izzie was free, Lilyan clasped her arms around her. Izzie stepped back and lifted the covers to expose Cassia's face and her huge brown eyes gazing calmly back at her. Without a word, the woman handed the precious bundle over to Lilyan. Laurel stood beside her and leaned down to kiss the babe's sweet, dear face.

Lilyan's joy came to an abrupt end when she saw Nicholas, Marion, and Samuel climb over the rail and onto the deck. The stoic expression on her husband's face stabbed like a knife through her heart. He held open his arms and she ran to him.

"You did not find him," she said, her face pressed against his chest, hearing the thunder of his heartbeat.

"No, *agapi mou*. But do not despair." He paused, pulling in a deep breath and letting it out slowly. "We know where he is."

"Un. Un," Izzie moaned. "May the Lord have mercy on him."

CHAPTER 14

Lilyan's knees wobbled, and if Nicholas hadn't wrapped his arms around her, she would have slumped to the deck. "Galeo? Galeo has our son?"

"No!" Laurel clutched John's arm.

Nicholas searched Lilyan's face. "Is he so terrible, this Galeo, that he incites this fear in you?"

Samuel grunted. "He's the *debil* hisself."

"Ma? Your cheeks are like chalk." Marion ran to her, his body trembling.

She locked eyes with his, the whites showing around his golden irises. "I'm fine, dear boy. Your ma is fine." Forcing a smile of reassurance, she ran her fingers like a brush through Marion's wiry curls and retied them with the ribbon at the back of his neck, knowing they wouldn't stay tamed for long.

She met Samuel's worried gaze. "You saw Paul? How? When? How was he? Did he speak to you?"

Samuel circled his straw hat in his hands, fraying its tattered edges. "I did. I seed him the day after we got word that you and Miss Laurel went missing." He wrinkled his nose and his eyes grew round. "I gotsta be honest, ma'am. When he crawled outta de woods with that monster dog, he was mighty poorly. Skin and bones. Cuts all over. Out of his mind with fever."

Bludgeoned by the pictures forming in her mind, Lilyan fought back a wave of nausea and clamped her arms across her chest. *A fever? A monster dog?* The second her mind formed those thoughts, she caught something out of the corner of her eye. *A flying dog!* At least it looked like a dog or a small horse, his legs dangling, his limp body secured in a swing being winched in from the side of the ship. The closer the mastiff came to the crew, the more he growled. Trying to make sense of what she was seeing, she watched them lower him to the deck.

"That's Cal, Mrs. Xanthakos," Samuel offered. "He saved your boy. Howling like a wolf, he done dragged that young'un through the woods to where the people was."

The yowling I heard as we were running through the woods. Was Paul that close?

"Gave Galeo's men what for when they parted him from your son." Samuel scratched a fingernail across the frayed edge of his hat. "They wanted to shoot him, but Izzie convinced them she'd tie him up and not let him loose. He won't hardly let nobody near him 'cepting Izzie and young Marion there. Seems to have taken a shine to him. I guess 'cause he's so much like his brother." He furrowed his brow into deep coils that glistened with sweat. "He's a mean dog all right."

Izzie harrumphed. "He ain't mean, Sam. Just hurt and scared."

Because the huge animal wouldn't stop snapping at them, crewmen stood as far away as they could, stretching up onto their toes to unlatch the swing; and when the last knot was untied, they jumped back. The dog crumpled into a heap, too exhausted to take advantage of his freedom. Marion sat on the deck and lifted the dog's big square head into his lap.

"Take care, Son," Nicholas warned, standing at the ready near Marion's feet.

The animal tried to lick Marion but drooped and stared up at Lilyan, his limpid brown eyes pools of misery that struck a chord in her heart. No one, neither man nor beast, deserved the abuse he had suffered. He was her hero, and she would treat him accordingly.

Was there someone near Paul who would show him some human kindness? Give him water when he thirsted? Bind his wounds? At home, he never liked to sleep without a lit candle in his room. Would someone provide him light in his darkness?

Lilyan inched toward the dog. "Where do you hurt, sweet boy?" She pitched her voice low, soothing.

She dropped to her knees and reached out to pet his fur, filthy with black mud and riddled with cockleburs. "I'm a friend. I won't harm you."

"Watch yourself, ma'am," one of the sailors hissed.

Ignoring the warning, she ran her fingers across his chest, which was so emaciated, she could have counted each individual rib.

She didn't take her eyes from the dog's black-masked face. "Cal? You say his name is Cal?"

Marion pointed to a makeshift harness strapped to the dog's broad shoulders and neck. "It's written right here on the cloth, Ma. Paul must have named him after Callum."

How fitting that her son had named his guardian in memory of their family's old friend and self-appointed protector.

Lilyan examined the straps made from a black hair ribbon and strips of cambric, ragged as if torn from a shirt. *Paul's ribbon. Paul's shirt.* She spotted the letters—CAL—sienna, all capitals, and squiggly as if written by a trembling hand, so unlike Paul's meticulous, elegant script.

"Looks to me like he wrote it in blood," commented one of the sailors gathered around.

Blood! Her heart tripped.

Cal lifted his massive paw and tried to move it toward his tongue, which lolled from his foaming jowls.

Lilyan picked up his foot, and he flinched when she turned it over. "Ugh. There's a black thorn buried in the pad. I can't tell how long it is, but the skin around it is hot and swollen. I've got to get it out before it festers. Someone, please, run and find Cooky and ask him to bring his medicine kit."

Captain Hawkins, who had been watching them from the poop deck, yelled, "Quartermaster, get the men back to work. We have a battle ahead of us."

The men quickly dispersed, and Nicholas, Laurel, and John moved in closer. Despite Cal's warning growl, Nicholas bent down on one knee and brushed his fingers up and down the mastiff's body. "No broken bones. Looks as if he's been out in the wild for some time. Lots of ticks and fleas."

Samuel took a hesitant step forward but remained at a safe distance. "Yes, sir. That's what the men was saying. Gone wild, some said."

Nicholas wiped his hand on his breeches. "Marion, bring soap and water. We'll bathe him. See if there are other injuries."

The entire time Nicholas was examining Cal, Lilyan cooed over the dog as if to a baby, and it didn't take long for the hound to fasten his soft brown eyes on her. A bucket of water, soap, and cloths arrived, along with Cooky's medicine kit, a tin of water, and tidbits of beef. Together Nicholas and Marion bathed the dog, bringing a shine to his apricot-colored, thick, short fur. They combed out the sand spurs and pinched the ticks from his skin. With a pair of long tweezers, Lilyan gingerly removed the thorn that, thankfully, came free in one piece. Cal braved the pain without a whimper, and once Lilyan had cleaned and bandaged his wound, he slurped water from a cup with one lap of his giant mastiff tongue, and gobbled down the beef she fed him with her fingers. He crawled to her and placed his head in her lap, looking at her with such adoration, she almost cried.

As if sensing her thoughts, Nicholas put a hand on her shoulder. "We owe him much. Besides, I see you have already opened your heart to him."

Cal didn't care for the bandage, though, and when he began to pick at it with his teeth, Lilyan waggled a finger at him. "Leave that be, Cal. It needs time to heal."

He immediately desisted, and when Lilyan rubbed his ears and told him what a fine fellow he was, he moaned, and his eyes lit with pleasure.

Nicholas chortled. "Let's see if we can get you to stand, big boy."

He and John scooped the dog up underneath his shoulders and haunches and stood him upright. Cal took a few tentative steps, favoring his sore foot, but when Lilyan stood, he pushed himself next to her skirts and plunked a massive paw between her feet.

Nicholas tucked a tendril of Lilyan's hair behind her ear. "He's claimed you. 'Tis the nature of his breed going back to the times of ancient Rome. He's all yours now."

Unconsciously scratching Cal's forehead, with the warmth from her newfound friend seeping into her legs, she watched a lazy wave in the distance swell and roll. "Until Paul returns," she murmured.

Nicholas became pensive, following her gaze. "I promise, *agapi mou,* I will do everything within my power…" His voice drifted away, and he cleared his throat. "God willing, our son will be in your arms soon."

That evening after supper, they stretched out in the cabin bed, Nicholas resting his head on his folded arms and Lilyan on her side, her arm draped across his chest. Cal stretched out on the floor beside the bed, his head resting on one of Lilyan's shoes.

She wanted to talk about Paul, to exorcize the worries that gnawed at her innards until they burned like an open wound splashed with alcohol. If she expressed her feelings to Nicholas, she knew he'd oblige by listening, but she also knew what it would cost him. Though he hurt as terribly as she did and agonized about the fate of their son just as much as she, he wouldn't volunteer those feelings. Would talking about the future assuage some of their fears? Give them some hope? She so wanted—needed—hope.

"You know Paul wants to be a doctor," she ventured.

He continued to look at the ceiling. "I suspected as much."

"I thought a while back he could be a successful artist. But his drawings and paintings, though quite good, are meticulous, more scientific."

"Yes. He's quite good."

She twirled the string tie of his shirt in her fingers. "So. It doesn't bother you that he won't follow in your footsteps and take over the vineyard?"

He unfolded his arms and slid one around her back. "I want Paul … I want all of our children … to do what's in their hearts. To be what God calls them to be."

"He wants to study medicine in Europe, but after all this, I don't know if I could let him g-go." She choked on the words, and the dam of emotions she had been holding back burst like an explosion of dynamite unlocking a log jam. Tears spilled down her cheeks. "I want him back, Nikki." Her voice broke, and her shoulders shook with her sobbing.

Nicholas held her close, his tears mingling with hers.

Cal sat up and laid his massive head on the bed and whimpered until Lilyan's crying subsided. She leaned up on her elbow and moved by the dog's pitiful expression, she reached over Nicholas and scratched the dog under his neck and cooed until he lay back down.

Lilyan snuggled back down next to Nicholas, drawing comfort from his strong arms, when there came a knock at the door. "It's Izzie, Mrs. Xanthakos."

Nicholas sat up. "Come in."

Izzie cracked open the door and stuck her head inside. "Thought you might want to spend some time with the babe."

Lilyan held out her arms, and Izzie walked across the room and handed Cassia to her. "I'll come back in a bit," she said, leaving the room and closing the door behind her.

They lay back on the bed and curled toward each other, knees touching, with Cassia tucked in between them. Lilyan caressed the babe's soft skin, delighting in her smile. Each time Cassia gurgled, Cal slapped his tail on the floor. It hadn't taken her long to learn what Nicholas meant when he said Cal had claimed her. Like a sentinel guarding the crown jewels, he never allowed more than one foot of distance between them. She had unwittingly tested his devotion when, seeking some privacy after supper, she had shut him out of the cabin. His harrowing, mournful howl had brought Nicholas and several of the sailors barreling down the galley way, primed for attack.

Lilyan swirled her fingertip around one of Cassia's springy ebony curls. "Isn't she beautiful? In these few short days, she has blossomed."

Nicholas burrowed his thumb underneath one of the babe's hands and marveled when she wrapped her fingers around his. "Yes. She's lovely. And what a solid grip for such a tiny thing."

His expression became thoughtful.

"What is it, Nikki?"

"I asked Izzie and Samuel if they'd like to come back to the vineyard with us. They both agreed. Said they've had enough of the sea."

"That's wonderful news."

"It is." He paused. "I was thinking … about Cassia. I know you promised her ma you'd take care of her. Treat her as your own. But…" He lay on his back, folded his arms beneath his head, and stared at the ceiling.

"Just say what you're thinking, Nikki."

"I don't want to tread on your feelings. You love this child. I know. But have you given any thought to how much Izzie and Samuel have become attached to her? Especially Izzie?"

She swallowed the lump in her throat. "I have. I even wondered if she would fare better with parents of her same race."

He turned back on his side and rubbed her cheek with a knuckle. "I don't know much about such things. I have witnessed children of mixed parentage being tormented. Called half-breeds and all manner of hurtful things." He dropped his gaze to Cassia. "But I have also seen whites take in Indians and Indians take in whites."

"When I look at this sweet babe, I don't see the color of her skin. I see a beautiful child that God has entrusted into our care." She leaned over and kissed Cassia's forehead and smiled when the baby let out a dainty snuffle. "If Izzie and Samuel live close by, we could see her every day. Couldn't we?"

Nicholas groaned. "More cabins to build."

Lilyan giggled. Poor man. Over the years, their family had grown by leaps and bounds. Originally, Nikki had built a compound with four cabins to accommodate his family; her brother Andrew and his wife, Golden Fawn; Golden Fawn's twin brothers; and Callum. He had built another for the woman who had cared for Laurel after she was kidnapped as a child.

They lay quietly for a while, watching Cassia succumb to sleep. The moment her pale, delicate eyelids blanketed the smile in her liquid brown eyes, Lilyan looked at Nicholas. The expression of love she found in her husband's eyes permeated her body. Her thoughts drifted toward their mountain home and their secret place, a slab of rock nestled between boulders beside a gurgling stream. On cool, late summer evenings, they would lie on that rock that had baked all day in the sun, warming their limbs through and through while cool breezes wafted across their bodies.

She closed her eyes, remembering those delicious sensations. "I yearn for our home. To have our family together again. Whole. Complete."

He curved his arm up over her head and caressed the curls that feathered around her forehead. "You share my thoughts, do you not, *agapi mou*?"

She opened her eyes and curled her palm to his jaw, drawing a circle on his cheek with her thumb. "I do. I ache with it."

His expression grew serious, and his eyes bored into hers. "I sense something in you I haven't felt since the evil one."

Bradenton. She sucked in a breath. They never spoke the name of the British officer who had tainted their lives with terror and remorse.

He pressed a finger to the pulse at the base of her neck. "Tell me about this Galeo."

She didn't know where to start. She worried her bottom lip as a jumble of visions—all dark, all chilling—bounced around in her mind: the captain's lascivious smirk upon their first meeting; his smugness when he replaced Laurel's cross with a gemstone necklace; his maniacal laughter at the pitiful man groveling at his feet and his apparent enjoyment watching the man hang; the gleam in his eyes as he looked up from kissing her hand, and the feel of those lips on her skin … She shivered.

"He is a man more depraved than the other one ever dreamed of being. So much so that upon our first meeting, the Holy Spirit sent a warning and positioned himself in front of my heart."

"Your words pierce me. Nothing else you could have said would have caused me more anxiety. Even during the atrocities of war, I can't remember coming across a man who embodied the level of malevolence you feel in Galeo." His voice shook and his Adam's apple bobbed. "What you and Laurel endured … What our son might be enduring…"

He bowed his head and whispered, "Dear God, give me strength. As David spoke to you upon the battlefield, 'Plead my cause, O Lord, with them that strive with me. Fight against them that fight against me.'"

He sat up and draped his legs over the side of the bed, resting his stockinged foot on Cal's leg.

"We fight the pirates tomorrow." His shoulders drooped, and he shook his head back and forth, studying his calloused hands. "These have become the hands of a vintner. Yet once again I find myself a warrior, and they must wield a weapon. 'Twas not what I had intended when I planned this grand adventure."

She crawled around the babe to the foot of the bed and then

157

sat beside her husband, clasping his hand and resting it in her lap.

"What will happen tomorrow?" She leaned her head against his shoulder.

"We will all meet here on this ship in the morning. I intend to ask to lead a small party to search for Paul. Hopefully, during the battle, the pirates will be too occupied to worry about guarding prisoners."

"You will take John? As he knows best where to search."

"Yes." He gave her a crooked smile. "Again we share the same thoughts."

"So, I am to say good-bye to you again. Send you off to fight, not knowing if you will return to me." She lifted their entwined hands to her lips and kissed the top of his hand. "The pain is the same as when we were newly wed and you would leave me to fight alongside General Marion. I filled my days with work until I was too tired to place one foot in front of the other, hoping the exhaustion would help me sleep through the night." She dropped their hands back into her lap. "It didn't work."

He freed his hand and draped his arm around her waist. "Those were dangerous, unsettling times."

A tremor shook his body, filling Lilyan with alarm. For years after the war ended, Nicholas' nights became so haunted he often woke, chilled and trembling. Many times he left their cabin to roam the woods, not returning until daybreak. She couldn't count the times he had stopped work in the middle of the day, strode back to the cabin, and silently guided her to walk out among the tall oaks and pines with him. He never spoke of his experiences in battle, and she didn't push him to share. She gave him what comfort she could, but worried about his thoughts growing taut like a festering blister, the pressure mounting, needing to be opened and purged and cleaned out before it could begin to heal, else it would burst open on its own, leaving an even deeper scar.

She had coped with memories of her own, not of actual battle, but the pain-filled faces and desperate cries of the wounded she had nursed back to health. It wasn't the blood and gore she remembered most—the oozing bandages covering what once were arms and legs—but the soulful questions: How will I work my farm? How will I care for my family? Will my fiancé turn away from me? And then there were those who gripped her hands, terrified as they faced death and breathed their last breath on Earth. As horrible as her recollections were, they could not compare with her dear husband's.

She rubbed circles across his shoulder blades. "Yes, dearest, they were unsettling times."

He stared at the floor. "We were different people then, Lilyanista. It was only the two of us. No children. No property…"

She knew what he was about to say and clamped her eyes shut.

"I've made arrangements so that you and the children will be cared for. In the event something should happen to me."

Her eyes flew open. "Oh, Nikki…"

He caressed her bottom lip with his thumb. "There are papers in the chest at the end of our bed at the cabin. A will. The name of my bankers. The deed to our vineyard. Some money. I spoke with your brother a while back, and he has agreed to take care of you. But it was a mutual agreement. I pledged to care for his family if anything ever happened to him."

"Dearest husband. I don't want to talk about such things. May we speak of something else? Like the cuttings arriving from Greece."

He smiled. "The new vines mean the future and hope for you. Yes, *agapi mou?*"

How well he knows me.

"Then we will speak of that."

With her cheek pressed against his shoulder, she closed her eyes and listened to him speak of his plans for the vineyard, his voice low and methodic with a hint of his Greek accent, calming her ravaged emotions. A welcome lethargy crept into her bones.

Izzie soon arrived for Cassia, followed by the children, who came to bid them good night.

Nicholas pressed a finger to his lips, warning them to silence. Looking back at his wife who had finally succumbed to sleep, her facial muscles relaxed and her rose-petal colored lips partially open, he gathered Laurel and Marion in his arms and kissed the tops of their heads. *Lord Almighty, you gave me these dear ones, and I thank you from the bottom of my heart. Please look after my family and guard us all from harm. Guide my path and lead me to my son, please, Lord. Bring him back among us.*

They woke early the next morning to calm seas and stood on the deck in awe as the rising sun chased away the stars and transformed the sky into a heavenly opal with bursts of purple, then pink and apricot and milky blue-green. Gathered near the mainmast, they prayed together with the children, Izzie, and Samuel.

Laurel broke away from them, walked to the side of the ship, and leaned against the rail. The gentle morning breezes teased the ruffles of her mobcap and rippled the ends of her shawl that draped across her elbows in a graceful *U*. John, who had studied her from a distance, strode across the deck to stand beside her. They lingered there, not speaking, gazing at the horizon. A gust of wind billowed her skirts, and she shivered. John lifted her shawl and tucked it about her shoulders and neck. He leaned down and said something Lilyan couldn't catch. With a subtle shift of her body, Laurel leaned into him, and he slowly curled his arm around her.

"She has made her choice, then?" Nicholas whispered into Lilyan's ear, his voice full of emotion, his accent heavy.

Several expressions made their way across his face—all varying degrees of resignation. Lilyan blinked away the tears pooling in her eyes. "I believe she has, Nikki."

"I reckon we best get to know this pirate if he is to be a part of us." He crooked his arm.

"Former pirate," she corrected, threading her arm through his.

Their much-anticipated conversation with John was cut short as representatives from each of the ships were piped on board. All looked distinguished in their varying uniforms, and all had the same grim determination on their faces. One particular face among them made her smile.

"Mr. Whitehouse," she called out.

Spotting her, Daniel Whitehouse hurried toward them, grinning. "Mrs. Xanthakos. Captain."

He bowed to them with a devilish glint in his amber eyes. He searched the deck, and, seeing Laurel and John, suddenly the warmth in his eyes turned cool. He tipped his hat and strode across the deck to join the couple. He and John stared at each other over Laurel's head, stationing themselves on either side of her like sentinels.

"Trouble?" Nicholas asked.

"Not if she's made up her mind. Which I'm sure she has. Though I think Daniel will always remain dear to her."

They watched the silent drama until the last group of men arrived. John and Daniel bade Laurel good-bye and joined Nicholas and Lilyan to gather with the others in the captain's wardroom.

A thin man who was seated at the head of the table, his jawline a rigid L as if cut from stone, pleated his forehead. "I wasn't aware that women would be present."

Captain Hawkins cleared his throat. "Now, Captain Talbert. No need for abruptness."

Nicholas took two strides to stand beside Captain Talbert, stiffened his spine, and frowned at him with a fierce gleam in his eye. "Captain Talbert, may I present myself. I am Nicholas Xanthakos, and this is my wife. It is our son, Paul, who was captured by the pirates. As his mother, it is her right to hear how you would assure the safety of her oldest child during the battle. Do you agree?" A heavy Greek accent made its way into Nicholas' challenge; a sure sign that he was in a temper.

Captain Talbert sputtered, his swarthy cheeks glowing red. He stood and bowed to Nicholas and Lilyan. "A pleasure to make your acquaintance. So sorry for the situation in which you find yourself."

Embarrassed for him, Lilyan smiled and returned his bow.

Captain Talbert motioned to the vacant seats to his left. "Mrs. Xanthakos, Captain, won't you be seated?"

The burly, red-haired man sitting across from Lilyan leaned forward. "*Captain* Xanthakos? Master of what ship?" he asked in a thick Scottish burr.

"No ship's master," Daniel spoke out from the group circling the table. "Earned his rank fighting alongside General Marion in the war."

The Scotsman's eyes gleamed with respect. "Good. A real fighting mahn, then." His rolled *r* emphasized the word *real*.

Captain Hawkins pushed back from the table. "Before we get down to business, let me introduce everyone. Captain McGregor, master of the *Saint Andrew*. Captain Talbert, the *Swiftsure*. And Captain Sumter, the *Lapis*. Robert Barringer, head of the Swansboro town council and colonel in charge of the militia."

Nicholas lifted an eyebrow. "Colonel Barringer? The same as fought with Marion's partisans?"

A smile crinkled the man's leathered skin, digging deep wrinkles around his serious hazel eyes. "Well met, Captain Xanthakos. My memory's not as it should be, but I do remember you now. Proud to serve with you again."

Captain Hawkins continued the introductions. "Standing behind Captain Xanthakos are Mr. Whitehouse, first mate of the *Lapis,* and Sergeant Major Hamilton of the North Carolina marines."

Each man gave a nod of greeting or made an informal salute.

Colonel McGregor looked down the line of men standing around the table until his stare rested on John, who was leaning against the wall with his arms folded across his chest. The colonel ran his glance up and down the claymore at John's side. "And who's this rock of a man who has the look of a Scotsman that's been through a battle or two?"

John unfolded his arms and stood straight. "John Cameron."

"Odd," said McGregor, rubbing his fingers through his bright red beard. "A Cameron wearing the McDonald colors."

"'Tis a story for another time," John said matter-of-factly.

Colonel Barringer frowned, his expression suspicious. "What is your connection here?"

"Until a few days ago, I was under the command of Captain Galeo."

"A pirate?" Captain Talbert yelled.

Nicholas put his hands up. "Former pirate. But most importantly, my friend."

"Anyone have a problem with this man?" Captain Hawkins asked.

Some grumbles and mumbles reverberated around the room, but no one spoke up against John. Lilyan released the breath she'd been holding.

Cooky chose that moment to enter the room with his assistant, both of them carrying platters of biscuits, sausages, tea, and tankards of rum. Lilyan accepted a cup of tea but politely refused the food. She wouldn't be able to swallow anything and feared she might not be able to keep it down anyway.

Captain Hawkins took a gulp of the rum and slammed the tankard onto the table, the pewter reflecting the light of the whale oil lantern swinging above his head and casting cross-shaped shadows onto the table. "Let's get to it. We must decide on a commander."

"You're doing a fine job, Hawkins. I say you continue," said Captain Talbert.

"Aye. I second that," said Captain McGregor.

The others raised their hands or spoke in agreement.

Captain Hawkins rested his arms on the table. "It follows, then, that the *Virginia* will be the flagship. Since the *Lapis* is new and untried, especially for battle, it will remain away from the fray, serving as a supply ship for the extra munitions, food, and medical supplies. Consequently, Captain Xanthakos' family and party are ordered to be transported to the *Lapis* as soon as possible. Do you agree, Captain Sumter?"

"I do. And, Captain Xanthakos, I'm putting Mr. Whitehouse in charge of your family's safety. You'll have no worries on that score."

John leaned forward and locked eyes with Mr. Whitehouse, his expression an unspoken challenge that he'd best follow through on his assignment.

Nicholas unclenched his fists. "Thank you, Captain Sumter. Mr. Whitehouse. I'm in your debt. I suspect now's the time to request about five men, John among them, to join me in a rescue party for my son."

"Only five?" Captain Hawkins asked.

"The smaller the group, the better," Nicholas responded, his jaw set as if to brook no argument.

Captain Hawkins smoothed out the map in front of him with his long, bony fingers. "As you say. Make your selection after our meeting."

For the next couple of hours the men constructed a meticulous plan for attacking the pirate ships and their lair. Lilyan's head swam with the details, but she had every confidence in the stalwart, determined group.

At the conclusion, a frail looking, fresh-faced young man with spectacles resting on his nose stepped forward, and with his prominent Adam's apple bobbing against the two forks of his white tabbed cravat, introduced himself as chaplain for the militia. A somber expression filled his charcoal-gray eyes as he asked to lead them in prayer. Those who had been seated at the table stood and joined the others, tucking their hats up under their arms and bowing their heads.

Lilyan felt the warmth of Nicholas' hand as he curled his fingers around hers. Her skirts were rustled by a movement beside her, and she opened her eyes to find John, his eyes filled with a yearning so powerful that her heart leapt with hope for him. She clasped his clammy hand, and they bowed their heads.

The chaplain's voice rang out loud and strong. "Lord, we pray thy blessings upon our endeavor. In the hour of battle, when all around is lit by the lurid cannonade glare and the piercing musket flash, when the wounded strew the ground and the dead litter our path, we pray that we remember that you are with us. That you, the awful and infinite God of the heavens, fight for us and that you will triumph Great Father. We bow before thee invoking thy blessing. We are in times of trouble, O Lord, and sore beset by foes, merciless and unpitying. O God of mercy, grant us wisdom and strength. Shower our leaders with your counsel. If we are defeated, O God of hosts, be our stay and our guide. If we triumph and vanquish, teach us to be merciful, though our enemies would not be merciful to us. Care for the wounded and sick. And in the hour of our death, guide us to the abode you have prepared for the blest. We return thanks to thee through Christ our Redeemer. Amen."

Wiping the tears that flowed down her cheeks, Lilyan lifted up a silent prayer for Nicholas and their dear son and for John that he would come to know Christ as his Savior. With Nicholas' hand warm and secure on the small of her back, she followed the men as they left the room without a word.

It wasn't until after noon that Lilyan found herself aboard the *Lapis*, standing at the rail with Laurel and Marion bidding a tearful good-bye to Nicholas. Her spine as rigid as the posts that secured their grapevines, she kept her eyes trained on the skiff transporting him back to the *Virginia*. Cal, as if sensing her anguish, pressed against her legs and nudged her hand with his head.

Her heart, already torn asunder, suffered another blow as she watched her precious daughter bid farewell to her own warrior. John was resplendent in his kilt, cambric shirt, tartan scarf, and claymore, with a musket and powder horn slung over his shoulder. His face a study of grim determination, he clasped Laurel's hands and brought them to his lips, kissing them with a reverence that caused a hitch in Lilyan's breath.

The couple moved to stand in front of her. "Ma, will you give John the family blessing?" asked Laurel.

Her daughter's lips quivered, and her fern-green eyes were shadowed by a sadness that filled Lilyan with deep regret. *How could I have spared her this? How can I fix it? But this is Laurel's life, and she must live it. The pain she suffers now will intensify the joy she knows later.* Two powerful forces—a mother's love and a mother's wisdom—warred within her.

The giant of a man leaned down for her to kiss both of his eyelids and then his lips. Clasping the sides of his smooth, recently shaved face that smelled of mint and bay leaves, she searched his earnest, warm brown eyes. "May God keep you safe while we are apart one from the other."

Laurel whispered the words with her.

Remembrances of too many other sad farewells formed like ghostly, distorted shapes in the aching cavern that was Lilyan's heart. Pressing her hand against the intense pain in her chest, she spied Nicholas as he stood in the skiff and waved both arms over his head before boarding the *Virginia*. She returned his wave and blew him a kiss. She draped one arm across her daughter's waist and rested a hand on Cal's head, waiting for John to board the *Virginia*.

Around five o'clock, with gooseflesh running up and down her arms, she watched the fleet of four ships armed with cannons and loaded with two hundred militia and marines weigh anchor and advance toward the pirates' lair. A strong wind pressed her skirts around her legs, and she glanced up at the white sails stretched taut in the wind and heard the creaking of the rigging as the ship rolled and surged forward.

In less than an hour, the battle would commence.

CHAPTER 15

The remnants of the *Lapis* crew stationed themselves on the starboard side of the ship, and like patrons anticipating the opening act of a macabre opera, they snapped open their telescopes.

Standing on deck, Lilyan craned her neck to view the lone sailor in the crow's nest. The man, bare-chested and barefooted, his shoulder-length hair bleached nearly white by the sun, leaned breathtakingly far over the rail that circled the mast and steadied a large telescope on its tripod. She cupped her hand over her brow and squinted toward the island at ships that appeared the size of Marion's toy armada he often launched in their rain barrel at home.

The cloudless sky shone as clear and blue as a morning glory. An occasional northern wind danced over the calm sage surface of the ocean, teased open the sails, and rustled the flag atop the mainmast. The quicksilver in the ship's thermometer rose no farther than seventy-five degrees. She'd cringed when Captain Sumter had pronounced it a perfect day for battle. Today, men would fight, suffer, and die. Shouldn't lightning clatters reflect the clash of swords … thunder of clouds echo the cannon reports … rain fall like tears shed for the lost?

At the first faint echo of cannon, Lilyan and Laurel joined the crew at the rail. Her heart racing, she patted Cal's head when he tucked himself next to her. There was too much to worry about—the safety of her dear husband, of Paul, John, and all the men risking their lives to clean out the pirates' den. She cast an anxious glance at Marion, who balanced himself on the rigging of the mizzen sail. With his usual exuberance, he waved to her until the sailor beside him admonished him to hang on and watch what he was doing.

"It's started," yelled the man from the crow's nest.

"Report what you see," ordered Mr. Whitehouse, who stood beside the captain on the poop deck.

"The *Saint Andrew* got off the first shot. A broadside, right to the midships. What crew there is on the pirate ship is running around like scared whalers."

Through her telescope, Lilyan could make out the *Saint Andrew* and watched in awe as the cannon belched huge smoke rings through the air. The crewmen nearby shouted with laughter and raised their fists in the air.

"Another volley from the *Saint Andrew*," said the man standing beside Laurel. He held out his telescope to her. "Would you like to see, miss?"

"Yes, thank you, Mr...." Laurel took the spyglass and trained it toward the cove.

The man pressed a knuckle to his brow. "Hinson."

"Look, just there." Hinson pointed the way. "The pirate ship's starting to list and buckle in the middle. Sinking fast. Depending on the depth of the water, with any luck, she might sink just enough to block one of the other two pirate ships."

"Can't make out the name of the one going down," one of the sailors called out. "The closest is the *Salamander* and t'other's the *Akantha*."

The *Akantha*. Galeo's ship. A shiver ran down Lilyan's back. Was Paul on board or was he locked up in the same building where she and Laurel had been imprisoned? A picture of her son, hurt, hungry, bound in chains, seared her mind like a bolt of lightning.

Guide my Nicholas to him, Lord. Please.

"The *Salamander's* firing back. I guess they woke up," Hinson said with a chuckle.

Laurel handed the telescope back to him. "But I heard that the *Salamander* had been stripped for careening."

"You don't strip the cannon for careening, miss. Just secure them good and tight. *Salamander's* shooting back. Giving the *Saint Andrew* a beating."

"The marines are disembarking from the *Virginia* and the *Swiftsure*. Not meeting any resistance just yet," came a call from the crow's nest. "They'll land in a few minutes."

Lilyan focused her telescope on the boats. Nicholas and his men were among the marines, but they were too far away for her to pick them out. At the *crack* of musket shots, she swung her telescope to the shore and gasped at the sight of pirates taking aim at the approaching boats. Sweat trickled down her back and rolled between her tense shoulder blades.

If only I could see Nicholas. She leaned so far over the rail that Cal clamped his teeth into her skirt and tugged.

She leaned back in and patted his head. "Thank you, Cal."

"*Virginia's* been hit," someone shouted.

"Damage?" Captain Sumter demanded.

"The stern. Not that bad. She can still maneuver," a voice answered from somewhere in the ship's rigging.

Lilyan glanced at Mr. Whitehouse whose attention was riveted on Laurel, standing with her arms clasped across her waist.

With every nerve in her body on fire, Lilyan paced behind the row of sailors who watched the fight. Cal took every step, every turn alongside her. She glanced up at the sails. If she'd been wearing breeches instead of her homespun dress, she'd climb right up there beside Marion. Better yet, she'd station herself in the crow's nest. If she were a man, she'd be in the middle of the fight. As it was, she had to settle for the duty relegated to women—waiting. But waiting wasn't something she did well. Besides, her time for action, to care for the wounded, drew nearer with every cannon volley and every musket shot. She clamped her eyes shut against the vision of mangled bodies. Thanking God that there was a doctor on board, she took her place again at the rail.

If only we were closer. I want to see.

In frustration, her mind's eye visualized Nicholas and John and the three other men in the rescue party hurrying up the beach near Izzie's hut, then skulking from one dwelling to the next, skirting the woods, and heading toward the main building. Would they sneak in the back entrance and up the stairs, checking each room as they went, including the one where she and Laurel had been held? She could see the trunks of clothing, her abandoned medicine kit, the place where the guard had passed out from the potion she gave him. Were they meeting resistance? Or had everyone run to shore to fight off the invasion? Where was Paul? Where was Galeo?

Laurel spun around, strode toward a crate, and sat down, pressing her hands to her cheeks. She looked so forlorn, Lilyan joined her, enveloped by the tangible tension that crackled in the air. Cal sprawled himself across their feet.

"Ma, when did you know for sure how you felt about Da?"

"Almost from the moment we met."

"I remember him telling us about that first time. Walking down a street in Charleston, he spotted one of the most beautiful women he'd ever seen. Only you were mad as a wet hen about something. You kicked a pebble so hard, it skipped across the street and struck him in the knee."

Lilyan couldn't think why she had been so angry. But she did remember the tingling sensation upon gazing into his warm, expressive eyes for the first time. "It was on our second meeting that I knew for sure I had met my soul mate. I remember it well. I regarded his face, so gentle, so concerned, and decided that I could trust him with my life." She sighed. "Something I've had to do more times than either of us would have wished."

"After you married, when he went away to fight in the war. Was there this terrible emptiness? An ache that clawed at your belly?" Laurel pressed her hands to her stomach.

Lilyan studied the tight muscles in Laurel's face and her eyes so full of worry—eyes much more mature than when the family's journey began. Her precious daughter was in love.

"You've described the feeling well, my dear." She curled her hand over Laurel's. "As soon as John returns, your pain will become a distant memory." How true she knew those words to be.

"I see in your John some of the same qualities that drew me to your father. A steadfastness. A rock-solid comfort in times of trouble. But there is a vulnerability about him. You must always remember his tragic upbringing and realize the power you have in your love for him, which can raise him up or beat him down." She sighed. "And it doesn't hurt that he is very handsome to look at."

Laurel's eyes lit. "He is. Isn't he?"

"Have faith, sweet one. Pray for his safe return and for the strength to endure the wait. God is good. He will never forsake you—"

"Fire!" the man in the crow's nest yelled. "The buildings are on fire."

Laurel clutched her throat. "Ma. What if Paul is inside one of them? Chained or bound. Unable to get out?"

Lilyan blanched at the thought and pulled her daughter close, draping an arm around her shoulders. "Oh, my sweet girl. Try. Try hard to think of them ... all of them ... returning to us safe and sound."

Mr. Whitehouse took the steps from the poop deck two at the time and strode across the deck to stand beside them. "It won't be long now. We should know something soon."

Laurel gave him a tremulous smile, and her eyes misted as she once again riveted her attention to the shoreline.

Lilyan closed her eyes and prayed. *Please, God, if Paul was in one of those buildings... Please, let Nicholas have found him. Please, let them be on their way back to me.*

"The *Swiftsure*'s been crippled. She's dead in the water," someone shouted. "There's a pack of dinghies headed for the *Akantha*. Pirates."

Lilyan stood and clicked open her telescope in time to see the boats reach Galeo's ship. Was he going to escape? Was Paul with him? Her dry tongue stuck to the roof of her mouth.

"They're weighing anchor," reported the man beside Marion.

With that announcement, Marion scurried across the rigging and down the mast and sprinted to Lilyan, almost stumbling across Cal's back.

"Paul?" was the only word he managed to speak.

At the panicked look on his face, Lilyan swept him into her arms. Bereft of words, she kissed him on the top of his head. Together with Laurel, they huddled close and watched in disappointment as the *Akantha* slipped from the cove unchallenged.

Mr. Whitehouse hailed the captain. "Are we to follow, sir?"

"No. As much as I want to." The captain slammed his fist on the banister running across the poop deck. "We've not enough manpower nor guns. We'll await orders. Meantime, beat to quarters."

"Boats ahoy," reported the man in the crow's nest. "Six. No, seven. The marines."

"All right, lads." Mr. Whitehouse addressed the crew who, responding to the pounding of the drummer and the whistle of the piper, scrambled to their battle stations. "Prepare to take on boarders."

Will Nicholas and Paul be among them? Please, God, let it be so. She and Laurel faced the opposite side of the ship to watch as, one by one, marines climbed up the rope ladder and swung themselves onto the deck until they covered every square inch of space. Lilyan's heartbeat pounded out each moment.

Laurel wrung her fingers. "Where are they?"

The words had just left her mouth when Lilyan spotted

Nicholas. She grabbed up her skirts and ran headlong through the marines, who jumped back to make way. Unable to slow her steps, she slammed into him and pressed her face into his open collar, melting her body into his, breathing him in.

"Dear husband, you came back to me," she whispered.

His arms enveloped her, and he rested his chin on the top of her head and sighed. That sigh and his thundering heartbeat spoke more eloquently than any words.

"Paul?" she asked, dreading the answer.

He unwound her arms from his waist, held her by her forearms, and gently pushed her away. Laurel and Marion joined them, and Lilyan noticed the nearby marines moving away to give them privacy.

Nicholas' usually brilliant eyes grew as dark as unburnished bronze. "He's aboard the *Akantha*, bound for..." He scraped his fingers through his hair. "We know not where."

All the color left Laurel's cheeks, and she reached out to him. "Oh, Da."

Nicholas swept his family into his long, warm arms, and with Cal circling them, hunting for his place, they stood a few minutes, drinking in comfort from one another and gathering strength to withstand their next ordeal.

Finally, they parted, and Laurel glanced at the remaining men making their way onto the ship. "What about John?"

"Injured," he said, and seeing the tears pooling in her eyes, quickly added, "but not seriously. He should be here any moment."

In her still lifes, Lilyan often flicked a brush of white next to the shadows of a flower, opening it to the sun and instantly changing the mood of the picture. So it was with Laurel's expression. Even her body changed; her spine was no longer wilting but stood tall like the stem of a sunflower, her head bobbing in the direction of the ship's rail. Studying her daughter's face, Lilyan knew the instant she spotted John, who slowly climbed over the side, his arm in a sling.

Laurel hurried to wrap her arm around John's waist as if, with her tiny body, she could bolster him.

John grinned down at her. "*A chuisle mo chroí.*"

Puzzled, Laurel furrowed her brow.

"You'll understand in good time, hen," John spoke gruffly.

Responding to Nicholas' expression that mirrored their daughter's, Lilyan gave him a brilliant smile and whispered, "It's Gaelic for 'pulse of my heart.'"

"He does love her, then." His words a statement rather than a question.

Before she could respond, Mr. Whitehouse sprinted up to them breathing heavily, his expression grim, his eyes somber. "Captain, if you please. Captain Sumter, Colonel Barringer, and Sergeant Major Hamilton would have a word with you and Mr. Cameron in the captain's cabin. I believe we're bound to intercept Captain Galeo."

CHAPTER 16

The *Lapis*, her full sails curved into canvas parentheses, skimmed the tranquil ocean like a skater gliding over a sheet of black ice.

On deck, Lilyan, Nicholas, Laurel, Marion, and John gathered around a crate that served as a makeshift table. The women sat in ladder-back chairs fetched from the cabins, and the men settled on kegs. The muted glow from the ship's lantern in the center of the crate lit their faces and enveloped them like a golden shawl. Beyond their intimate little circle, the full moon painted the heads and shoulders of the crew with a shimmering light, casting stark shadows as they moved about their duties. Stars sparkled through the fast-moving gray clouds like crystals beyond a gauze scrim.

Cal, seated in his customary place next to Lilyan, dropped his head onto her lap.

Staring at her husband, impatiently waiting for him to explain the plan to save Paul, Lilyan tapped her foot on the decking and scratched behind Cal's ears and underneath his neck. She had paced for hours while the men holed up in the captain's cabin. Her dear son's life depended on them, and now that she had her chance to ferret out their intentions, her questions threatened to stick in her throat. Once apprised of their decisions, could she accept them?

She had to find out. "What's going to happen?"

Sliding his hands down his thighs and clasping his knees, Nicholas leaned forward. "John, it was your idea. Why don't you explain?"

With a slight wince, John crossed his arms over his broad chest, stretching his rolled-up sleeves taut over his bulging arm muscles. "The way I figure it, because Captain Galeo's ship departed in such haste, he'll need provisions soon. He'll have to seek out a port. There aren't many havens left along the coast, though. He could put into Drunken Jack's Island or Murrells Inlet in South Carolina, but pirates were rooted out of those places years ago, as was done today."

He dug the heel of his boot into the decking. "I'm guessing he'll make his way to Savannah."

Paul's fate relies on speculation?

Lilyan furrowed her brow. "Guessing?"

John uncrossed his arms and clasped the edge of the keg he sat on. "Please realize, dear lady, I know the captain's habits well. I served as his first mate for years, and this is more than a hunch. It's something I feel … here … in my gut." He pressed his hand to his stomach.

Recalling her own premonitions and intuitions, Lilyan rubbed the back of her neck. "I appreciate what you're saying, John. Please, continue."

"Yes, ma'am. At its customary knottage, and if the weather holds, the *Akantha* should reach Savannah in five days. Our plan is to outrun them. Reach Savannah ahead of them, turn, and sail back up the coast, posing as a passenger ship. A plum, ripe for the picking."

"We can do that?" Laurel asked. "Outrun the *Akantha*?"

"Aye. I'm sure of it." He locked eyes with hers and paused as if unable to pull away.

Nicholas' gaze bounced from one to the other, and he cleared his throat, a wry expression on his face. "The plan, John."

"Right." John arched his lips into a crooked smile. "The *Lapis* can outrun the *Akantha*. She's new and she carries a lighter load. No cannon."

Lilyan, unhappy with the thought of confronting a heavily armed ship, knitted her fingers together, an imitation of the muscles in her stomach. "It's hard to believe that in this vast ocean, our captain can maneuver our ship to the right place at the right time to intercept the *Akantha*. In my mind, it would take a miracle."

"Captain Sumter's as skilled a navigator as I've ever seen, Mrs. Xanthakos," said John.

"Nonetheless, I'll be praying for that miracle." Lilyan unclasped her fingers. "And what is this other part of the plan about a ripe plum?"

John's eyes lit with a roguish glint. "We'll make ourselves into something Galeo can't resist—a vulnerable target. We plan to have a group of women walking about the deck—"

"But there are only three of us on board," Laurel interrupted.

John chuckled. "Some of the daintier among the crew"—he bobbed his eyebrows—"will don dresses and disguise themselves as women."

Laurel sputtered. "I should like to see that."

"Aye. I'm sure 'twill be a sight." John winked at her. "This is how I think it will play out. Since they will want to board us, they won't bombard us. Maybe shoot a few cannonballs over our bow to scare us. Our crew will run about like landlubbers, the captain will flag surrender, and Galeo's crew will hook into our ship and lay down some walking planks between us. Once they've planked us, that's when the marines, who will have stayed hidden, will board Galeo's ship and overcome his crew."

Lilyan tried to follow along and visualize John's descriptions. "And our son?"

John glanced at Nicholas, who encouraged him with a nod. "We're hoping to surprise them. To act so quickly, they won't have time to think about Paul."

"I don't know. So much of this strategy depends on guesswork, miracles, hope." Lilyan hated sounding so pessimistic. As a rule, she looked to the brighter side of things, but how could she trust her son's life to a plot that could have earned a home in one of Shakespeare's plays?

Some problems just gotta be worked out on the run, lassie. The words of her dear protector and friend surfaced from years gone by. She remembered one occasion well. She and Callum had followed a beeline into the woods in search of a hive rich with the most honey they had ever seen in one place. Except they weren't the only ones to discover the bounty. As they rounded a stand of trees, they spotted a huge brown bear intent on swiping the hive from the limb. When the bear spotted them, he reared up, bellowed, and then charged.

"Head for the river, lassie. You hightail it that way," shouted Cal. "I'll run t'other. Move in and out, like a figure eight. Might confound him."

They both made it to the river, where they jumped into the frigid water and swam to the opposite shore. That was definitely a plan concocted in the heat of things. But encountering an angry bear hardly equaled coming up against vicious pirates.

They continued their discussion for a while until Marion was drawn to a wand shoot target the marines had set up for knife and hatchet practice using a board from one of the mess tables. Watching him walk away, Lilyan noticed the stripe of tar running up and down the back of his shirt.

"Ugh," she groaned. "Another shirt ruined with a caulk line. Nikki, really, dear, you must tell him not to nap on the deck. He'll not have one decent shirt left. It's bad enough you let him run around barefoot like a deckhand."

Nicholas pulled a face. "He's a boy on board a ship, Lilyanista. Leave him be about his clothes."

She harrumphed but couldn't resist smiling at her husband's

comical expression.

After awaiting his turn standing at the head of a cluster of lanterns lighting the target, Marion drew his longbow and loosed a succession of blunt practice arrows. With each bull's-eye, the huzzahs of the men grew louder.

John clapped and yelled with the others. "Quite a marksman."

Nicholas grinned. "Quite. As are his mother and sister."

John guffawed. "Surely, you jest."

"Would you care to observe?" Laurel jumped up and strode up to Marion, who, with a huge smile, handed her the bow.

The puzzled expression on John's face as he followed closely behind Laurel made Lilyan laugh, and she curled her fingers into Nicholas'. "He's in for a mighty surprise."

Chuckling, Nicholas stood and offered his arm. They found a place among the marines, who, watching Laurel take her stance, stared in varying degrees of bewilderment.

"Can someone so dainty even draw the bow?" one of the marines whispered.

Their puzzlement soon grew to amazement as Laurel hit the center ring three times in a row. Her last shot, dead center, brought forth a roar of huzzahs so loud, Lilyan clamped her hands over her ears.

John cocked his head toward Lilyan, his eyes aglow with admiration. "I wouldna believed it if I hadna seen it."

If you win my daughter's heart, young man, there'll be no end to the surprises in store for you. After all, Laurel was a mountain woman, trained the same as her brothers to survive in a most times unforgiving land. She could hunt rabbits with her bow and arrow, skin and tan a deer and fashion the hide into moccasins, search out the juiciest bamboo shoots and forest edibles, and gather up herbs and plants to minister to the sick and wounded. Though genteel and feminine, she was no hothouse flower, pampered, coddled, and soft. She was a chamomile like her ma. A sturdy "rebel flower," which, despite its dainty appearance and sweet fragrance, springs back stronger each time it is trodden upon.

The marines, some still mumbling their astonishment at what they had witnessed, disbanded and made for belowdecks, seeking rest in their hammocks strung in rows from the ceiling beams.

After gathering her family to pray, Lilyan, followed closely by Cal, wandered to the side of the ship to gaze at the stars. Nicholas stood behind her, stretched out his arms on either side of her, and clasped the rail. With the warmth of his chest pressing against her back, she felt safe, at home.

He rested his chin on the top of her head. "Five days, Lilyanista. We will have him back. I know it."

She nuzzled her head against his neck and felt the pounding of his heartbeat against her shoulder blades. His familiar smell enveloped her, earthy like raindrops rolling off muscadine vines and soaking into loam-covered roots. She wanted to respond, but her words caught in her throat.

He took her by the shoulders and turned her around and kissed her on her forehead. "Have confidence, *agapi mou.*" He tipped up her chin with his fingertips and studied her eyes.

The tears that had pooled in them slid down her cheeks like a swollen creek after a heavy rain.

"Shh. Shh. Don't cry, dearest." He pressed the side of her face to his chest. "I know you've been through more than most can bear, but you haven't seemed yourself in the past few days. You're pale, and you've hardly eaten. Are you unwell?"

She pulled back and curled her hands around his. Should she tell him what she suspected? If so, her news would shine like a beacon in the midst of their gloom. She let go of his hand and traced the new wrinkles that marred the skin beside his eyes. No. He had enough to worry him. She would wait until she was sure.

"I'm tired." She sighed. "Worry for Paul is eating away at my innards, and I have lost the desire for food."

"Then let us rest, Lilyanista."

She would like nothing better than to pile up in bed and throw the covers over her head. On her way down the steps, she waved to members of the crew who called out wishes for a good evening. Before retiring, she visited the cabin two doors down to bid a good night to Cassia, Izzie, and Samuel.

The next two days followed quietly one after the other, with Lilyan and her family gathering on deck around their table and observing the marines clean their muskets and sharpen their knives and bayonets.

The second night after supper, a somber-eyed Mr. Whitehouse approached them and stood with his arms clasped behind him, his gold buttons reflecting the lantern light. He slid his glance from Laurel, to John, and back again.

With an artist's eyes, Lilyan had studied the young man's intense focus on the budding relationship between Laurel and John, and she saw past his valiant efforts to disguise his feelings. If she were to paint disappointment, she would look no further for a model than Mr. Whitehouse's set jaw and his brown eyes as bleak as a mountain pine struck by lightning; its seared, oozing scar left bare to the elements.

"Good evening, sir," she greeted him.

He bowed. "The weather favors us."

"It does that." Lilyan motioned to a nearby keg. "Won't you have a seat? Join us?"

He glanced over his shoulder at the helmsman. "Thank you, I will."

When he was seated, Lilyan leaned toward him. "John puts great store in your captain's navigating abilities. Do you have the same faith?"

"I do," he responded, his somber eyes open, trustworthy.

They sat in comfortable silence for a few minutes until an object on the table caught Mr. Whitehouse's eye. "Is this a lyre?" He stood and ran his fingers along the strings. "It resembles one, at least, but it's not the same." He glanced around their circle.

Laurel picked up the instrument and placed it in her lap, curving her arms around its box-like body and resting a pick on the strings. "It's a kithara. My uncle Theo, Father's brother, sent it to me from Greece for my tenth birthday."

She began to pluck out a tune.

"Sounds like a mandolin." Mr. Whitehouse began to hum along. "I recognize this one. 'When Jesus Wept.' It's one of my favorites."

He sang the words in a clear, strong tenor. As Laurel reached the refrain, which was a round, John joined in, a vibrant basso. The three of them blended their voices, and as they reached the close of the song, a group of marines and members of the crew gathered close and broke out in applause.

One of the marines stepped forward. "Do you know 'Come Thou Fount,' lassie? 'Twas a favorite of my ma's."

"My pleasure." Laurel straightened her back and proceeded to play.

Many present sang along, including Lilyan, drawing hope and comfort from the encouraging hymn. "Here I raise my Ebenezer; Here by Thy great help I've come; And I hope, by Thy good pleasure; Safely to arrive at home."

The words died on her lips, and she lifted up a silent prayer. *Dear Lord, like Samuel, I recognize you as my stone of hope, my help in troubling times. I praise you for bringing us this far and pray with all my heart that it is your will that we will arrive safely home.*

She opened her eyes and studied the faces of the men circled around them. Some seemed to enjoy the amity, and others had faraway expressions as if yearning for homes and absent family. The obvious joy they felt showed in their enthusiastic clapping at the end of the hymn.

"Miss Xanthakos, do you know another song by Billings called 'Chester'?" asked Sergeant Major Hamilton.

Nicholas laughed. "Of course. Every proper daughter of a patriot knows that one."

Smiling, Laurel strummed the opening bars of the lively tune.

When all the marines joined in a rowdy rendition of the fiery song, her face lit. They raised their fists in defiance as they sang the words so many patriots had sung during the war with Britain, "The foe comes on with haughty stride; our troops advance with martial noise; their vet'rans flee before our youth; and gen'rals yield to beardless boys. What grateful off'ring shall we bring? What shall we render to the Lord?"

They finished the song in a deafening crescendo, "Loud halleluiahs let us sing, and praise his name on ev'ry chord."

Sergeant Major Hamilton yelled out, "What a rouser! Let's give the young lady three huzzahs!"

The men followed his lead, clearly enjoying the impromptu concert.

"All right, men," said the sergeant major, "time to retire. Clean up after yourselves before you go. Leave the deck shipshape."

He spun around to address Laurel. "Thank you, miss, for lifting my heart and the hearts of my men. It was sorely needed. You play well."

A blush stole across Laurel's cheeks.

Lilyan stole a glance at Nicholas, whose face shone with pride. *Thank you, Lord, for this man who loves his children and is strong enough to show it.*

He grinned. "Especially 'Chester.' I knew William Billings—not well, but he was an acquaintance. He and I attended the same church. One evening I had the privilege of hearing him sing 'Chester' with two of his staunchest friends and admirers, Samuel Adams and Dr. Pierce of Brookline. They stood in the church choir and sang with such patriotic fervor, the place rang with their words."

Her eyes aglow, Laurel placed the kithara on the table. "That must have been special."

"It was, dear lady. Very special indeed. Thank you for returning that most pleasant memory to me."

The sergeant major's sentiments spurred Lilyan's own thoughts back to the turbulent times of the revolution when simply saying names like Samuel Adams stoked the fires of patriotic zeal.

He bowed. "And now I will bid you all a good evening."

The family spoke their good nights and settled into a quiet time, watching the sergeant major and his marines exit the deck.

"I'll take my leave as well," said Mr. Whitehouse with a bow.

"Good evening, Mr. Whitehouse." Lilyan watched him return to the poop deck, and then she turned to Marion. "It's time you were in bed. Take Cal with you, if you please."

"Aw-w-w-w, Ma!" Marion protested.

Nicholas stood and patted his son's shoulder. "You heard your ma."

Grumbling, Marion took Cal by his collar and turned to leave, his shoulders slumped.

"My kiss, young sir?" Lilyan held out her arms. She smiled at him as he sidestepped and reluctantly lifted his cheek for her kiss. "Pleasant dreams, dear boy."

Taking her place once again in the chair, she noticed an exchange of glances between John and Laurel, who scooped her arms forward as if encouraging him to speak.

John sighed in resignation and bobbed his head. "Mr. Xanthakos ... Nicholas ... might I have a word? In private, if you please?"

"You may." Nicholas cocked an eyebrow at Lilyan.

She had an idea of what was to come, but she wasn't sure. She shrugged and stood with Laurel, and then sat with her on a chest that was nearby but out of earshot.

"Is John asking for your hand?" she asked, keeping her voice low.

Laurel ran her fingers along the folds of her skirt. "Not exactly."

"Not exactly?"

Laurel worried her bottom lip. "Though I wish with all my heart that John was asking Da's permission to marry me, I believe he is, instead, providing him a list of every impediment he can think of."

Astonished, Lilyan cast a glance at the two men. Nicholas, arms crossed and casually leaning back on the keg; John, his back rigid, perching on the side of a keg and punctuating his petition with his hands. She had observed the young couple's growing romance with mixed feelings. Part of her enjoyed watching her daughter's obvious attraction to John, the soft glow in her eyes, the demure smiles she gave to only him. But another part conjured up hindrances of her own. She knew that eventually Nicholas would share the gist of the conversation with her, but her curiosity grew with each passing moment. What were they saying?

"What sort of impediments?"

Laurel worried her bottom lip. "The difference in our ages, for one. Eight years is not so much, is it? Da is nine years older than you."

The earnest plea in Laurel's mint-green eyes struck a chord in Lilyan's heart. "No. I don't think it a sufficient worry. Though I was almost twenty when your da and I married."

"My youth is another impediment, according to John. But Ma, I'm seventeen. Or … I will be in a week's time. Back home, Amy and Sara are married. Hannah's younger than all of us, and she's with child. Why is my age relevant when I know my own mind?"

"Your birthday is next week? How do you even know today's date?" So much had happened, Lilyan hadn't kept track.

"I asked Mr. Whitehouse. He knows from the captain's log."

How different their lives would be in seven days. Would they be celebrating … or mourning?

"Oh, Ma. Listen to me. My precious brother is out there–" she swept her hand toward the shore "—somewhere. Suffering only God knows what. I feel so petty speaking of my birthday. So selfish considering my own happiness and future at a time like this."

Lilyan gripped Laurel's hands and bounced them on her lap. "Dear, sweet girl, don't reproach yourself. Your happiness and your future are important to your da and to me. I know how much you love Paul and how you worry for him. Please, continue. What else has John to say?"

Laurel crossed one ankle over the other, exposing the toes of her dainty apricot slippers a few shades darker than her gingham overskirt. "He feels strongly about the vast differences in our upbringing. What he perceives as his rough, unpolished manners."

Lilyan smiled. "I believe him to have a kind heart and a gentle manner, especially toward you, my dear. Besides, manners can be polished."

"I would not dare to say such for fear of hurting his feelings. But I agree. And maybe Da would take that on." She held her hands out palms up. "Maybe by guiding and correcting the boys in his presence? Or by providing an example for him to follow?"

"That's a lovely idea." Lilyan could not have been prouder of Laurel's solicitude and her hesitancy to damage John's pride. "What else?"

Laurel balled her hand into a fist. "He says I'm too good for him. That once people back home found out about his past … about his being a pirate … their gossip would hurt me or eventually cause a rift betwixt us. He would not be the cause of any suffering for me."

"I admire his regard for you and his desire to keep you from harm. But do you remember what James says in the Bible about an untamed tongue?"

"We cannot praise our Lord and Father with our tongue and also curse men, who have been made in his likeness."

"God's word is clear in denouncing gossip as unchristian. So anyone who would do such is not a credible source and should be ignored. Would you be able to ignore any slights a gabble grinder would make about John?"

"I—I." The color in Laurel's cheeks grew red. "I should think I could try, though I might want to smash them over the head with my kithara."

Lilyan struggled against the laughter that pushed up through her body but lost the battle, and they both started giggling.

Once sobered, Lilyan took Laurel's hand again. "You have not mentioned the most important impediment."

Laurel squeezed Lilyan's fingers. "The difference in our faith."

"You are a lovely, Christian woman. The Holy Spirit resides in you." Lilyan pressed her hand to her daughter's chest. "Right here. And I imagine he would groan if you were to marry an unbeliever. We are called upon to be helpmates to our husbands and to submit to their final decisions. I think you would become discontent should you ever come to a serious disagreement. Though I feel that gossip would not cause a rift, I am convinced that John's disbelief would. Over time. I'm afraid it's the one impediment among all you've mentioned that would cause your father to refuse his permission. He would not want his daughter to be unevenly tied to another."

Laurel's bottom lip trembled. "John and I talked about that, and he confesses that, because of his experiences, he has many doubts. But he would be willing to listen. He's sharing that with Da and is placing himself under Da's guidance and teaching. If Da will agree."

Lilyan studied her husband, listening so intently to the young man who would take his daughter from him. Of course, he would agree. She knew he would consider it a high honor to encourage someone onto the path of righteousness.

She turned her attention back to Laurel, whose expression had grown soft watching John. Was theirs a true, enduring love?

"Laurel, you say you know your own mind. Are you sure this isn't an infatuation?"

"It is nothing I've felt before." She paused and furrowed her brow, considering her next words. "Do you remember Bradley? He was the first boy with courage enough to kiss me." She pressed her fingers to her mouth. "It was exciting and very daring, but it affected nothing but my lips. And then there was Lieutenant Clayton, who showed me such attention three years ago when our family met President Washington on his visit to Camden. He flirted with me terribly and took every opportunity to touch my person. Placing my hand into the crook of his elbow. Brushing my fingertips with his when he served me punch. Lifting my hair from my shoulders when helping me don my coat."

Lilyan's eyebrows shot up. They had watched over Laurel carefully, especially around the soldiers attached to their dear General Washington. If Nicholas had known the man was taking such liberties ... well ... there was no telling what would have happened.

"All of that and"—Laurel looked over her shoulder toward the helm—"even my latest pleasantries with Mr. Whitehouse. They were all ... how can I express it? Shallow."

Her expression became serious. "You know how it feels when we swim in the river near our cabin in the summertime? The water is inviting, like warm silk flowing across your skin. But when you plunge beneath the surface, the deeper you go, the colder the water is with a sharpness that jolts all your senses alive. A powerful undercurrent that could sweep you away any moment." She pressed a trembling hand to her chest. "That's what I feel in my heart for John. Warmth and comfort from his dear person. Coupled with the most wonderful tingling, exciting, enlivening sensations."

Lilyan's attention was drawn to Nicholas, from his handsome face, the strong column of his neck, to his muscular arms, his broad chest, and his long legs. She knew exactly of what her daughter spoke so eloquently. He was her rock, her comfort in the storms of life. And how often had her Nikki's embrace swept her along in a dangerous, exhilarating current? A tide of love deeper than the ocean upon which they sailed flowed through her body. Nicholas chose that moment to lock his eyes with hers, and as though he read her thoughts, his expression grew intent. And then he smiled, crooking his lips into an expression so meaningful her heart would trip.

Oh, Nikki, our daughter will know the same depth of love with John as we have.

Yes, agapi mou.

Such was the conversation with their eyes.

With great effort, she unlocked their stare and looked up at the billowing sails. Would that all her children were blessed with a loving marriage. With his jovial, adventurous, curious spirit, what type of woman would attract Marion? And Paul? So often serious, thoughtful, and caring for others.

What do you have in mind for him, Lord? Please, if it be your will, would you let him live and grant him the love for a woman equal to Christ's love for his church?

She shuddered, knowing the answer would reveal itself soon.

CHAPTER 17

"Sail ho!" came a call from the crow's nest.

Everyone on deck stood still, including Lilyan and Laurel, who had been searching through their luggage for clothing for the unfortunate sailors who had lost the lottery. It was the first ship they had encountered since skimming the coast, then turning back northward and reaching Savannah; a trip that had taken five, long days.

"Is it the *Akantha?*" yelled Mr. Whitehouse from the helm.

"Can't make her out just yet," answered a sailor who was climbing the ratlines.

Lilyan's back muscles drew up in painful knots as Mr. Whitehouse and Captain Sumter snapped open their telescopes. Cal took a step closer. Nicholas, John, and Marion, who had been studying together in their cabin, came bounding topside. Nicholas and Marion halted at the trunks while John strode up the poop deck stairs and asked Mr. Whitehouse if he could have a look.

John, his shoulders and spine rigid, put the telescope up to his eye and studied the faraway ship.

Finding the *Akantha* meant good news and bad—moving one

step closer to Paul and moving one step closer to Galeo.

Tell us, Lilyan shouted in her thoughts, her stomach aquiver.

"It's not the *Akantha*," John announced, his expression a mixture of relief and disappointment.

Everyone took a collective sigh.

Turning back to the task at hand, Lilyan scooped down into the bottom of one of the trunks that had been hauled up from the hold, a chore that had taken longer than expected, because she and Laurel had sorted out their short clothes. No need to cause even more embarrassment by exposing their shifts, petticoats, and stays to flap about in the wind in front of the men.

She unwrapped a gauze-encased bonnet and straightened back up to find one of the sailors struggling to fasten the hooks of the mauve crepe bodice he wore over a mantua skirt. The slender man was so tall, the dress stopped at his mid-calf, exposing his tattered breeches and his bare feet.

Avoiding eye contact with Laurel, she gulped down her laughter. "May I assist you, sir?" Her voice broke on her last words.

He yanked down on the bodice hem and grumbled, "No, thank you, ma'am. Don't seem proper, somehow. I can manage."

Her eyes dancing with mischief, Laurel held out a bonnet trimmed with violets to another sailor. "Would you care to try this on? It complements the muslin gown you are wearing."

The man jerked at the puff sleeves of his high-waisted gown, ripping the seams to make room for his bulging arm muscles. "That it does." He grabbed the hat and plunked it on his head, tied the ribbons under his chin, and started to stomp away, trying to maintain what dignity he had left.

Another of the unfortunate crew, wearing a lime-green quilted pelisse and matching travel bonnet, grabbed him by the arm. "It don't tie like that, you numbskull." He loosened the bonnet ribbons and tied them into a bow at the side of the man's face. "There. Better."

"I say." A stocky, red-bearded crewman sidled forward in a

glazed cambric Chinese print dress with a busk wedged into its bodice. "There's slits in the side of this skirt. I can reach inside and grab my pistols."

"I'm hiding mine under me apron," said another, patting the front of his white muslin pinafore.

Lilyan's shoulders shook with suppressed laughter, and she knew if she didn't leave the deck soon, she would burst. In an effort to help her keep her humor in check, she concentrated mightily on unfolding her favorite Brunswick jacket. The three-quarter length garment made of soft lamb's wool dyed the color of a robin's egg was her favorite traveling gown. At her nod, one of the sailors reluctantly stepped forward and allowed her to hold it up to him. He slipped it on, but his chest was so broad it stretched out the loose pleats in the back. Unable to look him in the eye, she placed a mobcap over his loose shoulder-length hair and arranged the ruffles around his unshaven face. For a final touch, she showed him how to tuck the jacket's hood around the mobcap. The entire time, his eyes darted here and there at the other sailors, his hands balled into fists, at-the-ready for a sly remark.

A deck hand waltzed up to one of the *ladies*, bowed, and then held out the crook of his arm. "Would you care for a turn about the deck, dearie?"

The *lady* punched him in the arm with a blow that sent him stumbling into the gunwales. "I'll dearie you, you swab." Advancing toward his prey, he stumbled over his skirts.

A group of marines, who had been watching silently, started laughing and pointing.

Another seaman approached and made a mock salute. "Can you not hear the quartermaster handing out our supplies as we come aboard? 'One pea-jacket and one cloth cap. A pair of cloth trousers, flannel over- and undershirts.'" He held out his hand like a tablet, checking off each item. "'A pair of drawers, shoes, necktie, and socks. A comb, knife, pot, pan, and spoon, one bar soap, clothes bag. And...'" He paused, adding to the impromptu drama. "'One straw bonnet with dainty little purple violets and streamers.'"

The marines laughed even harder.

"Belay all this sauce!" yelled the quartermaster, standing arms akimbo, a deep frown creasing his brow. "You were told the need for this action. We've got to fool the pirates into thinking we're a bride ship. Our lives depend on how well these men carry out their orders. Cut 'em some slack."

His sobering words convicted Lilyan. These men were enduring humiliation to help her family. To save her son. She would not forget again.

The quartermaster motioned to the *ladies*. "Stow those clothes for now, and everyone get back to work. While I'm at it: All of you, listen up. If you have shoes, put 'em on. Pirates are known for tossing caltrops afore they board."

"Pardon me, sir." Marion addressed the quartermaster. "What is a caltrop?"

"Devilish devices, laddie. About an inch tall, made out of iron or steel. They have four sharp points and look like a crow's foot. And no matter how you throw them, they land with one point up. Hurts like he—" Remembering his audience, he hunched his shoulders and turned toward Lilyan, a contrite expression on his face. "Beggin' your pardon, Mrs. Xanthakos. Caltrops do some mighty painful damage when you step on 'em."

Lilyan held up her hand. "No offense taken, I assure you. I appreciate your taking time to answer my son's question. I expect we'll run into all manner of new experiences and weaponry before we're done. It's comforting to know that we have someone as knowledgeable as you on our side."

"Thank ye kindly, ma'am." The quartermaster bowed and then strode away.

Nicholas, who had been sitting nearby in a chair, snorted. "I do believe your compliments made the man blush, my dear."

"I merely spoke the truth," she said with a smile and then looked pointedly at Marion's bare feet. "You heard the order, Son.

Put on your shoes."

"Aw-w-w," Marion said in a mild protest, but seeing his mother's stern expression, he left to find his shoes.

Later, with the peal of the ship's bell indicating three o'clock, the family once again gathered on deck. This time, Izzie and Samuel sat with them.

Lilyan cuddled Cassia in her arms, cooing. "Look at her little expressions. As sweet as confection. Isn't she marvelous?"

Cal sniffed at the swaddling clothes and sidled over to plop down by Marion, who was re-lacing the buckskin ties of his quiver.

"Cal isn't impressed," said Nicholas, who sat with John and Laurel around a keg that served as a table for their cribbage game.

They all focused on Cal's bored expression and the overly dignified lift of his chin. What started as a giggle grew into laughter, though born of nerves and fear, and it became so contagious some of the crew joined in.

"Sail ho!" The announcement splashed over them like a bucket of ice water.

John exchanged glances with Nicholas, who handed him his spyglass. Grim-faced, together they hurried to the rail.

"It's her." John spoke the words softly as he looked down at Laurel, who clasped his forearm.

"It's the *Akantha*," he repeated loud enough for all to hear.

"I knew it," came a voice from nearby. "We was followed by a shark this mornin'. In our wake, it was. Sure sign someone's going to die today."

Lilyan trembled. A crewman had spoken those very words the day they had come upon the slave ship. Many people died that day.

"Beat to quarters," ordered Captain Sumter.

Nicholas strode across the deck and stood before Lilyan, who handed Cassia to Izzie. He took her hands in his and kissed her palms. "Follow the plan. Take Laurel, Izzie, and the babe and go below. Keep Cal close."

Feeling the pulse racing in a vein in her neck, she gazed into her husband's golden eyes, now sharp with dread. She splayed her hand across his wide chest. His heart hammered against his ribs, pounding with a beat equal to the signal drummer. "God keep you safe, my love. Watch after Marion." Her voice faltered on her son's name.

He curved his hands around her cheeks and captured her lips in a kiss of desperation.

Will this be our last kiss? Lilyan took gulping breaths that could not ease her rising panic.

He drew away and touched his fingertip to her chin. "We will see our Paul this day," he whispered.

Laurel bade a tearful good-bye to John and gathered up her skirts, matching his long stride as they hurried to join her parents. Marion retrieved his bow and arrow and came to stand beside them, his jaw set, his eyes steely. They stood in a circle while Nicholas blessed them and spoke in a low, solemn voice. "We can do all things through Christ, which strengthens us."

A group of marines, heads bowed and huddled around their young chaplain, caught Lilyan's attention.

How many of those young, proud, determined faces would she see again after the battle?

"About ship!" commanded the captain.

"All right, ladies," yelled the quartermaster. "Time to dress. Keep your face turned away, Sellars. Don't want them shocked by that bright red beard under your bonnet."

Some of the sailors guffawed until the quartermaster stared them down.

Mr. Whitehouse made his way toward Lilyan and her family through the men now donning their female garb. "That's the captain's order to prepare for tacking. It will take us a while as we play out our charade. If they rise to our bait, they'll more than likely sail with us hank-for-hank." He caught the curious lift of Lilyan's brow. "Progressing with us. Tacking along with us at equal speed. When they get close enough, they'll fire a shot over our bow. That will be the sign they mean to board us." A muscle in the side of his jaw quivered. "Stay below, ladies. Don't come up till you're given the all clear."

With that, he pressed a knuckle to his forehead and returned to stand beside the captain at the helm.

Before leaving, Lilyan gave Marion a tremulous smile, amazed at his demeanor, even though his distraught sister clung to him. Almost before her eyes, her son changed from a high-spirited, rakish boy into a determined man, intent on a somber mission.

"God be with you, dear one," she whispered to him and unraveled Laurel's arms from around his neck. "Come, Laurel. We must take our place."

"Do us proud," Izzie called out to Samuel, who leaned against a musket as tall as he.

Izzie dropped her face into the sleeping baby's swaddling clothes to hide the tears that streamed down her cheeks.

Before the women took a step, John called out, "Wait. Just a moment."

Her insides tumbling over themselves, Lilyan watched him wrestle a ring from his pinky finger. He held Laurel's trembling hand, kissed the ring, and slid it onto her thumb, the only finger it would fit. He struggled to say something, but his larynx bobbed up and down, leaving him to speak his farewell with his eyes.

Laurel gulped and would have stayed, but Lilyan pulled her away, and holding on to Cal's collar, she led them down the stairs. There, in the stuffy cabin, she grabbed a fan to cool the sweat beads that had popped out on her forehead. They waited and waited, hearing only the occasional bump or clatter from topside. The walls of the cabin closed in, becoming a stifling prison. The ship's bell rang twice.

"It's five o'clock. Two hours. Two hours have passed." Lilyan groaned her impatience and perched on the side of the bed beside Laurel, who had clamped her hands into fists resting in her lap; her knuckles had gone white. Cassia, oblivious to everything, slept on a pillow at the head of the bed. Izzie remained rigid as a statue seated on the edge of a chair in the corner.

Lilyan jumped back up, stepped over Cal, and began pacing the cabin until a tap on the door sent a lightning bolt shooting down her spine. If she'd been a cat, she'd be digging her claws into the ceiling.

She yanked open the door, stopping the sailor in mid-motion of his next knock. "Yes?"

"Mr. Whitehouse says to tell you it won't be long now. Batten down your hatches." He saluted and walked away through a group of grim-faced marines gathered around the steps, clenching their muskets.

As soon as Lilyan closed the door, a deafening explosion brought the three of them to their feet. They huddled in the center of the cabin, swaying with the pitch of the ship as it began to slow down. The ship shuddered and jerked, tossing the women up against the wall. Izzie ran to the bed and scooped Cassia into her arms. To their astonishment, the babe slept through it all.

Lilyan wrapped her arm around Laurel's shoulders. "We must have rammed against the *Akantha*."

The jarring slam was followed by two loud bangs of wood against wood and then the bloodcurdling yells of the marines charging up the steps and across the planks. The muffled cracks and pops of musket and pistol fire came in rapid succession.

What transpired topside? Did Nicholas fight for his life? Were their numbers sufficient to overcome the pirates? And what of Paul? Everything had happened so quickly, she never heard a stated plan to rescue him. Had they even made a plan? Was Paul alone … afraid … listening to a war that raged overhead?

"I can't stand this." Lilyan wrung her hands. "I've got to see what's transpiring."

Laurel gasped. "Ma, you must stay here. We were told to stay put."

"I don't want to seem needlessly reckless, Laurel, but I simply cannot wait here while my son is left to cope alone. I'm going topside." She noted the panic in her daughter's eyes and patted her pale cheek. "I'll be careful. I promise."

She slowly cracked open the door, which Cal took as his signal to follow.

"No, Cal. Stay," she ordered.

He pushed against her legs and woofed his disagreement, but Lilyan opened the door wide enough to slip through and closed it in his face. His frantic scratching and whines followed her as she crept up the steps. Catching the distant clashing of metal against metal, she crouched at the top of the stairs and peered out. She wasn't sure what she was expecting, but an abandoned deck wasn't one of them. Still creeping, staying low, she made her way toward two planks stretched between the ships.

"Mama!" screamed an unfamiliar voice.

She cringed. The sound came not from one of her children, but from a dying man crying out to his mother.

Rough planks clawed at the folds of her skirt, and the tips of her fingers stuck to the tar holding the boards together. Reaching the side of the ship, she stood, and the scene that greeted her was something out of a horrible nightmare. Having spent their ammunition, the pirates and the marines, in menacing groups of twos and threes, were engaged in clashing sword fights and hand-to-hand combat. Broken, mangled bodies were strewn across the *Akantha*'s deck like ninepins in a deadly bowling game; bloody legs and arms bent at angles they were never meant to be. She found herself staring into the ferocious orbs of a burly man, his long, black beard plaited with yellow ribbons. He sneered, exposing two gold teeth. She found that she couldn't move nor could she take her eyes from him—until an arrow whizzed through the air and lodged in his chest. He looked down, puzzled, as if he couldn't believe what he was seeing, and then he keeled over face down, jamming the arrow out through his back. Stunned, she followed the trajectory of the arrow to discover Marion in the crow's nest, drawing a bow for another shot.

Apparently, in an effort to make more room for cannon, the pirates had removed the ship's side walls. Well-placed shoves sent many of the combatants straight over the edge of the ship, screaming as they fell into the sea.

Desperate, she scanned the carnage until she caught sight of Nicholas, his back to her, lunging across the fo'c'sle, thrusting his sword into the belly of his opponent. He turned just in time to fend off a blow from a pirate who charged at him, brandishing a boarding ax. Nicholas wrestled the weapon from the man's hand, stabbed him with a knife, and tossed him overboard.

She hitched up her skirts, and, using the gunwale slats and the rail as steps, she climbed up onto one of the boarding planks—where she made the mistake of looking down. There, in the narrow corridor between the two vessels, floated the bodies of scores of men whose blood had turned the sea red. She gulped down the bile that threatened to spew from her mouth. Trembling, too afraid to stand up, and ignoring the splinters that ripped through her stockings and bloodied her knees, she crawled across the narrow piece of wood and onto the *Akantha*. She spotted Nicholas again, and part of her desperately wanted to hail him. But he fought for his life. Refusing to put him in more danger, she determined to stay out of his line of sight. Two men, swords clashing, came upon her so quickly, she had to lunge herself over a bloody body to avoid being trampled. At that moment, a terrible chill ran across the back of her neck, so strong that she scrubbed at the skin. All around her were locked in mortal combat. There was no plan to rescue her son. It was left to her.

She took a moment to catch her bearings, her eyes darting here and there, searching for the entrance to the hold.

At last she spotted it, and focusing only on the grate partially covering the passageway, she stepped over bodies and around fighting men so intent on staying alive, she might well have been invisible. Clasping the side of the upside down cockboat in the center of the deck, she duck walked, her bloodied knees burning, to the top of the stairs.

Slowly, steadily, one by one, she maneuvered the steps until she reached the lower deck and relative quiet compared to the combat going on over her head. Once there, she soon realized that the *Akantha* was built differently from the *Lapis*. She was surprised to find herself among rows of cannon. She reasoned that the hold must be another deck below, but where were the steps? She grabbed a lantern madly bobbing from a hook in a beam, and she raced across a wide corridor, dodging cocoon-like hammocks lashed to the ceiling. At the end of the deck toward the aft, she found the stairs she sought. The next level was even darker than the first. The light from only a handful of lanterns didn't reach past the center of the cavernous room. Crates, barrels, kegs, extra cannon, and cannonballs secured in pyramids up against the walls; and the smell of burnt food, rancid water, and body sweat lingered in the air. The air was cooler but so thick and smelly, it was like breathing soup. She found a gaping black hole in the center of the room, from which a stench wafted so horrible, so debilitating, she cast up her accounts on the floor. Eyes burning, she bunched up the hem of her skirt and wiped her face. She pinched her nose and took gulping breaths through her mouth.

She leaned over and angled the lantern down a long, steep ladder.

Dear Lord, I don't want to go down there. Please, give me strength.

Every part of her body quivered in revulsion, but she knew what she must do. With gooseflesh running up and down her spine, she turned around, set the lantern on the floor, and stepped on the first rung of the ladder. After two more rungs, she clasped the lantern once more in her right hand, and curling her left arm around the slats, she slowly made her way down. Her last step off the ladder was into calf-deep, freezing water that smelled like burnt, rotten eggs and threatened to turn her stomach again. Worse than the bilgewater was the scurrying and scratching of rats and cockroaches fleeing the light. Woozy and nauseated, she stood for a few moments, took a step, and nearly stumbled over a pile of ballast stones. She lifted the lantern, searching one way and then the next, seeing nothing but the slimy black walls of the bilge compartment.

He's not here.

Slumping in disappointment, she heard a splash and shuddered as a rat swam past her and jumped onto a ledge about three inches above the water line. Watching it run, she thought she spied a flash of white.

"Paul!" she shouted and sloshed through the water toward the form curled up on the ledge.

She put down the lantern and gathered him into her arms, wincing at the coldness of his limbs. "Paul. It's Ma. I'm here. You're safe now."

But there was no response. It was then she noticed his pallor and the sharp jabs of his bony arms and legs as he lay across her lap, his head resting against her shoulder. He was emaciated, weighing no more than he had when he was eight. There wasn't a place on his skin that wasn't bruised or scraped.

She brushed his thick, greasy, lice-infested hair across his forehead. Why wasn't he responding? His chest was still, no sign of breathing.

A crushing fear squeezed at her heart as she slid her fingers down his arms to his wrists and then to the base of his neck seeking a pulse. Nothing.

"I am too late," she whispered against his cheek.

A grief as old as Eve whirled through her body and clawed its way through her ribcage and into her throat, and she began screaming and sobbing, rocking his body to and fro and massaging his angular shoulder blades. "I am too late. Too late."

Dear God, is my son with you now? With Ma and Da, Callum, Elizabeth, and Francis? How can I live without him? She clasped her neck. *Oh, the pain. I cannot breathe from the weight of it.*

At the moment her heart would have broken asunder, she noticed the lantern glow intensify, and she heard a voice within her head as clear as if spoken.

Do not grieve, daughter. He remains with you still.

She felt a flutter beneath her fingertips that were splayed over Paul's heart, like the quickening she had experienced when her son first made his presence known in her womb. With hesitant joy, she began to rub up and down his arms and over his body.

"Wake up, dearest. Wake up." She felt so giddy, she began to laugh, and tears flowed down her cheeks.

"He is alive, then," echoed a voice through the darkness.

Terror crept its way up her throat and burned her mouth with the acrid taste of sulfur.

Galeo.

CHAPTER 18

If possible, the dank, forbidding room grew colder, and Lilyan clamped her jaws together to keep her teeth from chattering.

Galeo trudged through the bilgewater, hopped onto the ledge, and stopped to make a bow. He bent low and swept his hat in an exaggerated arc, making a mockery of the gesture.

He donned his hat that was adorned with bright crimson feathers and crossed his arms over his chest. "I couldn't believe my eyes when you stepped onto the deck of my ship. If I hadn't been otherwise occupied, I would have applauded your bravery as you managed your way across the plank."

He squatted, bringing his eyes level with hers. "You, dear lady, are a gem among women. Unfortunately, you and your family have become an irritation. A thorn in my side, if you will." He giggled, a feminine, yet menacing, sound. "Ha! A thorn. Like my *Akantha*."

A feral gleam lit his eyes as he swept them over Paul, who was draped across Lilyan's lap. "Your son annoyed me like an itch I could not scratch. And he surprised me. Not a brawny fellow, he still withstood all the punishment I meted out. Believe me, I gave it my best. But he simply would not die. Having him thrown down here, I was sure I had seen the last of him. But no. There he lies, in the bosom of his adoring mother." He waggled his eyebrows. "And what a bosom, if I recall correctly."

Lilyan shuddered at his vileness and struggled desperately to shut out the visions of what this cruel monster must have done to her son. She knew him capable of anything. When Galeo pressed his hand on her shoulder, using it as a prop to stand, she tightened her arms around Paul.

Towering over her, Galeo curled his body toward her like a coiled snake ready to strike. "As I think on it, you both may be of use. You, my hostage. He, my leverage."

He held forth his hand. "Let him go, Lilyan, and come with me."

Her stomach lurched. "I refuse."

"I advise you very strongly to change your mind. Because if you don't—" He slipped a knife from the scabbard tied next to his sword. "I will snuff out, once and for all, the flicker of life he so desperately clings to."

She glanced down at Paul's dear bruised and swollen face and was moved to kiss his forehead. "You promise not to harm him?"

Her eyes raked his face. What was she thinking? Galeo, one of the foulest people she had ever encountered, would not keep to his word.

He pressed a hand to his heart. "I am wounded by your doubt."

It would mean nothing to this evil man to kill them both. But what choice did she have?

He sneered. "Ah. You are coming 'round to my way of thinking."

His uncanny ability to read her mind stunned and confused her, and she shook from the fear of it.

"It's your eyes, love. They are so expressive and mirror your thoughts."

She immediately shuttered her eyes with her lids and concentrated on Paul. "I'll come with you, but only if you remove him from this terrible place."

"I admire your gumption, but you are in no position to make demands."

She jerked up her head and studied his face, tired of playing mouse to his cat. Determined to turn the tables and demonstrate her own powers of reckoning, she chose her words carefully. "You desire me. More than you want to let on."

He blinked rapidly. "Your perceptive abilities are as remarkable as your lovely … face."

She sat straighter, adjusting Paul's body across her lap. "I'll come with you. Willingly. Be yours."

"In whatever way I choose?" He curved his lips into a lascivious grin. "I must warn you, my imagination knows no bounds."

She recoiled as if she'd been struck and felt the blood draining from her face. "In whatever way you choose."

He snapped his heels together and bowed again. "We have a bargain. Give him to me. You precede me, and I will carry him."

Even with his burden, he climbed rapidly up the ladder. Once in the storage area, he deposited Paul none too gently on the floor, and then crossed the room to reconnoiter the stairs leading to the cannon deck. Lilyan dropped to her knees and pressed her fingers to Paul's chest, rejoicing at the faint but regular beat.

As she started to rise, she felt the pressure of cold, sharp steel on her neck.

"Slowly, my dove." He shoved her body in front of his, one arm draped across her midriff and the other holding a knife to her throat.

His shirtsleeve reeked of gunpowder, blood, and bay rum pomade. Those smells, mixed with the foul odor wafting from the bilge, coupled with the pressure of his arm across her stomach, threatened to make her retch. She coughed and swallowed down the threat.

She clamped her hands around the arm holding the knife and pulled down, but to no avail. "There's no need for this, Galeo. I said I would come with you."

He pressed a kiss against her ear. "How I adore hearing my name on your lips. But you will understand the necessity when we reach topside. We do not as yet know who is winning the battle."

Her chest muscles tightened in alarm. That the pirates would prevail had not crossed her mind.

Halfway up the stairs, she caught a glimpse of Paul, who was lying so cold and still, she lifted up a silent prayer. *Heavenly Father, I ask nothing for myself, but for my son. You spoke to me and comforted me and let me know it's not Paul's time yet. Please, give him his health back and let him be strong again. As with everything, I ask this in your will and in the name of your son, Jesus.*

She had hoped her prayer would ease her burdens, but questions crowded in. What was God's will for Paul? God was the great physician, but would he choose to bring Paul back to health?

Her shoulders weighed down with her worries, she ceased her struggles and moved with Galeo across the room. After climbing several sets of stairs, they finally reached the galley way to the top deck. To Lilyan's mind, though she still heard a handful of blows and grunts and groans, the din of fighting had lessened. Galeo nudged her up the last two steps and clamped the knife tighter to her neck, piercing the skin. It stung, and it frightened her. Would he kill her outright or wait a while so he could fully enjoy terrorizing her?

Though it was near evening, the light shining around her blurred Lilyan's vision for a moment. She squeezed her eyelids and blinked away her tears to discover a group of marines slowly circling in on about a dozen pirates near the steps to the poop deck. To her relief, she spotted John sitting on the steps, resting his forehead on his claymore. Mr. Whitehouse, the sleeve of his uniform ripped away, was leaning over a uniformed man. She couldn't see his face but assumed he must be Captain Sumter.

Where was Nikki? She quickly scanned the deck area and spotted him slumped against the rail at the helm. Relief flooded through her, and she dropped her chin onto Galeo's wrist.

Nikki, who still had not seen her, jammed his fists onto his hips and his stomach lurched with each jagged breath. He straightened and looked down at the tattered, blood-soaked shirt that barely clung to his shoulders. Scowling, he ripped it off and flung it away. His shoulders drooped, and he leaned heavily again on the rail.

Lilyan frantically examined his exposed chest, which was bruised, but otherwise unharmed. The blood belonged to his enemies.

Her beloved was alive and with no critical wounds. "Nicholas! Thank God you are safe."

Her cry stunned the men around her into a standstill. Incredulous, Nicholas whipped his head up and took stock of her and Galeo before he vaulted over the rail and sprinted across the deck, sword in hand, weaving through and jumping over the fallen marines and pirates.

"Ah, the famous Captain Xanthakos," Galeo whispered in Lilyan's ear.

He waited for Nicholas to come within a few yards before shouting, "Stay where you are. This blade is poised over her jugular. It would take only an instant for me to kill your beloved wife." He studied several nearby marines who threatened to close in. "And that would be a shame for all, would it not?"

Nicholas scanned Lilyan, searching for injuries just as she had when she saw him. Seeming satisfied that, so far, she was unharmed, he focused his eyes on hers. The love she saw in them permeated her body, shored up her wobbly legs, and put an end to her trembling.

Reluctantly, he took his eyes from her face and stared at Galeo. "What do you want?"

Galeo laughed. "Forthright. To the point. I like that. Fine figure of a man, too. I wondered what type of man our Lilyan had taken to her bed."

Once again he bent his face low, and the heat of his breath on her cheek made Lilyan shudder. "You do not disappoint me in your choice of mate, my dear."

His words made Lilyan feel queasy ... dirty ... and she worried about the murderous fire that leapt in Nicholas' eyes.

"You don't like anyone else touching her, do you?" Galeo's voice was as slimy as the bilgewater that had collected in Lilyan's shoes.

Keep calm, Nikki. Don't let anger rule your judgment.

"I ask again, Galeo. What do you want?"

"Drop your weapon, for one," Galeo ordered, the steely edge returning to his voice. "Then have your men stand down."

Nicholas' sword clattered to the deck. "You heard him," he yelled out to his men.

The sailors, hesitant at first, held on to their weapons and grumbled among themselves. Mr. Whitehouse, recognizing the hold Galeo had over Nicholas, bent down and placed his sword on the deck. "We must do this. He will kill Mrs. Xanthakos."

"Probably gonna kill her anyways," came a voice from the group.

The grizzled whisper held some truth, and Lilyan braced herself.

"Belay that," said the quartermaster. "How many of you here has she cared for, sewed up, and bandaged? We owe her."

The crew reluctantly, slowly, dropped their guns, knives, and swords into a pile and backed away. Some of the pirates pushed their faces up close to the crewmen, crowding them, sneering and laughing.

"Now, have your men clear this deck. Throw the dead overboard," said Galeo.

Nicholas jerked his head toward the marines. "What of the wounded?"

"Do you truly imagine that I care? Throw them over as well." Galeo loosened his hold on Lilyan's waist long enough to grab a pistol from a corpse that lay at their feet.

As if posing for a portrait, the three of them remained still while the marines picked up the dead—under the arms, by the neck, or by the boots—and dragged them to the side of the ship, leaving trails of gore in their wake. It wasn't long before the deck boards were exposed once more.

Lilyan shook her head against the vision of more bodies floating in between the ships. Nicholas' cheeks turned pale, but she could tell from his glare that his mind was working to retrieve the upper hand.

Galeo's chuckle rumbled in his chest and vibrated against Lilyan's shoulder blades. "Now. You will kindly lead your men down to the hold."

Nicholas braced himself. "That, I won't do."

"Pity," Galeo spoke nonchalantly, and then without warning raised his pistol, cocked it, and aimed for Nicholas' chest.

"Nikki!" Lilyan's primal scream ripped through her throat.

An instant before the sparks lit the gunpowder, she pushed on Galeo's arm, thwarting the bullet, which grazed Nicholas' arm as he dove for cover.

At that moment, the high-pitched howl of a wolf rose in the air, echoing through the sails and sending gooseflesh across Lilyan's neck.

Ever a superstitious lot, the spooked pirates stared wide-eyed at each other.

"Unnatural," one stammered.

Another pointed toward the source of the wailing. "Banshee!"

The pounding of running feet set the pirates into a panic, and they closed ranks into a knot. At the click of nails against wood, they all turned, almost as one, to find Cal bounding across the plank. Flying through the air, he lunged his massive body toward Lilyan and Galeo and clamped his fangs into the captain's wrist. Galeo dropped the knife, and his shrieks of anger and frustration rang in Lilyan's ears. In one seamless motion, Cal shoved her aside, reared up on his hind legs, and pressed his paws against the screaming man's shoulders.

Lilyan slammed onto the deck and fought the black spots that whirled in front of her eyes. She looked up to find Cal, gnawing at Galeo's neck, turning his squeals into sickening gurgles. As if dancing, Cal led the captain the few feet to the exposed edge of the deck and pushed him over.

Cal's triumphant howl spurred the marines into action. They wrestled weapons from the pirates, pushed them against the side of the ship, and made them kneel with their hands over their heads.

Warm, loving, familiar arms circled her waist and would have lifted her had she not shaken her head vehemently. "Nikki, it's Paul. He's below. He's alive. You must go to him."

Nicholas pressed his cheek against hers. "Yes, *agapi mou*."

He turned on his heel and took off running. "John," he called out over his shoulder. "To my wife, please."

One of the *Lapis'* crew slipped past Lilyan and peered over the side of the ship. "Sharks is bearing down on him. Can you believe it? The Shark gettin' eaten up by a shark."

Dazed, Lilyan felt herself being lifted into a pair of powerful arms.

"So, there is justice in this world." John pushed his words through his grinding teeth.

Lilyan teetered on the edge of a bottomless, black pit. "John ... do you see P-Paul?" Dizziness invaded her head that buzzed with a thousand bees.

"I do." John lifted her up higher onto his chest and gasped. "Ach! What did they do to him?"

The horror in his voice nudged her over the brink and into darkness.

CHAPTER 19

Lilyan came awake the following morning in their cabin bed on the *Lapis*. She had slept so hard she felt fuzzy-headed and was slow to sort out the weights that pressed on her legs and across her body.

She was curled on her side next to Paul, who faced away from her toward the wall. She wiggled her toes and felt Cal sprawled across her and Paul's feet. When she tried to turn onto her back, she realized that Nicholas lay sideways with his head and arms draped across her body.

"Nikki." She patted his arm, and he grumbled. "I must use the necessary."

He groaned and sat back in the chair he had pulled next to the bed, rubbing his face with his hands. "Sorry, my sweet. Let me help you up."

He started to rise but sat down quickly, pressing his hands to his back. "Oh. My spine's been ridden over with a caisson full of cannonballs."

She sat up and cupped his cheek, stubby with a two-day old beard. "Did you sleep in the chair all night?"

"You both were so cold." He looked around her at Paul. "He hasn't moved. Not one muscle."

She twisted around and blanched at the sight of Paul's bald head. Gingerly, she caressed his scalp that was crisscrossed with more scrapes than she could count and a bruise the size of her palm at the base of his neck.

Nicholas stretched his arms over his head. "We hated to do it, but his hair was so filled with vermin, we thought it best to shave it."

The night before, when she came to aboard the *Lapis*, Nicholas sent her off to bathe away the stench of the *Akantha*. Laurel, a most loving handmaiden, cared for her as she would her own babe. She tenderly removed the splinters from her knees, washed her hair, scrubbed her with her favorite lemon-scented soap, and disposed of the soiled dress and shoes. Lilyan didn't care that Nicholas had paid a fortune for the shoes. She knew every time she saw the toes peeping out from her skirts, her thoughts would be thrust back into the living nightmare her son had endured in the bowels of the *Akantha*.

Nightmares. Would she suffer those? And Paul? Though unconscious, did he wrestle his memories?

In the cabin two doors down, Nicholas and Marion had immersed Paul's battered body in an oak bathtub filled with warm, soapy water. The filthy water needed changing twice.

After he placed Paul beside Lilyan in their cabin bed, the haunted look on Nicholas' face and the tears in Marion's eyes told the gruesome tale more poignantly than any words could have. Though they hadn't gone into detail, what her husband and son did say about Paul's battered body made her ill. Thankfully, from what Nicholas could determine after a thorough examination, Paul suffered no broken bones, but many of his lacerations were puffy, red, and septic.

Late in the evening, before consenting to Laurel nursing the wounded and before allowing herself to sleep, Lilyan had demanded and received assurances from John that he wouldn't leave her daughter's side.

And now, after a restless night, she lingered by the bed and took the opportunity to examine her son closely, tracing her fingertips over his still, cold limbs. She grew concerned about the bruise on his neck, but his barely audible breathing and comatose state worried her the most. He must have water and food soon, or his fragile heart would give out. Reluctantly she turned away, and after tending to her needs, she removed a dress from a hook on the wall.

Nicholas took it from her. "Let me." After sliding the homespun garment over her head and down her body, he kissed her forehead and then helped her lace the bodice.

When he turned her to knot a kerchief around her shoulders, she noticed deep grooves in the cabin door. "What happened there?"

"Cal happened. Trying to get to you when you left to board the *Akantha*. We bandaged him the best we could."

She spun around and sat on the bed, examining the bandages on the dog's paws. "You poor dear." She leaned over and kissed the top of his head. "You're my hero, sweet boy. You saved my life."

Cal lifted his neck for her to scratch it and then scooted up the mattress to lay next to Paul's back.

"And he rid the world of Galeo." Nicholas shuddered. "I hate to speak his name. Evil man."

"Then let's make a pact never to say his name again."

"Done."

"Nikki, will you turn Paul over?"

Cal waited patiently for Nicholas to gently settle Paul onto his back and rearrange his nightshirt and the covers. Once that was done, the languid dog stretched his long body into the crook of Paul's arm.

Nicholas patted Cal's shoulder. "That's a good boy. Keep him warm."

Lilyan stood beside her husband, and the two of them surveyed their son's damaged body.

Feeling vulnerable, she leaned closer against Nikki's rock-solid hip. "He's with us again."

"Yes." He pulled in a deep breath and let it out slowly. "Would that he comes awake soon."

Drawing comfort and strength from each other, they stood silently. Lilyan visualized their deep love for their child curling out from their hearts like finely hatcheled flax silk and weaving a cocoon around his body. But love alone would not mend him.

Pressing her fingers to her forehead, she broke the sad silence. "We must think of a way to give him liquids. He will die soon if we do not." She struggled to speak the last words.

"Spooning a few sips—broth or water—at the time wouldn't do?" he asked.

"No. In his present state, the muscles in his throat can't work on their own, and the liquid might go down the wrong way. It could cause him to cast up his accounts."

"Could we massage his neck?"

"No, he still might strangle." She snapped her fingers. "I have it. I remember something Golden Fawn told me about feeding someone who is unconscious. We need about a half-foot of something hollow and smaller around than my little finger. Golden Fawn used a hollow reed." She tapped her forefinger into her palm. "Then some honey and warm water."

Nicholas furrowed his brow. "Tell me how you would apply it. I can't picture what we'll be doing."

"We'll hold Paul's mouth open. Press the tube against the side of his throat and let the honey mixture slide down the tube. We must make sure the tube is correctly situated so as not to cause him to strangle or gag."

"I see. Like a mama bird feeds her chicks." Nicholas opened the door to the cabin. "I'll start searching, and I'll send Marion to Cooky for the honey."

After Nicholas left, Lilyan fussed with the bed covers and then sat in the chair.

"I don't know if you can hear me, dearest, but we are all—even Cal—working so very hard to help you heal. I pray every waking moment that God will be merciful." She caressed his forehead and traced his nose, lips, and chin with her fingertips. "Try, Paul, try to make your way back to us."

Her conversation turned to Cal's heroic deed and the death of the pirate captain, whose name she refused to acknowledge. Even in her thoughts, she wouldn't give that man a name. Each time she mentioned Cal's name, the languorous dog opened his eyes halfway and snuffled.

She spoke of their plans for feeding him and then turned her words toward plans for the future.

"I know you want to attend medical school in Edinburgh, but I've been looking into options. After all that has happened, I hope you will reconsider studying in Europe. Which is … so far away."

Much too far away.

"I don't want to meddle in your business, nor would your father and I impose our will upon yours, but there are two fine American schools offering doctorates in physic and in medicine. One in New York and one in Philadelphia." *Still too far away.*

"Do you remember volunteering to help deliver Cassia? Though I refused your offer, it was so dear of you to ask. Is that something you would care to do in your practice? If so, I hear both schools offer courses in midwifery." She sighed. "How our world is changing. Though I cannot imagine a woman desiring a man to deliver her babe. Even someone as gentle as you, my dear boy."

She took in a ragged breath and studied Paul's ghost-white face spattered with black and blue patches, some turning vivid green and purple, others faded to a soft gray. She was so desperate for him to awaken, her body ached with it.

"I'm chattering, I know. But I'm praying that something I say might catch hold of your interest. Or your ire. Or your amusement."

Nicholas entered the cabin and tossed some objects onto the mattress. "You wouldn't believe how everyone pitched in to find an instrument we can use. One man hollowed out a chicken bone with a rigging needle, but I think it's too jagged. Another searched through straw packing in the hold, but it's too old and crumbled into pieces. The captain offered his pen quills, but they're too short."

"Will this do?" He held up the stem broken off a clay pipe.

She studied it a moment and nodded. "It just might."

Armed with the pipe, they took turns holding open Paul's mouth and laboriously, drop by drop, administering what amounted to a few teaspoons of honey and water. Finally, her neck and arm muscles aching, Lilyan determined they should rest. Hoping it wasn't her imagination, she thought she saw some color in Paul's cheeks and mentioned it to Laurel when she and John came to check on them.

Despite John's doubtful look, Laurel smiled.

"Ma?" Laurel asked. "It's a beautiful day. The seas are calm, and there's a nice breeze blowing. Could we take Paul…?"

"I – I," Lilyan looked to Nicholas. "What are your sentiments?"

Nicholas considered a moment. "It might help. Yes." His expression brightened. "I think it might."

John left and returned minutes later with a stretcher, and they set about transferring Paul's emaciated body as gently as possible onto the canvas frame lashed tautly between two poles. Nicholas would have carried his son in his arms, but he feared breaking his fragile bones.

On deck, they secured the stretcher on top of two large kegs and gathered around smaller kegs for the family to sit on. Many of the sailors stopped their work, some to nod their sympathies, others simply to stare.

The quartermaster approached Lilyan and handed her something from behind his back. "Found this in the supplies. It's clean." He glanced at Paul's battered head and grimaced. "I heard he might need it."

Lilyan unfolded the cotton skull cap and slipped it onto Paul's head. "Thank you, sir, for your kindness."

Marion lay on the boards beside Paul's stretcher and gazed up at the fluffy white clouds hanging low in the cerulean sky. "Paul, I wish you'd open your eyes. There's a raccoon straight overhead." He moved his finger as if sketching.

Laurel pointed too. "I see it."

Lilyan studied the clouds. "Yes. And look, to the right. It's Neptune rising from the sea."

It wasn't long before they all took turns playing a game of cloud pictures, laughing and urging Paul to open his eyes and join in the merriment. A nearby deckhand strained his neck and stared upward. He pulled off his cap and scratched his head. His puzzled expression made Lilyan chuckle.

The family had finished the game only a few minutes when the marine chaplain moved to Lilyan's side and bowed. "Mrs. Xanthakos. There are some faithful among us who would like to express our sympathies. And"—he paused to look back at his men—"we who would ask your permission for a healing prayer service."

The chaplain's earnest request brought tears to Lilyan's eyes and formed a lump in her throat that prevented her from speaking.

She threw a pleading glance at Nicholas, who stood and bowed to the chaplain. "We would be most honored."

The chaplain nodded to his men, who congregated in a circle, resting their hands on each others' shoulders. Many of the crewmen removed their hats and stepped closer. Lilyan took one of Paul's hands, and Nicholas the other. Mr. Whitehouse and Captain Sumter, who had recovered from his wounds, completed the group. When she noticed John standing at a distance, his expression aloof as if a curious spectator, her heart sank. Laurel clasped her hand, and she sensed her daughter's disappointment.

A stillness like a soft, downy blanket descended upon the group. A wind curled gently through the slackened sails, causing the rigging to creak, reminding Lilyan of her rocking chair on their cabin porch back home.

The chaplain lifted his face to the sky as if basking in the sun. He waited so long, Lilyan wondered if he would ever speak. And then, to her amazement, the silence came alive with the presence of the Holy Spirit. He stirred her heart, invigorating and powerful like flash lightning dancing through low-lying violet clouds, and at the same time peaceful like wind rustling through a giant cathedral of pines on a still, moonlit evening. Laurel gripped her hand. She must have felt it too.

"Our most dear and heavenly Father. You are the giver of life. In you are only good things. In you are mercy and love. In you are freedom from worry and freedom from pain.

"You spoke to us through your servant Matthew who told us of your son, Jesus, as he went about Galilee, teaching in the synagogues and preaching the gospel and healing all manner of sickness and all manner of disease among the people. Through Luke, we know that many followed Jesus, who received them and healed those that needed healing. And Lord, thy servant James instructed us to pray one for another that we may be healed. And that the fervent prayer of a righteous man is effective and has great strength.

"You, Lord, are our medicine. Your words are truth and life. You, Lord, are the greatest physician. You heal. You protect. You care.

"We come before you, most humbly, to beseech your mercy for the Xanthakos family, who, not through words but through deeds, have shown that their hearts belong to you."

Lilyan heard her daughter's stifled sob and squeezed her fingers that slipped from hers to be replaced by much larger, more calloused ones. John had joined them. To fight her own tears, she focused on the chaplain's next words.

"As you know, their son Paul was most cruelly wounded and suffered greatly at the hands of unspeakable evil. Father, Thou redeemest our life from destruction and crownest us with loving kindness and tender mercies. Comfort this young man upon his sickbed. Ease his suffering. Restore his mind. Ease this family's suffering. We submit that no healing is too hard for you, if it be your will.

"May we ever remember that recovery is only a reprieve, and that someday we will go to our rest in the Lord. May we, therefore, secure the righteous path and live with eternity ever in our view. Amen."

Lilyan opened her eyes to meet Nicholas'. The muscles in his throat bobbed, and he blinked away his tears. She smiled at him and breathed deeply, filling her lungs with air for the first time in a long while. Looking into the confident, earnest faces of the young men gathered around them, she felt refreshed and renewed. And somehow, optimistic.

CHAPTER 20

Two weeks later, sitting in a pew box of their small Presbyterian church in Charleston, Lilyan recalled the optimism she had felt after the healing prayer on board the *Lapis*. Her initial buoyancy had lessened somewhat as Paul still showed no signs of consciousness.

At first, she had resisted leaving the house, where the family took turns keeping watch in the somber parlor they had converted into a sickroom for Paul. At times, she and Nicholas stood over him together as they had when he was a babe in his cradle watching with eyes of hawks as his chest rose and fell.

Glancing around the white-washed walls of the sanctuary, she was glad she had come. The simple, austerity of the sanctuary suited her mood. The only decoration was a plaque on the wall on which were carved the words, "Nevertheless, it was not consumed." She wondered what God had in mind for Paul, and though she believed his plan would be for eternal good, she still had many questions. Like the burning bush, would he make Paul one of his miracles?

Marion, who sat between her and Nicholas, started to fidget, pulling at the collar of his once immaculately tied cravat. He looked splendid and grown-up in his dark blue waistcoat and buff leather breeches. For once, his hose remained pristine white, and his shoes were unscuffed.

In an unusual gesture for his more *economic* nature, Nicholas had splurged on finery for his entire family, including John. Lilyan had to admit they made a handsome family. Nikki's brown double-breasted coat with two rows of shiny brass buttons and matching breeches molded his fine physique and drew brazen glances from women they passed on the street. The moss green of Laurel's muslin dress accentuated her lovely eyes and made her hair shine like burnished copper. John had chosen a severe black waistcoat and matching pants that contrasted with his stark white vest and necktie. He had pulled his auburn hair into a black ribbon. The effect was altogether breathtakingly handsome, though she wouldn't let on that sentiment to Nikki. Not to be outdone, she wore a high-waisted dress of calico print, with an ecru lawn scarf that crisscrossed her chest and tied in the back. She had woven a matching bandeau through her loose curls. Paul's new attire hung in an upstairs wardrobe in their house, awaiting his recovery.

Wiggling around, Marion pulled a feather from his breeches pocket. It was a prized raven's feather he planned to fashion into fletching for one of his arrow shafts. Without a word, Nicholas took the feather and slipped it into the open collar of his coat. Marion sighed and dropped his head.

Lilyan leaned down and whispered, "Patience." She peeked over his head and shared a warm glance with Nicholas. "Something very exciting is about to happen."

Intrigued, Marion stared from one parent to the other and then leaned forward to sneak a quick look at Laurel, seated between their father and John.

The minister raised his voice, "I call forth John Cameron and Elder Nicholas Xanthakos."

Nicholas and John stood to exit the pew box.

"What?" Laurel whispered.

John smiled down at her, touched her lips with his fingertip, and stepped into the aisle. As the two men walked forward shoulder to shoulder toward the pulpit, Laurel threw an astonished look at Lilyan, who nodded her reassurance.

The minister opened his Bible. "Hear the words of our Lord Jesus Christ: All authority in heaven and on earth has been given to me. Go therefore and make disciples of all nations, baptizing them in the name of the Father, and of the Son, and of the Holy Spirit…"

With these few words from the Gospel of Matthew, the emotions that played out on Laurel's face—bewilderment, amazement, and realization—made Lilyan's eyes mist.

The minister continued, now quoting from Ephesians, "There is one body and one Spirit, just as you were called to the one hope of your calling, one Lord, one faith, one baptism, one God and Father of all, who is above all and through all and in all."

Also realizing what was occurring, Marion sat up straight and grinned at Laurel, whose tears now rolled down her face.

It came time for Nicholas to speak. "On behalf of the session, I present John to receive the sacrament of baptism."

"John," said the minister, "do you desire to be baptized?"

"I do," John answered in a voice loud and clear.

The minister turned to Nicholas. "As his sponsor, do you promise through prayer and example to support and encourage John to be a faithful Christian?"

Nicholas turned to the young man with whom he stood eye to eye. "I do."

Lilyan gripped Marion's fingers. Her chest ached from more emotions than she could name, and she had to make herself pull in a deep breath.

"Don't cry, Ma. Baptisms are happy times. Right?" Marion whispered.

Pushing back a lock of hair from his forehead, she smiled. "These are tears of joy, sweet boy."

Marion bobbed his head toward Laurel and snorted. "I'm

bookended by weeping, happy women."

My son's receiving his lesson in women well.

Her attention back on the baptism, she heard the minister ask, "Do you, as members of the church of Jesus Christ, promise to guide and nurture John by word and deed, with love and prayer, encouraging him to know and follow Christ and to be a faithful member of his church?"

"We do," Lilyan spoke with conviction, proud to hear her children add their voices to the others.

As the sacrament continued, Lilyan thought back to the first time she and John had spoken of religion and believing. He'd talked of his abusive father, his mother's death, and the life of deprivation and degradation he had lived. He had intimated about some terrible things he had done. With Nicholas' guidance, he had finally realized and accepted that God would forgive all for the asking. Her heart was near bursting with delight for him and for her daughter.

They had come to the point in the sacrament where John kneeled while the minister scooped water from the baptismal font and sprinkled it over John's bowed head. The symbolism of that gesture never failed to fill Lilyan's body with awe, bringing every pore alive. That it was happening to the man her daughter adored increased her joy tenfold.

John stood, and the minister placed his hand on his head. "John has been received into the one holy catholic and apostolic church through baptism. God has made him a member of the household of God, to share with us in the priesthood of Christ. Let us welcome the newly baptized."

The congregation stood, and Lilyan, whose heart was so light she felt she could float on air, spoke the traditional words with them. "With joy and thanksgiving we welcome you into Christ's church to share with us in his ministry, for we are all one in Christ."

Nicholas and John, tears sliding down his rugged cheeks, faced the people as they sang the final hymn and received the benediction. Marion whooped and pushed his way through the people crowded around to receive their new brother in Christ. Lilyan slid over and stood by Laurel, whose body trembled with excitement.

"Isn't it glorious, Ma?" she said through quivering lips. "He is one of us."

One of us. Splendid sound.

"And." Laurel tilted her head, her face lit with a smile. "No more impediments."

Lilyan threw back her head and laughed out loud. They stood together waiting patiently for the crowd to disperse, leaving the Xanthakos family alone in the sanctuary.

John, his face beaming with the radiance of a hundred candles, his eyes for Laurel only, walked down the aisle and assisted her from the pew. He escorted her to stand in front of the church. On the way, they passed by Nicholas and Marion, who came to stand beside the pew box with Lilyan. When Lilyan saw John drop to one knee, she tried to choke back a sob but was defeated in her efforts and fumbled in her reticule for a kerchief. Nicholas stepped close, draped his hand across her back, and gave her his handkerchief.

Marion rolled his eyes. "More happy tears." He grinned at his father and winked. "I think we're going to need a rowboat before all this is over with."

Nicholas chuckled and clapped his son on his shoulder. It wasn't long before Laurel and John strode down the aisle to meet them. Laurel's face was aglow as she held out her hand and showed her family the ring John had slipped on her finger. It was the emerald ring John had given to her aboard ship before the fight with the pirates. He'd had it sized, and the gem glowed brilliantly against Laurel's creamy complexion.

Nicholas, his countenance fluctuating between poleaxed and happy, studied the ring. "'Tis only a few shades darker than your sparkling eyes, dear one."

Laurel threw her arms around his neck. "I'm so happy, Da."

Nicholas held her to him a few moments and then let her go, his eyes misty and glistening like amber. He clasped John's hand and pulled him into a bear hug. "You've made us all very happy, son."

Lilyan motioned for John to lean down so she could cup her hand around his jaw and kiss his forehead. "We're proud to have you with us, dear."

"Huzzah!" Marion yelled, yanking at his tie. "Now that it's all over, may I take this off?"

"Wait till we get home, you ruffian," Nicholas said with a smile.

Outside on the steps, Laurel bade her parents to take advantage of the grand weather and enjoy the city sights. "John, Marion, and I will return home and care for Paul. We'll send word if there's any change. And no arguments. You need time to yourselves."

Her daughter spoke with such authority, Lilyan caught a glimpse of how she would manage her own household. Nicholas, who must have had the same thoughts, shared a comical glance with John, and they both shrugged.

After everyone hugged each other good-bye, Nicholas held out the crook of his elbow to Lilyan. "Shall we take a turn about the city?"

She curled her arm through his. "Lead on."

They'd been walking toward the bay only a few moments when Lilyan asked, "Nikki, do you recall the healing prayer aboard the *Lapis*?"

He guided her across some rough patches in the cobblestone street. "I shall never forget it."

"I was moved by the chaplain's reminder that healing is only a reprieve and that we will all die someday."

He patted her arm. "I may sound selfish. But though heaven sounds glorious, I hope the Lord grants us more time together. Here. With each other. With our children."

"Me too, dearest. And when we do go to see our Lord, I hope we go together. I cannot imagine my life without you."

Nicholas smiled down at her. "Let's not speak of parting. It's a glorious day. Let us drink in the sights and smells of this beautiful city."

For too long her shoulders had felt hunched over like a shrub on the shore bent and battered and ravaged by storm winds. The glimmer of expectation that lit her husband's troubled expression, though bittersweet, was infectious. She absorbed it and stood straighter. Was it possible for their renewed hope coupled with the teeming life of the city to permeate their home and entice Paul back to consciousnesses?

A seagull squawked overhead, and Lilyan laughed, caught up in her husband's sudden burst of enthusiasm. Nikki's laughter matched hers, making her realize how long it had been since she had heard that delightful sound. On the heels of their recent ordeal, it felt good to laugh again.

It felt even better to be standing on dry land, dressed in the latest finery the port city had to offer. The appreciative stares of passersby only made her smile, as she and her husband both knew who they belonged to.

With revived spirits, they strolled arm in arm down a wide avenue that approached the mercantile area of town with rows of shops lining Elliott Street. Each of the long, narrow, three-story structures was painted a pale hue, reminding Lilyan of festive pastel ribbons in a nosegay. Families lived in the upper two stories, with the businesses taking up the first floor. The outside kitchens, servants' quarters, and slave huts crowded into the long, narrow backyards.

They passed a baker standing on the stoop of his shop and hurried past the cloud of flour he swept into the street. Lilyan sneezed and then giggled when the baker waggled his bushy eyebrows at her.

She had grown up in this city and enjoyed the thriving, bustling area of town where one could purchase muslins and linens from the fabric shop at No. 8 or view the delightful fashion dolls in the window of the French seamstress at No. 12. Hats, gloves, and gossip were the main wares of the milliner at No. 14. When they passed the apothecary shop, she made a mental note to return later to buy supplies to refurbish her medicine kit. Tantalizing aromas of nutmeg, cloves, and cinnamon drifted out from the sundry store.

Nicholas lifted his nose in the air and breathed deeply. "Um-m-m. Cinnamon. Do you think you could bake some bread soon? That's what you were doing one of the first times we met. Remember?"

"I do. I wrapped up some cinnamon bread for you, and you wondered if that was what heaven smelled like." The pleasant memory returned as if it had been yesterday, instead of almost twenty years.

"I was speaking of you, Lilyanista. Not the bread."

Her heart tripped, and Lilyan missed a step and was glad of Nicholas' arm clasped tight around her.

He chortled. "It's good to know that I can still … excite … you, my love."

He would soon know what excitement she had to offer. She had contemplated the effect her announcement would have on their already overwrought family, but it wasn't something she could keep to herself much longer. She hoped her news would draw them even closer.

They reached the end of the street and the harbor that was dotted with a row of warehouses and long stretches of wooden docks where a myriad of boats of all shapes, sizes, and colors were moored—dinghies teetering with kegs and chests, longboats full of fish gleaming in the sun, and shrimp boats draped with V-shaped nets. The building housing Lilyan's wallpaper shop lay straight ahead. Once used as a warehouse for her father's trading business, it had two bubble glass windows on either side of the entrance door for displaying wallpaper samples and Lilyan's miniature portraits. Her shop was closed for the day, but although she had long ago turned the everyday running of the business over to her former apprentice, she had kept a key. She pulled it from her reticule and handed it to Nicholas, who unlocked the door.

Inside, she made a complete circle, taking in the organized piles of samples and the tidy front counter. With Nicholas following, she walked to the back of the building and into the workroom. A barn-like area, it held shelves stacked with paper and cloth samples, jars of paints, boxes of brushes, carving knives, and blocks of wood for stenciling. She closed her eyes and breathed in the familiar aromas of linen paper, glue, linseed oil, turpentine, and freshly whittled cedar wood. Some might consider the smells acrid and pungent, but they were as pleasant to her as cinnamon was to Nicholas.

She opened the back door and stepped out onto a deck that jutted out over the water. A gust of warm air ruffled the water into caps that danced across the harbor catching the sun like fireflies. Cupping her hand across her brow, she gazed out to sea allowing melancholy memories to wash over her.

Nicholas stood behind her and pressed her body against his chest. "You're remembering about the prison ships, aren't you?"

She nodded and traced the scar on her right arm. "It's where we started. And to think, if Andrew hadn't run away to fight. Hadn't been captured and put on that ship. We may never have met."

He turned her to face him and tapped her nose with his finger. "That's where you are wrong, *agapi mou*. God would have found a way for us to meet, no matter what choices we made."

She pressed her hands to his chest and then straightened the high collar of his jacket, moving her gaze up his chin, across his full bottom lip, and then she locked eyes with his. "Sometimes, Nikki, I fear my heart will burst open trying to contain all the feelings I have for you."

He tipped her chin and kissed her, sending charges of lightning throughout her body.

She stepped and took his hands in hers. "My love, there's something I've needed to tell you. But because of everything"— she shook with the memories—"I—that is…"

Concern clouded his eyes. "Yes?"

"I'm with child."

He whooped and threw his hat up in the air. He grabbed her and swung her around, and then, remembering her condition, put her down gently.

This time his kiss was gentle. Tender. "My heart stopped for a moment. I wasn't sure what you were going to say."

He grinned wide and his eyes sparkled, making him look so young Lilyan caught her breath. "You are happy with the news, sir?"

"Happy? I'm beyond such a humdrum word." He laughed again. "When?"

"I believe in time for Christmas."

"What adventures the babe has already experienced." He splayed his fingers across her stomach. "Our *pirate child*, then."

She covered his fingers with hers. "Oh, dear. When you put it that way, I quake with anticipation."

"No worrying. Remember, each day has enough troubles of its own." He embraced her and kissed the top of her head. "The babe will make a splendid Christmas gift."

Lord, will our Paul live to enjoy the gift too?

She stepped back and fiddled with the scarf tied at his neck. "Nikki, let's go tell the children."

"They will be overjoyed, I'm sure. Perhaps such good news will stir something in Paul." He held out his hand. "Come. Let's make haste."

They left the shop, and Lilyan had to pick up her skirts to keep up with him as he hurried them down the crowded streets. Turning the corner to their house, she heard such a din spilling out into the street, she frowned at Nicholas, and they picked up their pace.

The front door was wide open, and Cassia's screeching, ear-piercing screams greeted them at the steps. Marion sat on the bottom step of the stairway, his head in his hands. John, obviously consoling Laurel, tried to pull her hands from her face as she wept.

"Don't cry. Please, don't cry, dear lassie," John begged, draping his arm across her shoulders.

In her haste, Lilyan almost tripped, and Nicholas grasped her elbow. They stopped, and their glances collided.

Oh, Nikki, what awaits inside? Death? Sadness? Pain?

I know not, my love, but whatever it is, I am here for you. We will face it together.

As they crossed the threshold, Cal pushed his way between them and stood in the parlor, lifted his head in the air, and let out a howl that made the hairs on Lilyan's arms stand up.

Dread washed over her. She wobbled, rubber legged, into the room to find Izzie, standing beside Paul's bed, sobbing, her apron pulled up over her head. Cassia, lying on the bed and cradled in the crook of Paul's arm, was crimson faced and pumping her legs.

Lilyan pushed Izzie and Cal out of her way and pressed her hand on Paul's chest. "He's still breathing. Thank God."

Not dead. Intoxicating relief shot through her body, and her knees almost gave away. She clutched the edge of the mattress to keep her balance.

"What is going on here?" Nicholas yelled, startling Cassia and making her squall even louder. He frowned at Cal, who was still adding his voice to the ruckus. "That's enough, dog."

Cal immediately ceased howling and plopped down on his haunches.

Lilyan pulled the apron from Izzie's face. "What happened?"

Izzie rested her arms across her stomach. "I needed to check on de bread. In de outside kitchen. So I laid de babe beside Mister Paul, thinking she'd be all right. I wuzn't gonna be gone long." She picked up Cassia and started cooing and rocking her back and forth until she stopped crying and started snuffling.

"Then I heard this almighty loud screaming. Enough to wake the dead, it was." Her face broke into a huge smile, exposing her gums. "I ran in here and seed Mister Paul, his eyes open, lookin' round all confused like. He asked me who I was. Scared de life outta me!" She caressed Cassia's cheek with her fingertip. "Mr. Paul helped bring this littlun into the world, and she done returned the favor. It's a wonderment. It is."

Lilyan's gaze rested on the sweet babe who had already made a home in her heart and now gained a forever place among the Xanthakos family.

Marion, who had been hanging back in the doorway, started laughing, "He spoke, Ma."

Laurel joined in the laughter between her hiccups.

"First it's caterwauling, now it's laughing," Paul said in a hoarse whisper. "Is this the madhouse?"

As one, they all turned and stared at him.

Lilyan ran to him and pulled him into her arms. "Paul. Oh, Paul. My son. My dear son."

Nicholas ran to the other side of the bed and leaned over them, his eyes brimming with tears. "You gave your ma quite a scare." His voice cracked. "I'm so proud of you, my boy. You withstood more than most men could have."

John stepped close to the bed. "Paul, I'm John Cameron, your sister's intended."

Paul held out his hand. "A pleasure to meet you." Shaking hands with his soon-to-be brother-in-law, he glanced at Lilyan with a stunned expression. "Exactly how long have I been unconscious?"

Everyone laughed, and when Lilyan finished kissing every inch of Paul's face, she slid her arm underneath his back for him to slowly, painfully rise up on one elbow.

His expression grew serious. "Ma? Can we go home?"

Home. A beautiful vision took form in Lilyan's mind. With a good wagon and sturdy horses, they'd arrive in plenty of time for the harvest. Nicholas would return his sword to its place over the mantel and tend his grapes, running his calloused hands across the tops of the burgeoning trellises, his eyes as clear and bright as the golden muscadines. In the evenings, Laurel would play her kithara, and she and John would sing. Marion would roam the woods, his longbow slung over his shoulder, and Cal trotting alongside. Paul would sit on the front porch reading his new medical books Lilyan had purchased from the apothecary.

Lilyan would paint and make pottery and wait for her new babe to make its presence known. And every day, maybe twice a day, she would climb to the mountaintop, lift her face to the sky, and thank the good Lord for his tender mercies.

EPILOGUE

November 16, 1836
Asheville, North Carolina

Exhausted, Lilyan slumped onto the tufted satin bench at her dressing table. Turning her cheek to the mirror, she brushed her fingers below her temples and over the cocoa-colored blotches intensified by their porcelain background.

"I'm seventy-five," she whispered.

If God would allow it, would I do it all over again? Everything?

Her eyes traveled down the pale blue veins pulsing underneath the wrinkled skin on her forearm, stopping only an instant at the faded dusty rose of her scar. She held her hands out in front of her. *Still my best feature.* With skillful, brilliantly colored brush strokes, they had brought to life on canvas the wonders of nature so abundant to her beloved South Carolina: lavender orchids hidden deep in the swamps; sable brown cattails that rustled in the marshes along the coast; and waxy, white petals of magnolias that canopied the streets of Charleston. Her long, slender fingers had caressed her husband's dear face, cradled their precious babies, and tenderly bound the wounds of sick and injured soldiers.

These same hands had bludgeoned the life out of another human being.

A chill crept down her spine, and she reached for the shawl

draped across the foot of her bed. A pain shot down her left arm as she pushed up from the seat and wrapped the shawl around her shoulders. Leaning on a cane, she shuffled to the window and drew back the lace curtain. Stragglers still mingled on the lawn. Everyone she cared about had attended the party, except for the one person she most wanted. She breathed in deeply and let the air out slowly, clasped her shawl closer around her neck, and made her way back to the dresser. She looked again into the mirror and studied her eyes, remembering how Nicholas used to say they glowed like fiery emeralds when he would smile and beckon her into his arms. She pressed a hand to her chest.

What a silly old woman I am. My heart still skips at the mere thought of him. I must write to him.

She dipped a pen into the inkwell and began her letter.

Beloved,

We celebrated my birthday today. What a joyous time it was having our clan, children, grandchildren, and great-grandchildren, gathered close once more.

Caroline, in her own strong-willed fashion, spent months planning the affair, sending out missives to her brothers and sister. Not surprisingly, although our children are grown, they continue to dote on their baby sister. They respond to her every wish with the same adoration they felt when she was born.

What a time that was. I shall never forget how incredulous you were to find that you were to be a father again. Time has been unable to erase the memory of the tender glow in your eyes as you kissed our daughter's soft cheeks for the first time.

But today was a bittersweet occasion, my darling Nicholas, for it marked another year without you by my side.

I grow weary of this body with its aches and pains, which serve as a constant reminder that I have more days behind me than ahead. It seems only fitting, therefore, that my thoughts often wander to the past.

In my heart abides a treasure chest of memories. It is a place I visit often. Reaching in and carefully unwrapping the keepsakes that reside there, I savor the essence of you. The warmth of your thumb tracing circles in my palm. The salty smell of your hair after bathing in the ocean. The padding of your footsteps as you tiptoed across our bedroom to close the window on stormy evenings. The deep rumbling sound of your laughter when the boys tipped over their canoe. The tears you shed when we received news of the death of our dear President Washington.

God has granted me all these blessings, and I shall be eternally grateful to him for the gift he gave me in you, my soul mate, my other half. But, oh, how I long for the day when I will be with you again.

I must go for now, my dearest. I am very tired and must rest, but I will take up my pen this evening before I retire.

Lilyan slid her pen back into the inkwell and rocked a blotter across the words that had spilled from her heart. She began to pull the pins from her chignon and dropped them into a tortoiseshell bowl, freeing her hair to spill down her shoulders. There was something comforting about performing this ritual—something she had done so often, she could have done it with her eyes closed. Indeed, she remembered, there had been several occasions in her life when she had done just that. Only then, her thick, curly tresses had shone like fire reflected in a polished copper kettle. Time had relaxed the curls into soft waves, and experience had faded the red-gold to the pale white-apricot color found only in the rarest of pearls.

She picked up the comb that had decorated her hair, and cradling it in the palm of one hand, she stroked her fingers across its inlaid turquoise stones, then down its three teeth made from ebony bear claws. Golden Fawn had fashioned it for her many years ago.

She rose slowly from the vanity and walked to the rocker beside her bed and eased herself down. She touched the string of pearls at her neck. Nikki had given them to her in Charleston the night before they had sailed on their adventure to North Carolina. So much had happened in the thirty-six years since then. She had forgotten much, but, oh, the things she remembered. One of those memories caused her so much heartache, she could hardly bare it. In the center of the family cemetery lay her beloved Nicholas, who had passed away quietly in his sleep five years previous.

A tear rolled down her cheek, and she stirred to wipe it away, but her hand wouldn't move. She was tired. Down-to-the-bone weary.

Nikki, I miss you so.

I'm here, agapi mou.

At the sound of the warm, familiar voice, her heart leapt and then tumbled back into place with a dull thud.

Are you ready to come home, Lilyanista?

Oh, yes.

***

"Grandmother," Allison called softly from the bedroom doorway.

"Shh, dear. She's sleeping," Caroline Ravenel answered, following her daughter into the room. "You turn down the covers while I get her gown."

Caroline walked to the armoire and pulled out a cream chiffon nightgown, placed it on the foot of the bed, and walked around to kneel beside her mother.

"Dearest. Let us help you to bed."

It took her only a moment to realize that her mother had stopped breathing.

Allison ran around the side of the bed. "What is it, Mother? What's wrong?" Her chin quivered.

"Grandmother's gone, isn't she?" The words spilled from her trembling lips just as the tears began to spill from her eyes.

Caroline wrapped her arm around her daughter and, stifling her own tears, she tried to console the inconsolable.

Allison scrubbed her wet cheeks and reached out to touch one of the papers strewn across the bed and onto the floor. "What are these?"

"Letters. They're letters grandmother received and ones she wrote to PawPaw but never mailed. She showed them to me once."

Allison looked up at Caroline with solemn, soulful eyes so full of sorrow that it wrenched at her heart. Allison had been Lilyan's favorite. There had been a deep and abiding connection between the two of them. Everyone in the family was aware of it, but it was such a special relationship, no one resented it.

Caroline cupped her daughter's cheek. "Let's gather them and put them back. We'll sit down and share them together soon. Would you like that?"

"Yes."

They bundled the letters together in the ribbon and placed them in the chest.

Allison closed the top gently. "She's with PawPaw now. She must be very happy. She loved him so very much." She pondered a moment. "And God will be there too. That will be nice. She loved him very much too."

Unable to speak, Caroline nodded.

Allison trailed a finger across her grandmother's hand. "She wouldn't want us to be sad. We're to enjoy each day God gives us, right?"

How did my young daughter become so wise? Caroline caressed her mother's cheek. *Of course I know how, dear one.*

Dear Reader,

It's my fondest hope that you have come to love Lilyan and Nicholas and their family as much as I. If so, I thought you might like to know what became of them.

Paul waited a year after their Outer Banks adventure to recover his health and then left the vineyard to attend medical school in Philadelphia. A year after graduation, he married Sylvia, the sister of one of his classmates. Several months before Lilyan's death, they, along with their four beautiful, red-haired girls, returned to Asheville and set up a medical practice ten miles away from the Xanthakos vineyard. Throughout her childhood their oldest daughter, Elizabeth, spent many summer days with Lilyan tromping through the woods searching for mullein roots and wormwood to soothe her youngest sibling's cough and bronchitis.

Laurel and John married in Charleston a week after his baptism and moved into a cabin in the family compound. John was a natural vintner, much to Nicholas' delight, especially since none of his boys were interested in carrying on the family business. Laurel and John had five children, three strapping boys and two lovely girls, all with voices like angels and who loved to sing hymns. On cool, autumn evenings sharing a vibrant quilt that rivaled the leaves floating down to blanket the dark, vibrant earth, Lilyan and Nicholas sat on their porch and basked in their grandchildren's serenades that echoed through the valley.

In 1804, struck by wanderlust, Marion was almost inconsolable at being told he was too young to join the Lewis and Clark expedition. Her only child to inherit her artistic talent, he offered his services to two expeditions to the Pacific Northwest, and returned from both with pictures and yarns that brought much laughter and awe to the family's after-supper gatherings by the fireplace. His pictures were eventually published in a book acclaimed not only as a scientific accomplishment, but as a work of art. One of Lilyan's favorites was his rendition of a chamomile that looked so real, so alive, people imagined they could smell its sweet apple aroma. He was married for a brief time to a charming, bright woman he met while hunting in the forest. They argued over whose arrow had killed the deer. She and their babe both died during childbirth. The day of Lilyan's seventy-fifth birthday, with his eyes gleaming, he told his family about meeting Kit Carson, a trapper and mountain man who was considering guiding an expedition to the Far West.

Caroline, their "pirate" child and the sister her brothers called "the bossy one," married into a prominent Charleston family. At the age of twenty, her oldest boy Gerald answered the siren call of the sea. Her daughter, Allison, was a sensitive child with huge mint-green eyes and red-gold hair. She carried a sketchbook with her everywhere she went. Lilyan knew she shouldn't have favorites, but...

Nicholas gave Izzie and Samuel a plot of land in the southwest corner of the valley to farm, as they were not allowed to purchase property. Though Cassia lived with them as their child, she visited Lilyan every day, asking repeatedly for the story of how her brave mother had brought her into the world. At eighteen she married a Cherokee man, and when President Jackson ordered the removal of the Cherokee to Oklahoma in 1831, Lilyan and Nicholas hid them and many of his relatives in the caves on their property. What a terror-filled time that was. Nicholas traveled to Washington to protest the mistreatment of the Cherokee, but greed prevailed.

And what of Cal? When they first brought him to the mountains, he spent much of his time on the porch and guarding Lilyan's every step. With each passing day, he expanded his territory, first the compound, then the vineyard, then the forests surrounding the valley. He took to visiting the nearby Cherokee village and garnered the name of *Little Horse*. During the day, his wolf howl echoed for miles through the mountains, but he always returned in the evenings to plop down beside Lilyan's rocking chair and lay his big head across her foot. He was her faithful guardian for ten years, and at his passing was buried in the family cemetery along with

Andrew and Golden Fawn, who had succumbed to the influenza epidemic of 1820, and near the two children born to Lilyan and Nicholas after Caroline.

AUTHOR'S NOTES

Baby's Heartbeat
(Mentioned in Chapter 6) A baby's heartbeat can be heard most clearly through its back. At seven months, babies usually lie upside down on their backs and to the left of the abdominal midline, so from week 28 look for the back lower than and to the left of the navel. Baby Cassia's heartbeat (120-160 beats a minute) was faster than her mother's (about 100 beats or less per minute).

Busk
(Mentioned in Chapter 17) A busk was part of a woman's corset, made of thin wood, ivory, or bone that was slipped into a pocket of material and tied in place at the front of a corset to keep it straight and upright. Busks were often carved and decorated, or inscribed with messages, and were popular gifts from men to their sweethearts.

Caraco Jacket
(Mentioned in Chapter 10) Several of the females in the pirates' den are wearing caraco jackets. These were thigh-length, fitted jackets worn over a petticoat (a simple two-paneled skirt gathered at the waist). If worn with the front open, then a stomacher was added or it was fastened with ruching strips (a strip of pleated lace, net, muslin, or other material for trimming or finishing a dress, as at the

collar or sleeves), or fastened with stays (strings or lacing strips). The women with the pirates often would not bother to lace the strings.

Careen
(Mentioned in Chapter 11) To careen was to take a wooden ship to a shallow area of water and pull the masts to the ground, exposing the bottom so that it could be repaired or scraped and cleaned of seaweed and barnacles. The growth on the bottom of ships slowed them down and made them harder to steer, so careening had to be done every two to three months. It was the most dangerous and vulnerable time for pirate ships.

Cassia
Cassia in Hebrew means *to bow down the head*. An aromatic bark, it was known as *the poor man's cinnamon*, because it had a similar fragrance to cinnamon, but was not as costly. It was an ingredient of holy anointing oil used to anoint priests, kings and their garments, and will be the aroma of Christ's robes when he returns to us (see Psalm 45:8 and Exodus 30:24). The ingredient of cassia reminds us of the suffering servant who in his body was the sacrifice for the world. The brokenness of his body was the sweet fragrance to the Father that he had won the human race back to himself (Ephesians 4:8).

Diamond of the First Water
(Mentioned in Chapter 1) Nicholas calls Laurel "a diamond of the first water," a term of the time that meant beautiful. In the gemstone trade, first water means "highest quality." The clarity of diamonds is assessed by their translucence; the more like a pure drop of water, the higher the quality.

Farthingale
(Mentioned in Chapter 10) These structures or hoops were made out of various materials including whalebone and willow. They were worn underneath dresses to hold the dresses out from the

body. The women with the pirates wouldn't have been concerned with such modesty; the clingier, the better.

Going to the Account (articles of piracy)
(Mentioned in Chapter 9) When a pirate made a voyage, he knew he'd be performing illegal acts and would be accountable for his own acts with the law. Pirates signed articles of "prey, no pay," which meant they worked for free if their ship took no prizes.

Hammock
(Introduced in Chapter 3) Sail makers issued each sailor a hammock. A Royal Navy hammock was 72" x 36" of No. 12 cotton, with 16 hitched eyelets (grommets) at either end, and with two cord-covered brass rings that hooked onto clews hooks fastened into the ship's beams. Sleeping in a hammock took practice. It was difficult to get into and harder to stay in. New sailors usually spent their first few nights falling out of their hammocks. When one sailor started to fall, he'd grab a hold of the next sailor's hammock, tossing him out as he grabbed for the next hammock—knocking everyone out like dominoes. It was a favorite prank for mates to loosen or cut the hammock riggings sending the poor victim crashing to the floor. Apprentice seamen were issued the following: one pea-jacket, cloth cap, pair of cloth trousers, flannel over and undershirts, pair of drawers, shoes, necktie, socks, white duck pants and frock, comb, knife, pot, pan, spoon, one bar soap, clothes bag, and a badge. According to tradition, when a sailor died, his mates would sew him up in his hammock, making the last stitch through the nose to make sure he was dead. Holystones, which were used to scour the deck, or cannonballs were tied around the deceased's ankles for ballast, and then his body was laid on the top of an 8-man mess table, and given up to the sea.

"Come, Thou Fount of Every Blessing"
(Mentioned in Chapter 16) Lilyan, her family, the crew, and the

marines sing this hymn written by Robert Robinson when he was 23. As a youth, he led a notorious gang, but upon hearing George Whitfield preach, he became a believer. Later in life, he drifted from the faith. Once, when travelling on a stagecoach, a passenger was readying a hymn book and read his hymn aloud and said how wonderful it was. His reply: "Madam, I'm the poor man who wrote that hymn many years ago. I would give a thousand worlds to enjoy the feelings I had then."

I often wondered what "here I raise my Ebenezer" means in verse 2 of this hymn (and it has nothing to do with Scrooge). Ebenezer means "stone of help" and is simply a monumental stone signifying the great help God gave to the person raising the stone and an acknowledgement of God's blessings. (see 1 Samuel 7:12)

"Jesus Wept"
(Mentioned in Chapter 16) William Billings composed the hymn, "Jesus Wept," and also wrote the rousing song, "Chester," sung so often by the Patriots of the Revolutionary War that it rivaled "Yankee Doodle" as an anthem of revolution.

Kithara
(Mentioned in Chapter 17) The cithara or kithara was an ancient Greek musical instrument, a version of the lyre or lyra. In modern Greek, the word kithara has come to mean "guitar." It had a wooden sounding box composed of two resonating tables, either flat or slightly arched, connected by ribs or sides of equal width. At the top, its eight strings were knotted around the yoke or to rings threaded over the bar or wound around pegs. The other end of the strings was secured to a tailpiece after passing over a flat bridge.

Mock Trials, Captain Kidd Trial Transcripts
(Mentioned in Chapter 10) Life aboard a pirate ship could get

boring, roaming the oceans in search of a prize. To help the time pass, crews would stage mock trials. I discovered a fantastic site that has the transcripts from the trial of Captain Kidd.

http://captainkidd.org/Trial%20&%20Execution.html

Red Legs
(Mentioned in Chapter 9) Jamie (aka, John) is described as a Red Leg. It was a nickname for Scottish sailors of the day. Scottish men were known to wear kilts year round with nothing to protect their legs from the sun and harsh elements.

Slave Ships Throwing People Overboard
(Mentioned in Chapter 1) For example: the British slave ship *Zong* threw fifty-four sick and dying women and children into the sea. Two days later forty-two male slaves were thrown overboard; thirty-six slaves followed in the next few days. Another ten, in a display of defiance at the inhumanity of the slavers, threw themselves overboard. On 22 December 1781, the *Zong* arrived at Black River, Jamaica, with 208 slaves on board, less than half the number taken from Africa. *The King's Bench Trial Reports.*

Scuttlebutt
There was a lot of gossip aboard pirate ships, and scuttlebutt was the equivalent of gossiping around the water cooler. The "butt" was a barrel of fresh drinking water, and the "scuttle" a hole in the barrel through which sailors would draw water. Sailors would go to the butt for a drink and linger to chat with others.

Swansboro
In 1783, Swansboro (originally spelled Swannsborough) was incorporated as a town. During the American Revolution, a warehouse at the mouth of the White Oak River supplied the Continental army with salted beef and pork and barrels of salt. A

British blockade greatly reduced the importation of salt, making its production of critical importance. In answer to the blockade, several salt works were established in the Swansboro area to produce salt from sea water. Throughout the war, vessels from the port of Swansboro engaged in privateering, and a military company from the town (then called "Bogue") patrolled the coast.

Woolding
(Mentioned in Chapter 9) Woolding was a form of torture favored by the pirate Captain Morgan and his men. A piece of cord would be tied around a prisoner's head and around a stick. The stick would be twisted until the victim's eyes popped out of their sockets. The Spanish invented this torture, which they used during their Inquisition.